The Sensual Mirror

The Vassi Collection

Volume IX

The Sensual Mirror

Marco Vassi

OPEN ROAD

INTEGRATED MEDIA

NEW YORK

ISBN 978-1-4976-4083-2

This edition published in 2014 by Open Road Integrated Media, Inc.
345 Hudson Street
New York, NY 10014
www.openroadmedia.com

to Sheryl who made it possible

If they see
breasts and long hair coming
they call it woman

if beard and whiskers
they call it man:

but, look, the self that hovers
in between
is neither man
nor woman

O Ramanatha.
Dasimayya

What we need is a mixed diction.
Aristotle

Introduction

Were the Sixties put on earth so that Marco Vassi could happen? Or was Marco Vassi put on earth so that the Sixties could happen? To read his classic works of erotic fiction and his masterpiece of autobiographical fiction, THE STONED APOCALYPSE, is to realize that the man and the era were created out of the same fire and primordial elements. It is not, however, enough to say that Marco Vassi was a child of his age. It could just as accurately be said that the age was Marco Vassi's fantasy, a fantasy so intense and compelling that it is impossible to read any of his books in one sitting: one must either jump into a cold shower, relieve oneself sexually, or go for a long contemplative walk to reflect on the profundity of his insights into human behavior.

Vassi had done many things before he became a writer, but writing was not one of them except for some translations from Chinese and critiques of manuscripts submitted to a literary agency where he was employed for a few years. He had also tried numerous identities on for size as he acted out and lived out the experiences that were to pour from his mind like water raging over the spillway of a dam. When in the late 1960's "Fred" Vassi announced that he was embarking on a journey, his friends knew that it was not to a place but to a state of mind.

The state of mind was what came to be known as The Sixties, and anyone seeking to live in that state must enter it through the vision of the author of these works. In cartographic terms it was a journey from the East Coast to California, a trip that resonates with meaning for every student of The American Experience. Speaking metaphorically, however, it was a trip into the heart of life, love, laughter, horror, and sweet pain. Fred Vassi came back Marco Vassi, having recreated himself in the name of the intrepid voyager to the ends of the known world hundreds of years ago.

Heart fecund with all that had happened to him, he started writing the work that was eventually to become THE STONED APOCALYPSE, a book that captured in coruscating words what others of his generation were capturing so brilliantly in music.

With no source of regular income he tried his hand at what were then popularly known as sex novels, a genre of tame pornography that pandered to the fantasies of repressed males still mired in postwar inhibition. With the wide-eyed innocence and self-deprecating humor that characterized every venture he undertook, he showed them to me, his friend and a fledgling literary agent. He merely hoped to raise a few dollars with them. I told him that they were the most incredibly arousing works of erotic literature since Henry Miller, and arranged for them to be brought out by Olympia Press, Miller's publisher. Critics and reviewers confirmed my assessment. What distinguished his books from the rest of the pack was the application of Vassi's intelligence. He knew that the mind is the most erotic organ of all. He termed this fusion of mind and sex organs "Metasex."

For Marco Vassi, the liberation of sexual emotions, paralleling the liberation of so many others in the late 1960's and early 1970's, promised a new age of beauty, love, and honesty, and he lived his vision to the hilt—quite literally. For a long while it seemed to him impossible that this vision did not rest on the bedrock of reality.

But, in the words of Robert Frost, nothing gold can stay. The bloody hand of Vietnam and the corrupt fist of the Nixon presidency crushed the fragile beauty of the flower generation. The unbridled commercialism that became the 1980's captured and exploited the butterflies of Woodstock, enriching half of them and killing the other half with sex, drugs, and rock and roll. Finally, the horror of a new scourge, AIDS, visited death upon the bodies of those who had dreamed of eternal love, irresponsible fun, and self-realization. It was then that Marco Vassi awoke from his dream of The Sixties. When he did, the virus had entered his blood. The first malady of any consequence to come along, in this case pneumonia, conquered his defenseless immune system and made short work of him.

Marco Vassi's body died, but not the body of his work, which lives again in these new editions. Like a rainbow over a bleak landscape, his dream of The Sixties shimmers above the depressing, sordid, and tragic decades that succeeded his. And ultimately, it triumphs over them.

Richard Curtis

One

For Julia Gordis evening had always been the most beautiful part of the day. She still remembered the long hours of twilight when she had sat on the back porch of her home in the small Missouri town where she'd been raised. She cherished an image of her grandmother in a rocker, usually shelling peas or knitting or doing something else useful with her hands. The family dog lay mournfully on the grass, peering into the encroaching shadows, whining at the spirits which moved among the nearby trees. When she was a teenager and responsible for household duties, the time was spent in the kitchen with her mother, preparing the evening meal. The two women circled each with random purpose, like acolytes at a loosely organized sacrifice, performing a ritual of food. By then her grandmother had died and her father fallen into his terminal silence, his only communication a sourly mocking glance out from the depths of whatever pact he'd made with his soul. The dog, his coat now mangy, his eyes rheumy, slept in the corner next to the potato bin. The sadness of the hour and the intense loneliness of the house screwed Julia to an almost insupportable anguish. As the day died, she died, and when the meal was finished and the dishes washed, she ran to her room to surrender to an orgy of unhappiness, detailing the process in her diary between the bouts of weeping and attempting to calm herself by swimming in the cool white indifference of the ceiling. At twenty, her attachment to dusk had reached such levels of romantic meaning that she arranged to lose her virginity at precisely the moment when the light sighed and embraced the darkness, when the earth acknowledged the vastness of the universe in which it was nothing more than a mote. Afterwards, while the boy attempted endearments and reassurances, she gazed with abstract moodiness at the quality of the color of the blood on her thigh, feeling as though it were the night which had been her true lover.

Her marriage to Martin at first obscured and then exacerbated her need for her evening mood. During the first year they had been so busy adjusting and romping in erotic exploration that she forgot to be melancholy at all. There had followed the year in Europe, eleven months of nonstop excitement, movement, change. But when they settled in New York and she began her job, the old pattern of daily seasons reasserted itself. Except that now she never seemed to have any time alone. She arrived home at five-thirty or six and usually wasn't out of the shower five minutes before Martin came back. Punctilious in his responsibility, he always helped to make dinner. For a long while their life was so nicely tuned, so perfectly regulated, that she felt awkward suggesting to herself that she was growing more and more unhappy.

When they reached the Period of the Deadly Bicker, as she later referred to it, she complained about her lack of solitude and Martin, obliging as ever, made it a point to come home an hour later each night. She found it impossible to explain that it was as foolish to structure a time within which one might indulge a certain sensibility as it was to put a fence around a forest and call the area a wilderness. Other factors entered in, of course, other pressures, other tendencies. And when the breakup finally took place, through all the depression and relief, through all the catalogued changes of failure, the one signal clarity in Julia's consciousness was that muted trumpet of twilight, the liberty to lock the door and be ravished by the cosmic poignancy of loss, loss without an object, without a name.

Now she lay in her tub, awake and dreaming. The bathroom itself had undergone a transformation since Martin had left. The place was more casually disordered, more strewn with bits and pieces. A huge poster showing a closeup of Bob Dylan's face was tacked to the ceiling. The paper had been wrinkled by the heat of showers and baths and that made the face look old, like a drugged lecher leering at the naked woman beneath. Incense sticks burned in a holder on the windowsill. The floor was littered with clothes in the disarray that occurs when one lives alone and can let the environment totally reflect the state of one's mind. On the hamper next to the tub sat a squat bottle of wine and a joint. Julia had already drunk a glass of wine and was preparing to get stoned. It wasn't unusual for her, since she was alone again, to spend one or two hours in the bath each evening, drinking, smoking, reading, drowsing, periodically letting half the water out and replenishing the rest with hot.

She had turned twenty-nine the week before, and on midnight of the day itself had burst into tears because Martin had not called. She knew he wouldn't and really didn't want him to, but part of her still clung to certain primitive sentiments, or what used to be called girlish ways. Now she smiled wryly at the memory, wondering how long it would take to forget him completely, simultaneously sad at the realization that such a time might indeed come. The long black hair, which usually hung down between her shoulder blades, floated around her shoulders like a web of seaweed. Her breasts also floated, the nipples like the tips of icebergs, signposts of the hidden mass beneath the surface. She was a trim woman, a few inches shorter than Martin, her weight never going above a hundred and ten pounds. One of the things that had attracted him to her from the first was his admiration of her natural physique. She never exercised formally, and yet her skin tone was flawless, her muscles firm, her posture easily erect. In all, she maintained the lithe sophistication of a dancer.

She lit the marijuana cigarette and inhaled deeply, her eyes closed. Her classic beauty was never more powerfully apparent than at moments like these, when she was relaxed and inward, not projecting the glamor which she herself usually mistook for her true style. Her lips especially, combining the fullness of sensuality with the tension of intelligence, caused men to stop and smolder. It was a pornographic mouth, lush with lewd suggestion yet vulnerable with perpetual innocence.

She smoked again, and sighed. The narcotic effect of the herb began to work its magic on her nervous system. Synapses calmed down, circuits closed their switchboards, stereotyped stimulus-response engrams grew sleepy at the wheel and pulled off the highway to nap. And with the domino dalliance in domination of her brain, the sharp concerns of social consciousness drifted apart, like friends saying goodnight as they hied off to different trains going to different towns.

Julia sucked at the cigarette until it was a tiny ember at the tip of a blackened stub so small she had to to hold it with the very edges of her fingernails, at which point she tossed it into the toilet bowl. She had reached a very high level of toxicity very quickly and was ready to let the ensuing psychophysical chaos overwhelm her. It was clearly a process of losing control, but it is only in that loss of control that the chronic spasm and contraction called personality or character can be undone and the formless life force find expression.

With Julia, the falling apart was manifested primarily in two places; the brain and the cunt. She felt the usual gross changes, the increased heartbeat, the dryness in the mouth, the slight lowering of temperature in the hands and feet, the contraction of tiny blood vessels in the eyes. But through all this, two throbbing realizations claimed her attention. Her point of view, her ego, was becoming more and more diffuse. And she was randy.

The events of the day, just a few moments ago so neatly ordered along the lines of chronological sequence and personal importance, now tumbled around in her memory like a basketful of clothes in a dryer. Her seven hours at the office covered the center of the porthole through which she idly gazed at her thoughts, much as a large sheet will dwarf and swallow up shirts, socks, towels and panties. The other dramas flashed intermittently.

The face of Eliot Dawson, her boss, appeared. A short beefy man with thick fingers and rough skin, the latter the product of inbred genes and many years of gin, he was, when Julia first met him, the most unattractive man she'd ever sat at dinner with. He had turned up in an obscure village along the coast of Yugoslavia, having dinner in the same restaurant that she and Martin had found simply by virtue of its being the place that was there when it was time to eat. They had parked their van and, with the help of a phrase book and the fact that the owner knew several words in English, had settled at their table when

Eliot walked in. They could see the gleam of his Mercedes as the door swung out behind him. It wasn't too long before it became obvious that they were all Americans, and Martin's invitation for the other man to join them was practically obligatory.

What Eliot Dawson lacked in looks and surface appeal he more than made up for in power. Personally worth between ten and fifteen million dollars, he ran a small company, virtually unknown outside the narrow field in which it operated, that bought and sold used coal mines. A property might be considered played out and be selling for very little. Eliot's engineers, either finding a new vein or in touch with a new process of extraction, would recommend a purchase. But the final decision was not made on the basis of technical reports alone, for Eliot flew to each site and walked over it and through it, his nose literally twitching, as acute as a dowsing rod. He bought more on the basis of hunch than of science, and he wasn't wrong more than one time in ten. When he sold, then, his profit was counted in the hundreds of thousands of dollars and his labor had involved nothing more complicated than the movement of a few men and the typing of a number of sheets of paper. He owned his own small jet, a helicopter, and suites of offices and apartments in New York, Paris, and Houston.

The three of them had got quite drunk and Eliot was not at all subtle in his alcoholically ponderous desire for Julia. She was both flattered and disgusted and might have been moved to respond if he had been less physically unattractive. Martin, sensing that there was no threat, cajoled and egged the other man on. This was something that Eliot, despite his drunkenness, understood the reason for and resented deeply. Later, when Julia went to work for him, he began a serious and ultimately successful campaign to get her into bed.

"Eliot," she said out loud, slurring the name, using it to no end, without meaning, intonation, or implication. It was just that, from her stoned state, she suddenly saw him as a caricature in the cosmic theater. And then, like a soldier's boot crushing a flower, the memory of the night before stomped on her mind. The darkness, the needle on the stereo stuck in a groove, she face down and sweating on her bed, and Eliot above her grinding his cock into her flesh.

A chill went through her and she shuddered, causing the hot water to ripple against the black porcelain of the tub. Her mind foundered and grasped at recollection to pull itself together again, and the first thing it grabbed was the encounter with the groper in the subway that morning. Having her ass and breasts felt by anonymous hands was one of the trivial ambiguities of life in the city. Occasionally she was sidled against by someone either so repulsive or intrusive that she grew angry. Once she made a scene, whirling about and shouting, "Take your hands off me, you creep!" causing the poor man, a portly business type in his fifties to close his eyes and pretend he had disappeared in a puff of smoke. But most mornings it was not unpleasant, all comfy amidst the bodies, the brain not yet fully awake, breakfast digesting in the belly, the lurching of the train providing a compulsory rhythm to which everyone in the cars was forced to dance. Then a whisper of knuckle or a bit of tactile insouciance from a fingertip were all part of the sensual stew. It rarely went further than that, but this morning had been a decided treat, a perfect parody of woman's magazine fantasy of a perfect experience. He got on at 96th Street, and by the time they reached Times Square he was actually massaging the space between her buttocks while she tensed her muscles ever so slightly in response. His skill was admirable and she never did get to see his face.

That would feel good now, she thought.

She shifted her weight and slid down a few inches further into the water. Waves lapped around her shoulders and throat. Her breasts bobbed lazily. Small tight currents played beneath the surface, making Julia aware of her buttocks and thighs as sentient wholes. She took a deep breath and some complex tension in her diaphragm let go. For the first time all day she came in touch with her body, knowing herself as a body, sensitive, delicate, capable of pleasure. Her usual state was like that of everyone else in the civilization, continually covered, armored. In clothing, in the formal distance of social convention, and in the subtle defenses she maintained against psychic abrasion, all of that stood witness to the fear that had been implanted from earliest infancy on. She had come to feel about presences and glances the way she judged caresses: they were enjoyable and tolerable only if presented with the utmost finesse and awareness of the neurotic personality which guarded the gate to surrender.

That was the one real pleasure of marriage, she thought. *At the end of a day there was someone to be naked with.*

It had been almost two months since she'd know that kind of relief, the undressing, touching, fingering, licking, and sucking. The relaxation, in short, however momentary, from the relentless aggressive alienation of daily life. Even when her sex life with Martin had become utterly predictable, there was something thrilling about simply being naked with a man, kissing with open mouths and reflex tongues, and then actually *doing it.* No matter how mundane, it was always fresh. Her hole going wet and grainy, mewling, obscene, as blind as a black orchid sweating in a greenhouse, and the phallic stem stirring the juices with indifferent vigor while the two people attached to the process made sounds, bit and bucked, thrashed about and fell into swoons. There was something sublimely dirty about the thing; it was such a straightforward illicit delight, so ugly and so transcendent.

"It wasn't wrong, it wasn't wrong!" she said to herself all at once, thinking of the night before, of her raging need to have a man inside her, of Eliot's raw strength, and then the phone call, Gall's worried voice.

Julia roused herself and leaned forward to pull the plug, letting water out of the tub. As it drained, she shivered again, and thought she heard a sound in the next room. The apartment held its breath and peered in upon itself through her consciousness now as alert as that of a mouse in a room with a cat. The silence of inanimate presence pressed against the noisy consciousness of animal life. Julia shook her head. It was nothing, only her imagination or a stray noise from the street. The only actual sound now was that of the tiny whirlpool doing its dance of dissolution into the copper drain. Julia sat motionless, spectator and actress on the stage of her life. Martin's absence had become palpable for a moment, and for a few seconds she feared breaking down into tears and self-pity. She was alone, a lively corpse taking a bath.

And all the manifest universe, for that instant, served as little more than scrollwork around the mirror of self-absorption.

Rousing herself from the posture of fixation, she put the plug back in and turned the spigot to let more hot water into the pool that had become her life raft. She was tripping freely, the push given by the marijuana continuing to swing her loose from the moorings of any fixed viewpoint, so that considerations about her job, memories of her husband, and the tingling recall of the morning's groper could not claim her attention for more than a brief cycle of development. She let the water run until the bath was almost scalding, turning her skin pink. In the rising steam, she saw Gail's face.

Gail was her oldest New York friend, and Eliot's lover for more than a year. Their relationship had quickly assumed that cinematic intimacy which marks closeness in our time, a way of being together which combines conversation about the most intimate matters with a brassiness of style, resulting in a tinny authenticity. Gail was coming over for drinks at eight and Julia was going to have to tell her what had happened or not tell her, two equally unpleasant possibilities.

"I can't deal with that now," she said to herself, and closed her eyes and slid back into the water, letting the heat take her away, away from all linear thought and concern for three-dimensional realities. She drifted gently, by degrees, into a soothing trance. Her senses disconnected from the associative centers of her brain. She still saw and heard and felt, but none of it registered, none of it meant. Her state went beyond even pleasure, for experience itself would have been too active, too brutal a process.

Thus, when a deep and familiar throbbing began in her belly, it carried no more import than the faint sound of traffic from ten stories below. And when the movement infiltrated her loins and crept past the walls of her cunt, slithering inside like guerrillas taking command of a forest while remaining invisible to the enemy army, she did not stir. Only a fantasy formed in her mind and she rose from her oceanic oblivion at random moments to watch the screen, much as a couple might catch glimpses of a movie between prolonged spasms of necking.

It was an astral masturbation, and its manifestations reached with measured slowness toward the physical. At first, her body made no gross movements at all. Her hand did not ease between her thighs nor did her fingers slide into folded moist places. Even at her most frustrated, Julia rarely masturbated, for she found erotic tension much too interesting to discharge in a bit of theatrics which had no audience. She knew that the modern liberated woman was supposed to masturbate and to find ideal pleasure, even identity, in the act, but Julia had always considered it a petty satisfaction, bereft of imagination, humor, and conversation. One had to be stupid to masturbate, she thought, unless it were done with someone else there. Her last attempt, two years earlier, had ended when, at the point of orgasm, she opened her eyes and saw herself reflected in the mirror which backed a closet door next to the bed. She looked like an arthritic acrobat trying to do a backbend as she pumped her hips spastically at the ceiling while rubbing her clitoris vigorously with the middle finger of her left hand. The grotesque visual once and for all imprinted its message of silliness on the act and two subsequent attempts had never got past the squirming stage. Of course, Martin's almost daily assault left little energy for languor, and so the whole issue had faded out of awareness. But now her two months without sex made more keen by the morning's groper and the previous night's appetizer with Eliot inclined her toward perceiving the value of something she had been too ready to dismiss.

She became formless, pure breath, and her subconscious perked like coffee on a hot stove. A boy, who had pulled her panties down when she was six and put his finger as far inside her as anatomy and bravery would allow. Sitting on her grandfather's lap eating an apple and feeling a hot tingling in her bottom. Her father glancing at her one night as she passed him in the hallway on the way to the bathroom; she was wearing a gauzy nightgown and nothing underneath, and when his eyes locked on her breasts her stomach clenched. The professor of anthropology who had been the first to take her anally, and then had free-associated in her ear throughout the entire time so that she had trouble paying attention to what went on between her buttocks. The first time she tasted sperm, sucking Martin a month after they had been married and suddenly seized by the hunger to have him fill her mouth.

And then even the images disappeared and she became pure physiology, a smorgasbord of functions. Heartbeat, circulation, vegetative pulses, plasmatic oozings, neurological twitchings. From the depths of inwardness a spark of pure erotic awareness was struck and a flame begun. In the region of her chest, in the vital center near the heart, a fire started to burn. It was sexual and spiritual both, and yet neither, for it was at the source of all manifestation, the source from which all levels of creation spring. She felt an intimation of reality itself, void, resplendent, having come upon her unexpectedly, unbidden, and during a period of bathtub catatonia. Yet Julia could not identify the state, for all her education had trained her to view that thing commonly called God as a mythic figure or an abstract concept. All she now knew was that her whole body had become a single yearning, a scorching poignancy, a cry for return. The heat in her body and the heat around her body, the divine flame and the prosaic hot water, were one and the same, and had the momentary dissolution of ego state been other than the result of a temporary conflux of circumstances, she might have sipped longer at the sweet satori.

But her focus snapped back with the harsh abruptness of a door's being opened into a dark bedroom and glaring white light's falling upon half-closed eyes. Julia sat up in the tub, lifting gallons of water with her, like a ghost trailing mists as it rises from the grave. For a few seconds she was in a blind panic. Shreds of thoughts flapped through her mind like demented bats, her skin screeched its protest at the sudden contact with the air, her heart thudded like loose baggage banging against the hull of a heaving ship in a storm. The room seemed to spin wildly about and for a moment she was certain she would faint. The fear of splashing back into the water, sliding down, her mouth and nostrils filling up, a sputter and a gasp, and then the harsh drowning, filled her all the way into their fingertips and caused her to grasp the sides of the tub. She held on for a full minute until she had regained her inner balance and began to calm down.

"That's pretty strong grass," she said out loud, happy to hear her voice.

She reached forward and pulled out the plug again, then sat hunched over, her breasts against her thighs, her arms around her shins, until the tub was completely empty. For a long while she could not move, and it took no little effort to stand up, draw the curtain, and start the shower running. She soaped herself vigorously but when she came to washing between her legs she was surprised to notice the secretions that had oozed from her cunt. She parted the lips and a brief flow of viscous fluid, pearly white, seeped from the pink petals and edged toward her thigh, to be stormed upon and swept away in a turbulent stream of water. She caressed her clitoris experimentally and her knees wobbled. She had built a charge of erotic energy far more powerful than she had been aware of.

Suddenly she wanted to be lying on a rug, her back lacerated by bristly animal hair, her legs hung wide, while a strong man moved with inexorable slowness and majesty into her, screwing her to the floor and soaring with her off the edges of brilliant precipices.

"Fat chance," she muttered as she stepped out of the tub and stood drying herself in front of the full length mirror, viewing herself with exaggerated scrutiny, wondering by what alchemy she might become a seething volcano of lust erupting to the beat of a man's steady want. Once again she was troubled by the notion that an itching in her crotch could, amplified and ramified, transform her into a pornographic movie.

She stepped out of the bathroom and into the apartment proper, originally three medium-sized rooms that had been converted into a single space by tearing the inside walls down. It had seemed a good idea when they moved in, flushed as they were with togetherness and the prospect of more spacious living. The total lack of privacy had, however, over time, proved deadly, and they reached that point, known by so many couples, where the mere presence of the other felt like sand in the eye.

But with Martin gone, the place was quite impressive and more than adequate. Sixty feet long by twenty-five feet wide, with windows on three sides. It was on the tenth floor of a turn-of-the-century building in Washington Heights. The views were of the entire lower two-thirds of the island of Manhattan with its spires and smog, of the Hudson River and the Jersey miasma behind it, and of the George Washington Bridge, path to the open spaces to the north and west. When the sky was clear, the sun set right through the four main windows, as it was now doing, turning everything golden. Julia stood there for several minutes, transfixed.

It's worth it, she thought, *the loneliness, the insecurity, even the randiness. All of it is worth it just to have this solitude.*

She gazed over the expanse of the apartment, its uneventful features and sparse furnishings made magical by the extraordinary light. From the kitchen against the far wall to the bed and bureau against the other, with the middle space filled with floor pillows, some chairs, a television, stereo and odd pieces, the place had the air of a stage set on which a bit of off-Broadway theatre was about to be enacted.

Julia glanced at the clock. It was six-forty. Gail was due in an hour and twenty minutes. Julia went to the clothes closet, picked out a semi-transparent nightgown and shrugged into it. Then she fixed herself a vodka and tonic and sat down to try to figure out what she would tell her friend.

Martin threw off his towel, stretched, and stepped into the steam room. At thirty-five, he owned a physique that made most men wince in secret envy. He was fairly tall, a bit under six feet, and his entire life, from the age of fifteen, had been devoted to physical exercises. He had majored in Physical Education in college and earned a Master's Degree in Gymnastics.

His body type was closest to that of a swimmer, lean, lithe, the muscles flat and smooth. He had no sympathy for the bulk attained by weightlifters, knowing it to be detrimental to the most efficient functioning of the body. His own preference was for the parallel bars where he twirled himself about with lazy precision, belying the terrible strength necessary to accomplish the repertoire of rolls, twists and balancing postures.

He slid the glass door shut behind him and moved into the dense white cloud of heat. At once all his muscles relaxed. This was the most precious moment of the day for him. For the past three years he had worked as Manager of the West Side Health Spa, one of the dozens of emporia catering to the sudden compulsive interest in fitness among the office workers of Manhattan. It was as though, as the city itself continued its long slide into full decay, large numbers of people began to seek salvation in the care and grooming of their bodies.

The job itself required very little in the way of physical exertion. He planned exercise programs, interviewed prospective members, and exerted a general influence over the staff, mostly out-of-work dancers and actors. It was something he had seized upon when he moved to New York with Julia after their year in Europe. It did not provide the satisfaction of infusing young boys with a sense of the beauty of the body, but it paid more than three times as much as teaching and did allow a certain pleasure of prestige. In any case, he was forced to agree with Julia that it would be pointless to return to small town life and attempt to pick up where they had left off.

The other advantage of his current position was that he had use of its fairly sophisticated facilities. He worked out every evening, an hour before closing, serving as an incentive or a discouragement for those members who were there to watch him in his narcissistic dance through space. Then, when everyone but the staff had left, Martin, sweating and happy, went to his office, shut off the Muzak, and strolled to the steam room where he sank into the tingling oblivion of athletic exhaustion.

Now he lay down on the raised tile platform, sighed, and let himself melt. It was the single most exquisite experience he knew. More profound than sleep, more subtle than drink, more satisfying than sex, the utter abandonment of focus following the period of formal intensity provided Martin with the enjoyment of a state he could only describe as bliss. At such times he often drifted into a deep trance within which vast movements occurred. Awesome galaxies of obscured meaning drifted past brilliant rays of pure light which seemed to emanate from the very source of creation itself. Or memories of childhood might skip across the screen of his adult consciousness. Yet he was completely without a vocabulary with which to appreciate, and thus distort, awareness.

This night, as he let go, as his fingers uncurled, and the subliminal tension in his eyeballs dissolved so that he stopped the habit of looking which usually persists even with the eyelids down, a vision of Julia arose like a specter from the grave to embrace him with icepick anguish. The history of their relationship skimmed across the surface of his memory.

When they met she was teaching English at the same school and their nodding acquaintanceship, lunches, dating, sleeping together and marriage had followed a pattern totally without surprises. The surprise came afterwards when Julia began to manifest a sharp restlessness that Martin had never suspected in her. She began to complain about the small town they lived in, the tedium of spending the bulk of one's time with teenagers, and the meaninglessness of processing students year after year like cars on a conveyor belt. There was nothing in which she said that he hadn't given thought to, but she had imparted an urgency which he found compelling.

Their years in the city had been tumultuous, beginning with finding a new apartment and ending with their final fight about Martin's desire for a child. Instead of enjoying their marriage, they merely defended it or held on to it. And finally, they abandoned it. The breakup had come two months earlier when, in classic style, Martin packed two suitcases, and three boxes of belongings into a friend's car and moved to a hotel.

The door to the steam room slid open and was quickly closed. There was a slight drop in temperature as a bolt of cool air was sucked into the space. Martin was abruptly pulled from his reverie, something which ordinarily annoyed him. But now he welcomed the interruption, for thoughts of Julia invariably ended in upsetting fantasies, seeing her with another man or getting mugged or raped. He turned his head to one side to face the door.

"Sorry to disturb," a soft melodic voice said.

"Oh, Robert," Martin replied. "It's you."

"It usually is," the other man said.

Robert's tall thin body suddenly emerged from the hot white

cloud. He was the yoga instructor at the spa and by this time the only one who had been there longer than Martin. Teaching yoga was his chosen profession so, unlike the other employees, he manifested a certain professionalism which Martin appreciated. The two men had developed that kind of intimate anonymity which acts as social currency in most work situations. Over a period of time they had accumulated a great deal of feeling for the texture of one another's lives and had learned to read each other's moods with almost complete accuracy. Yet, neither knew the other's exact address. Their central conversation revolved around a discussion of the various virtues of yogic versus calisthenic approaches to fitness. And whenever they finished talking about the matter on the level of physiology, Robert would add, "But the yoga that you see, the actual postures and movements, is only the vehicle for something else. It isn't an end in itself." He had steadfastly refused to discuss that aspect of it further, saying that it would reveal itself when Martin was ready.

Aside from this, what he considered a tone of surperiority in Robert's attitude, Martin liked the man well enough, and even felt drawn to him. His involvement with his relationship to Julia, however, absorbing to the point of obsession, had kept him from fuller contacts with anyone else, including Robert.

"You do the corpse pose better than anyone I've ever seen," Robert said, referring to Martin's posture on the slab, lying on his back, legs apart, arms at his sides. "Sometimes I'm afraid you'll get into it so deeply that I'll come in here and find only your body remaining." He sat down on the lower tier just below where Martin lay.

"That's happened, you know," he went on. "A few Masters have done it just to show off. Lie down in the middle of the morning in front of a room full of students, tell them that he was going to leave the body permanently, and then, in the prime of health, just close his eyes, reduce his breathing, and die."

Martin involuntarily pulled himself up to a half-sitting position. Robert's laconic description had acted like a puppeteer's string pulling him to a state of vacant attention. Death was something he thought about only in terms of the effect it would have on other people. The concept, unexamined, was encrusted with images of funerals, grieving family, friends who quickly forgot, and the choking smell of too many flowers kept in a small room for several days. Its metaphysical implications never grazed him for he had always been too healthy to truly feel its immediate presence. The idea, just implanted by Robert's offhand report, that one might choose simply to cease to exist, and to do it as a sort of object-lesson for students, to do it whimsically and consciously, assaulted him with all the force of an outrage.

"That's just another one of those extravagant tales, isn't it?" he asked.

"Oh no," Robert replied, "there have been several well-documented accounts. One as recently as four years ago."

"But that's just a form of suicide!" Robert protested, swinging himself up to a sitting position, his legs dangling down over the edge of the platform.

"Only if you make a distinction between life and death," Robert said. "To one who has understood the true nature of reality, there is no difference between the two."

A peculiar thing took place in Martin's mind. On one level he responded with his usual cantankerous refusal to accept anything which fell outside of Aristotelian logic. A was A, had always been A, would always be A, and could never be B. Yet, on another level, some tension in him relaxed and a delicious vision stole through him. He saw himself sitting in the steam room and yet, somehow, disappearing. The thing he called himself was, miraculously, not operating. Yet nothing changed. His body continued to function, Robert continued to exist, the walls, the steam, the club, the city, the planet, the entire universe, went on completely unchanged. For an instant he *saw* the truth of what Robert had said. It made absolutely no difference to anything whether one was alive or dead. Everything went on as before.

The sheer unacceptability of it, however, almost immediately drove the vision from his mind. The abrupt voice of rational cynicism reminded him, in a raucous whisper, that the essential difference between his condition now and the condition of his death was that in the latter he would be *dead,* an eternal state of nothingness. On the brink of that panic Martin pulled himself together and returned solidly to his sense of himself as a body. He weighed a hundred and sixty-three pounds, he was sweating, he was thirsty. This was real. Robert was an amiable nut who was filled with Oriental gothic tales, not to be taken seriously.

The two men sat silently, side by side, one above the other, for some time. The space was without sound except for an occasional drop of water falling from the ceiling and the periodic whoosh of fresh steam erupting into the room. Each began to sweat copiously, the pores of the body opening and water running out, cleansing, purifying. Each entered a deep, meditative mood, aware of little else besides breathing and the automatic functions of the body. Heartbeat, muscle tone, thought, circulation, balance. They entered a mood of kinesthetic sobriety, much like two truckers who spend an evening hunched over their beers, yet without the truculence, the simmering secret search for a target.

Finally, Martin surfaced. "Do you really believe that?" he asked, "I mean, about life and death being the same thing?"

Robert uncoiled his rounded back and stretched his arms up. His spine cracked in four different places. Martin could almost see the sparks of energy from the spots where the cartilege was dislodged. He momentarily wondered whether the phenomenon was healthy and ran quickly through the memory log of his physiology studies, but couldn't retrieve anything pertinent.

"It's not a belief," Robert replied, his voice very low with relaxation. "It's not like saying that black is white. Of course, from one level of perception, they are vastly different states. I guess what is meant is that a person should view both with equal indifference, not try to hold on to life as being more meaningful than death."

"You sound like you're not sure."

"Well, I'm still a student. I've had glimpses into the truth of this teaching, but I'm very far from being a realized man." He chuckled, to himself, as though at some esoteric joke. "Very far indeed."

"Come on!" Martin protested. "I've seen you practically crawl up your own asshole. You do things with your body that I'd never even dreamed of doing. You look like much more than student to me."

"On the level of hatha yoga, the development of physical harmony and strength, I am already an adept, that's true. But as I said, that's only the vehicle for something much more profound."

"The life and death thing?"

Robert did not answer for a long time. Martin could almost hear him thinking. The yoga teacher stood up and his head disappeared into the mist so that when he spoke the voice seemed to come from a headless body.

"Has something happened in your life recently?" he asked. "Forgive me for prying, but it's just that I sense a significant change in you. I've been wanting to really talk to you for a long time, but you were somehow closed at a very deep level, even though you've always been friendly enough on a superficial level."

For a moment, Martin was taken aback, and then he shrugged. "I shouldn't be surprised if it shows, especially to someone who's spent a lot of time with me for almost three years." He ran the middle fingers of both hands into the hallows of his eyes and wiped away the film of perspiration which was at the very edge of condensing into drops.

"My wife and I split up two months ago," he went on. He had no conscious intention of saying more, but found the words sliding out from between his lips. "There wasn't even a cause, I mean, nothing that you could bring up in a divorce trial, although she refused to have a baby for four or five more years and that became an arguing point. I guess it began to go sour when I let myself be swayed by her restlessness and quit my job. I was happy as a teacher. But there was the excitement of Europe and, when we got back, the appeal of the city. I'd always lived a kind of sheltered small town life and for a while I got drunk on New York. Julia began making a fabulous salary working for a man we'd met in Yugoslavia who told her she had all the makings of a high-powered executive. I got this job and began making more than three times what I earned as a high school instructor. So we lived high off the hog. And . . . I don't know, I guess in the busyness and glitter we just lost sight of . . ." His voice trailed off. "Well, maybe we didn't really have a common vision to begin with. And it just took five years for us to realize it. We reached that point of not communicating. We found excuses to stay away from the apartment. I began to suspect that she was having an affair. And I began to think of having one myself. And then one evening we got into another argument over having a child. I said I wanted one. She said she didn't I don't imagine that was anything more than a symbol. But the anger provided us with the energy to do what we needed to. I packed my bags, and moved into a hotel."

Martin sat silently for a few minutes, his perspiration now coming as much from his outburst as from the steam. Then he wiped his forehead and laughed, a harsh brief expulsion of air. "It's peculiar," he said, "summing up five years of my life in a paragraph."

"Babba says that when we die we see that our whole life has been nothing but a brief thought."

"That's an odd form of consolation," Martin said.

"It's just his way of reminding us that this drama we live out from day to day is not very important."

"What else is there?"

"God," Robert said.

"Another odd form of consolation."

"Sometimes it's reassuring, sometimes it's not. The point is that it's a reality. In fact, it's the only reality. There is only God. And within that, there's just a grab-bag of details, none intrinsically more interesting than any other."

"You really believe that?" Martin asked. "Again, it's not a matter of belief. You either see it or you don't."

"And do you see it? Do you see God like that? What is it, a kind of screen on which we're the movie?"

"That's one metaphor. Every religion, every person, has their own image of God. But the great teachers remind us over and over again that any image we make of God is not God. God isn't a thing, or a person, or even an experience. God is . . ." Now it was Roberts turn to fall silent. He turned and walked to the other end of the steam room, becoming completely invisible.

"God is . . .?" Martin repeated.

"God is," Robert concluded. "That's about as far as language can go. After that, there is only realization, actually knowing yourself as God. And for that, you can stand on your head for a thousand years and not necessarily come any closer to that truth."

"Then why bother?"

"Because it's possible," Robert replied, his disembodied voice wafting through the steam. For an instant Martin sensed a peculiar parallel to the experience of Moses talking to a burning bush. "There are people who have realized themselves as God, who live as God."

"Jesus," Martin offered.

"He was one. Buddha, Lao Tzu, Krishna, Ramana Maharshi. There have been quite a number."

"Who's around today?" Martin asked, openly cynical.

"Babba is one," Robert said simply.

"Babba. You've mentioned that name a couple of times now. Is he one of these Indians whose pictures you see plastered everywhere?"

Robert did not answer and Martin waited several minutes before speaking again. He was beginning to feel the effects of the steam deep in his body. It was almost like getting drunk. He had told Robert about his breakup with Julia and now the two of them were discussing God. It was rather strange, and interesting, and exhilarating. Martin felt a loosening in his solar plexus, the beginning of a relaxation of a knot that he now saw must have been a very long time in forming.

"Excuse me," he said at last, "I didn't mean to insult your teacher."

"Oh no, no, nothing like that," Robert replied. "I was just wondering whether . . . well, whether you might not want to come with me tonight. I'm going to Babba's. It's an open meeting."

Martin's instinctive response was to refuse. For years he had trained himself to turn down all forms of invitation, counteracting his impulse to step out into relative chaos. Numberless times he had felt the calloused hand of routine grab him by the shoulder when he would have preferred to fall into a space of unstructured time. During his daily workout and subsequent steam a kind of lilting melody would play, like a randomly fingered turn on a shepherd's flute, luring him into a night of pathless pleasure. Such a course was almost invariably festooned with vague intimations of erotic surprises, but it was not sexual liberty per se he really desired; simply the liberty itself, the chance to be guided only by chance.

Now he hesitated and felt the weight of all the times he had denied himself access to the void, to the formlessness of virgin encounter. Going with a yoga teacher to see an Indian holy man was the least likely thing he might have imagined himself doing when free of the need to report home each night. But because it offered itself in the context of his perception of the pattern of refusal, he decided that he would do it.

"I don't know . . ." he said, extending himself tentatively.

"It's at nine o'clock," Robert said. "We'll have time to have dinner and talk beforehand."

"What do people do there? Maybe I won't fit in."

"Oh, there's nothing to do. We sit around. Sometimes we sing. Sometimes we are just silent. Then Babba gives a talk and answers questions."

"Well, all right."

Just then there was a loud knock at the door of the steam room. A false falsetto voice called out. "Can I turn the steam off, or would you two rather stay all covered up and cozy?"

Freddie, one of the attendants, was an overtly gay man of twenty-four, short and chubby. He generally gave the impression of being asexual, so his homosexual veneer was taken as an artifact of identification to keep himself from facing his essential lack of desire or desirability. He was destined, if he maintained the same manner long enough, to evolve into a classic auntie, possibly complete with frills on his cuffs. His bit, acerbic and fluffy, ranged from the irrelevant to the amusing and was irritating only when one was obsessed with a task or had a headache. He had been at the club a year while he took courses in watch repair. His goal was to own a shop which handled rare and antique clocks.

"Turn it off, Freddie," Martin called out.

"Can I peek?" Freddie shrilled.

"If watching a conversation turns you on, come right in,"

Martin said as he slid the door open. He had padded quickly
to the sliding door and pushed it aside precisely to give the
attendant a start.

But Freddie was waiting for him, and Martin found himself
no more than a foot away from the theatrically leering man.
Freddie slid his glance down Martin's front until it came to rest
at his crotch.

"Some conversation," Freddie said turning gracefully on
one heel and sauntering away. "I've read all about that body
language."

Martin smiled after the retreating figure. Unable and unwilling
to probe the complexity of Freddie's persona, he took the man
totally at face value, which served perfectly as the adjustment
which allowed them to work in the same place with a minimum
of friction. The chubby man's style was so consciously outrageous
that it never would have occurred to Martin that it was a valid
and viable way to speak the truth of one's plain perceptions.
Never having been in contact with any urge to fondle another
man's genitals, Martin could only view the suggestion of such a
thing as a baroque form of humor.

At that instant, Robert put his hand on Martin's shoulder.
Martin winced violently, his entire right side evincing a sharp,
momentary spasm.

"Oh, sorry," Robert said, "I didn't mean to startle you." He
pulled his hand back gently.

"Oooohhh wheeeee!" Freddie trilled as he waddled down
the tiled hallway into the locker room. He was by this time
projecting his inner states to a vast audience far more sensitive
and appreciative than anything one might ever expect at the
Palace.

Martin and Robert stepped into the walkway. "Well," Martin
said somewhat briskly. "Shower and then close the place down.
The night crew will be here to clean up in a few minutes."

"I'll meet you out front in fifteen minutes then?" Robert asked.
"What sort of food do you like?"

Martin shrugged. "I don't know. It's your show. Why don't
you choose?"

Robert smiled, and the two men went into the shower room,

taking a stalls at opposite ends. As Martin lathered his body, and sluiced the perspiration from his skin, he thought of a snake shedding, of that delightful process whereby the accumulations of a year are simply eased off one's body. *If it could only be that easy for people,* he thought, and suddenly, unaccountably, a feeling of happiness bubbled from his solar plexus and up into his chest. The water cascaded over his head and down his face and he opened his eyes to find that the shower room seemed five times brighter than it ordinarily did, as though a brilliant new bulb had just gone on.

All the while, Robert, who knew that there wasn't anything existing which isn't miraculous, had visions of the cosmic snake swallowing its own tail. He said the name "Babba" to himself, barely whispering, and then smiled.

The conventional world had lost all reality for Gail Goddard. All that mattered was the shimmering aura of color that surrounded her perceptions. The dominant tone was blue, a bright mantle of light which blessed everything she saw the way a summer sky without clouds transforms the earth beneath it. She sat in the back seat of a taxi and felt as though she were being wafted aloft on a glider, skimming mountain peaks on cushiony thermals. Her nipples rubbed against the inside of her blouse and her thighs chafed pleasantly against each other. Her entire body sang with the vitality of youth and well-being.

She was twenty-seven years old, as thin as a model, with just a touch of plumpness about the buttocks, a soft swelling that lifted men off balance when they looked at her but which caused her no little grief in trying somehow to remove it. Her yellow-green eyes sparkled in a face that would have driven Botticelli to his canvas to capture the high cheekbones and androgynous mouth, the upper lip firm and precise, the lower lip suggestive of a pout.

She inhabited a mood of total euphoria, one which her day at school hadn't been able to faze. She taught fourth grade in a public school in Williamsburg, Brooklyn, a Hassidic neighborhood lately inhabited by Puerto Ricans. The sidewalks resembled a divorce court, with the two ethnic groups arguing why they should be allowed to live separately even though they shared the same block. The ultra-orthodox Jews sent their children to their own schools, so among Gail's charges, thirty-two eleven-year-olds, many barely spoke English. Her job often involved a good deal of screaming and threatening, for she had not yet reached that level of maturity which elicits spontaneous respect from children. Also, she felt she had to uphold the official educational dogma, and so dutifully taught the uncomprehending urchins all about the French and Indian War, the formal structure of the United States government, and other bits of esoterica.

Were it left to her, she would ground them firmly in the scope of the English language and mathematics, and devote the rest of the time to music and dance and games. Yet she was too unsure of herself to be so daring, and in any case, such radicalism would have cost her her job. So, like all her colleagues, she acquiesced in the stupidity.

After classes, she'd returned home and spent the afternoon literally fluttering about, bathing, getting a bit high, staring out the window, playing with her cat. She was going to see Julia at eight, and until then had nothing to do but think about the extraordinary event of the night before, Eliot's proposal of marriage.

It had been a year since she'd met him in Julia's office. She'd been somewhat put off by the short, squat man with his blunt fingers and vulgar staring at her breasts. But at the same time, something in her had tingled. Perhaps it was the wealth he controlled, or some unworked-out fantasy about being whisked about the world in a private jet. The speculation about prostitution, which visits most people who are honest with themselves, had struck her sharply, given that fact that it could become a reality, and it carried more clout than she'd expected. She was old and knowledgeable enough to understand that her probable destiny, given the way her life was moving, held nothing more fascinating than becoming a spinster schoolteacher, or the wife of a high school principal. Unless she were rescued by some utopian adventure or a pleasant bit of wickedness, she had many dull years to look forward to.

When Eliot came on to her, directly, strongly, holding out

a promise of promises, she found herself responding to the potential behind the invitation. He took her number, called her two days later, and that night she was lying on his bed, looking at herself in the mirror fastened to his ceiling, as he reamed her wildly and piled into her like a fullback blasting into a line. That much she was prepared for, but what took her totally by surprise was the tenderness that followed. Her orgasm had been hard and fierce, a grinding affair which had her tucking her cunt down between her thighs, contracting her buttocks until they were rock hard, and offering Eliot nothing but a simple hot hole to fuck. Her pelvic resistance was offset by the wealth of expressiveness showing on her face. He had to fuck her for more than an hour to get past all the obvious defenses she threw up around letting go. It was a game he enjoyed more than any other. It was always a bit strange for him when beautiful women went to bed with him. He knew that they were usually mesmerized by his wealth, but he didn't understand how that translated into the odd forms of abandon they manifested once they were both naked. He did not have the capacity for abstract thought which would have uncovered the connecting factor: the same force which drove Eliot to power and money revealed itself in his love-making, a kind of sensitive brutality almost irresistible to vulnerable women.

Gail's attitude had been, "Let the son of a bitch work!" She found herself curious about what he would be like, what it would feel like to have all that energy exploding inside her. But she wasn't going to give anything away. Ironically, by holding back, she gave everything away. For Eliot knew how to go after a woman, how to punish and how to caress, how to thrust and how to hold back, how to tease and how to satisfy. And he was tireless. And a true enjoyer. He moved into her from a score of different angles, moving until he could feel the juices flowing in her and then, before she could reposition herself, would shift direction and speed, catching her off guard, probing yet another stretch of her secret cunt. All the while his hands and eyes glutted themselves on the feast beneath him, the naked breasts, so bold and defenseless, and her priceless ass, lean and lush.

The part he liked best was pressing his lips against her mouth and catching her moans in his throat. After a long time, she began to break up inside. Her legs parted and rose into the air, her arms circled his shoulders, her tongue flooded his mouth, her eyes flew back inside her head, and she pumped her hips steadily and wantonly into his pistoning cock. When she began to come he felt the beginnings of his own orgasm. They held on to one another tightly and then let go, forgetting who was tall and who was short, who was beautiful and who was ugly, who was rich and who was poor, who was man and who was woman.

Later he was solicitous, kind, even making them both a midnight snack, and over coffee they talked about their lives, openly, simply. The magic of sex had worked its wonders once more and two people who had been anonymous creatures now saw one another as intimates.

When Gail woke up the following morning, she suffered an emotional hangover. There were several minutes when she might have pushed herself out of bed, dressed, and left without a backward glance, glad to have had the experience and even happier to be finished with it. Eliot lay on his side, his face darkened by a one-day growth of beard, showing his age in the texture of his skin. She slid over to the far side of the bed and sat on the edge of the mattress. Something caused her to hesitate. She felt his eyes on her back and knew he had awakened also. He rolled over toward her. She half turned. It was a very naked moment. They did not have the excuse of nighttime intoxication; of the wine, of the adventure of exploration . . . the almighty first time. They knew each other's smells and blemishes and evidences of mortality. They had heard each other's stories. They had served as handles for each other's fantasies. They were even, and could quit clean, without blame, without bad feeling, without any imbalance.

But something drew her back, some shifting heaviness in her chest which had her sagging back, falling by degrees onto the sheet, her face coming to rest on his thigh. She shuddered, closed her eyes, and took his cock into her mouth. As she went down on him, he ran his fingers through her hair. She blew him until he came and she swallowed his sperm, the first man with whom she'd done that in nearly a year.

They saw each other heavily for two or three months after that. She wasn't taken for a ride in his jet, but she ate at restaurants she hadn't known existed, places which had no sign out front and no prices on the menu. She got to know what it felt like to drive to East Hampton in a Bently. Expensive trinkets collected on her dressing table. When he gave her a brooch worth eight thousand dollars she knew she had crossed a definite line. And it took nothing for him to slip a folded packet of hundred-dollar bills into her hand and say, "Why don't you treat yourself to something beautiful, Beautiful?"

One morning she could no longer hide from herself the fact that she was hooked. She liked the sensation of floating about on a magic carpet of money. She liked the flow which surrounded powerful people. She liked the way he fucked her.

"All right," she said to herself, "I'm a kept woman. I've had fantasies about it, and it's happened. Now what?"

Then the game began to get really interesting. For while he had her, she also had him. He had developed an addiction for the taste of her, and he followed that through with the same practical ruthlessness which marked his business dealings. One night he slid beneath her, his mouth sucking at her cunt, and asked her to pee on him. She had grown faint and for the first and only time in their relationship, made a mistake. She was thrown into a scene for which she had only a hearsay scenario, and so she told him to beg for it, which she guessed might be what he expected. He had pushed her off him so hard she landed on the floor, flying five feet from the middle of the bed. The fall knocked the wind out of her and when she opened her eyes he was standing over her. His face was a frightening mask.

"You get to me," he said, his fists clenched. "And I'm a little crazy about you. So much so that I want to drink your piss. Which is as weird for me as it must be for you. But don't you ever lose your respect for me. Even if I'm licking your asshole, don't you lose your respect for me. And I'll return the favor."

An illumination filled her then, and she felt something which she had forgotten could exist, that sudden direct perception which brings another human being into powerful focus. She could see him with total clarity, down to the lines of his thought.

To have called it love would not have been accurate, but in terms of the complete emotional awakening she experienced, the effect was the same.

"What if he asks me to marry him?" was her first thought. And immediately upon that came the certain knowledge that Eliot wanted a child.

But no mention was ever made of that, and the moment of naked encounter was slid into the pouch of the past and never referred to, even telepathically. Months stretched into a year, and as Gail chugged to Julia's apartment in the rusted Checker cab, fourteen months had passed since the night Eliot first took her out. Their meetings had become somewhat routine. He was out of town about a third of the year. During those times, she was free to do what she pleased. When he was in the city, however, it was tacitly understood that she was on call. He might see her four times a week, or not at all for ten days. Without an explicit agreement ever written down, she understood that she should be home no later than midnight on any night when they didn't have a firm date, in case he should want her at the last minute of his day's schedule. This in itself was not an overly irksome bind, for in any relationship the details of time and space must find some agreement. And when two people are fond of one another, considerate, and genuinely in touch, their desire to be together authentic, what might be a frustrating responsibility becomes a pleasant discipline. Since the night when Gail realized that she and Eliot had feelings for one another which subsumed all the differences of age and looks and wealth, an attitude of forgivingness spontaneously arose in her and bathed all their dealings with a soothing oil.

Then, the night before, Eliot stood her up. He was to have picked her up at her apartment, a place he disliked intensely because it was so small, so inconveniently placed in relation to his usual route of movement, and because it was so, as he put it, "poor." Two hours passed beyond the appointed time, and she began to go through that well-known misery of worry born between anger and fear. She called his Madison Avenue penthouse, but there was no answer. Even his manservant was not home. She speculated that he'd been called away on business, but he would have phoned. The only alternative was that he had been seriously injured or killed. She was astonished, and laughed out loud, when she saw that her first thought upon considering that he might be dead was the hope that he'd left her a lot of money in his will.

As it was, she accepted nothing from him on any sort of regular basis. The gifts and treats were fine, but she insisted, despite his urgings, that she keep her job, her apartment, and her general lifestyle, including the way she dressed. The ermine stole hung in her closet. She wore it occasionally, around the house, after showers when she needed something to serve as a housecoat. She knew by untaught intuition that if she became financially dependent on him the resultant bondage would destroy them both.

When three hours had passed she was beside herself with agitation, talking out loud to herself, cursing Eliot, praying for his safety. Finally, she had called Julia, who seemed distant, involved in her own problems, and who offered her nothing but cliches, a litany of probabilities. But the voice was comforting, and the reassurance of an ancient context, the embrace of women when men are off to war. Julia was at the point of telling Gail for the tenth time that Eliot was *probably all right* when Gail heard the lock snap in the front door, and saw Eliot walk in.

Now that he was there, now that he was palpably safe, the tension between worry and anger cracked, and all the energy that Gail had been using to keep her fears at bay was suddenly released to roar full force into the more violent wing of feeling. At once she was furious, vindictive, mean. Now no excuse of his could possibly suffice to placate her. He had offended her beyond words, and she would tear him apart.

None of this proceeded as a conscious process, nor was it immediately apparent in her behavior. She simply looked at him while he removed his jacket, his tie, kicked off his shoes and loosened the top button of his shirt.

"He's here," she said into the phone, her voice level.

"Oh, how wonderful," Julia said. "You see," she went on, "you did all that worrying for nothing."

"Yea-a-ahhh," Gail drawled. And then, after a pause, giving

Julia the warm back draft from the malevolence she was beginning to thrust at Eliot, she said, "Thanks an awful lot, love. I'll talk to you tomorrow."

When Eliot finally glanced over at Gail, he knew he was in for it. What made it worse was that he was guilty, in large letters. And in a way that was totally beyond his ability to expiate. He had been with another woman, but the woman was Julia.

He and his secretary had already had a fling, more than a year ago. It had run its course within two weeks, and had included three nights of pernicious ass fucking, acting out the slave-master undercurrent that informed all their daily business vibrations but which they were too civilized and too fixed on fiscal efficiency to get mired in. They rationalized the affair as a necessary blowing-out of gaskets, the way a person who drives a car in the city all the time will occasionally take it on the highway and run it at a hundred miles an hour just to give the engine its head, let it feels its power, and blast an the accumulated soot of mediocre speeds from its metal chambers.

When they met for the final night, they decided that that would be the final night. Julia's guilt over Martin, the potential havoc that an emotional storm might have on the business, and the fact that they enjoyed the carnal combat a bit too much for comfort, brought them to this reasonable conclusion. But they had tasted blood, and both sensed that one day they would return for another bite, if only a quick one. Often, when Eliot watched Julia move past his desk, a taut curve in a tight dress, he remembered her kneeling under him, sucking at his cock with her asshole, her buttocks opening and closing like spastic clamshells. And she caught his glances in the pit of her tight hole, twitching momentarily at the thought of all those millions of dollars' worth of raw force distilled in a hard cock and mean mind reaming her until she fainted, overwhelmed and corrupt.

That afternoon had proved the destined time. Julia was sending off the horny news that there was no longer any man in her bed. Eliot had known about the formal breakup, of course, but it took a week for the impact of the fact to hit them both, and almost two months to detonate. And when it did strike, they fell like soldiers before machine guns. Eliot, who hadn't been thrown off balance in twenty years, allowed himself the mistake of not even calling Gail to cancel their date.

He couldn't stay at the office or go to his own apartment because Gail would be calling both places, and even he wasn't callous enough to be fucking Julia while his mistress and her best friend was ringing the phone. So, when the space between him and Julia got so thick that they could barely talk, he offered to drive her home after work. She accepted, her knees a bit weak. And they were on her bed, drinking coffee and relaxing after a two-hour fuck when Gail called, using the special signal— two rings, hang up, then call again—that Julia had given to her friend because she wasn't answering the phone to anyone else.

"Oh Lord, that's Gail," Julia had said, realizing for the first time that she was not only putting herself in a situation in relation to Martin should he find out, but also to Gail. She was in bed with her best friend's lover. Yet she felt compelled to pick up the receiver.

As Gail spoke, spilling out her worry, Julia understood the deeper horror of the situation. Eliot had stood her up in order to accomplish this tryst. As her eyes narrowed, Eliot saw that he was in double jeopardy, and should Martin find out, it would be triple. He and Julia carried on a conversation in gestures and eye contact as he dressed and maneuvered his way out of the apartment. He sped to Gail's place and found her still on the phone when he arrived. He saw from her look that Julia had not told her the truth, so he was off that particular hook. But he now had to face Gail's anger. And he was wise enough in the ways of the world to know that she would use this incident as an excuse to unload on him every resentment she had garnered for the past year.

"A beast of a day, darling," he shouted out with gruff forced humor. The best tactic was to smooth over any reference to the fact that he had kept her waiting for three hours. They both knew it, but any words calling attention to it would merely serve as detonator for the explosion. He needed to buy time and space. The first to allow her to go through some changes on her own before focusing on him, and the second to take a shower. For if the fight went as these things usually did, it would end spontaneously in a fuck. But he still had vaseline and Julia's secretions in his pubic hair and on his fingers. It might go unnoticed, but that was taking a very big chance. He was prepared, as a last-ditch concession, to admit that he'd had another woman, a prostitute he would say, but preferred not having to go that far.

"I suppose you're going to explain," Gail said. Her voice was fingers stuck to an ice cube tray pulled right out of the freezer. Her eyes were those of the captain of a life raft looking down as he clubbed your fingers off the rim because your weight was dragging the boat down. She had all the force of moral righteousness behind her, that quality which has launched crusades and bloodbaths of all kinds. His crime had tied him to the post and she was flicking the whip to test its power of attack.

He was caught edging back toward the bathroom. He was so far off guard that he imagined his smell carried across the room and that Gail was already picking up the aroma of an alien beast.

It's so fucking feral, he thought. *We pride ourselves on our sophistication and intelligence as human beings but the only thing we get from our big brain is the ability to deal with our biology in a more shifty way.*

"I'm sorry, darling, you know I am," he said, knowing that his best tactic would be to soften his posture, to move toward her, to say in body language what could only be exacerbated by words. But there was the smell. He couldn't afford to get too close.

"It's like being a teenager again," he said to himself. "Be home by nine o'clock, don't stay with that rough crowd, do your homework, brush your teeth."

"I'm an awful mess," he said out loud. "I just have to have a shower before anything else." And then, with a stroke of virtuoso daring, "Would you be a sweetheart and make me a drink? I'll just be a minute." And before she could recover from his request, before she found the pacing once more, he had zipped away and was inside the bathroom with the door latched behind him.

She glared at the door for a few seconds, and then went into the kitchen to prepare a vodka martini. The first broadside had ended without any serious damage on either side, and was more like a skirmish than an outright battle, having the flavor of two battleships feeling each other out before getting down to serious warfare.

Gail smiled grimly to herself as she made the drink, acting out the ritual of tumbler, ice, alcohol, and lemon. Part of her couldn't help but be relieved that he was back; her worry had been genuine. But now he had to pay for making her worry, and she was to be allowed to whip him until her anger was drained. Afterwards, she knew, they would make love. It was perfectly obvious to her that he had been with another woman. Its very transparency, in fact, provided the edge of amusement that kept her anger from total venom. She knew that he was at that very moment washing off the traces of the crime.

Gail wasn't jealous of Eliot on the level of superficial encounters. She knew the sort of appeal he had, and the amazing resources of erotic energy. During an average day, he would come into contact with several high-powered attractive women, or young impressionable secretaries. *It's odd,* she pondered, *one thinks of a secretary as somehow being in a different category from a woman, as though it were a species all its own.* She knew that Eliot loved her, insofar as he was able to love, given his enormous defense against feelings. He often reminded her of the little boy who, at the end of the cowboy film, is disgusted that the hero kisses the heroine instead of his horse. She would have been threatened to the core if she had had any suspicion of his approaching a serious relationship with someone else; but when she imagined him with a woman, it was always in the form of a conquest; and that gave her a small sexual jolt between her legs. No, her state of mind at the moment was not rooted in jealousy, but in simple indignation at having been left waiting and worrying.

Eliot's passage was not so straightforward. He was in potentially very serious trouble. If Gail ever learned that he had been with Julia, there was no telling how violently she might react. A brief image of her rushing at him with a kitchen knife flashed through his mind. Or she might just collapse, which would be more difficult to deal with. Gail sitting woodenly in a chair, her eyes vacant, her jaw slack, the sorrow of double betrayal turning her skin to chalk held far more terror for him than any histrionics of anger ever could. But that was only the beginning. For after her came Julia. She had not known that he had a date with Gail at the very moment she was arching her buttocks and inviting him to penetrate her and drive her to that form of shameful glory which we call the orgasm. Their meeting was touchy enough, but they tacitly excused one another on the grounds of prior agreement, and the fact that they had already proved they could fuck without its spilling out into their lives. Besides, there had been a sense of fitness in their getting together, a karmic balancing that could not be defended on rational grounds. But when Gail called, and Julia learned what the situation was, the vibrations in her apartment began to fog all visibility beyond the strong message that he had better leave at once. His only salvation with Julia lay in his certain knowledge that she would not hurt her friend by letting her know what had happened. But she could and probably would make life very difficult for him at the office for a few days. As he soaped his crotch a second time, feeling foolish about doing it, he tried to take a quick inventory of exactly how vulnerable he was to Julia. He shuddered. She had enough on him to send him to jail for ten years. Not that he had ever done anything blatantly crooked, but that more than a few of his deals resulted in safety variances being waved via judicious gifts to mine inspectors. He just knew that a prosecuting attorney would consider the payments bribes, and that was an ugly word for which people were arrested and put in prison.

And beyond all that was his awareness that he wanted to see Julia again, that his desire for her, which had been filed under "inactive" for so many months was blazing again. Leaving her place was difficult for more than one reason; when the phone had rung he was just beginning to feel the second erection, one that would last for hours, and was starting to smile at the visions of opening Julia up beyond anything she'd ever experieiced before, even with her athletic husband who, Eliot was convinced, didn't understand about dirty sex and clean sex. That was the real source of Eliot's appeal, more than his money and sheer staying power; ultimately, he was a back door man, burning his way into women's secret gardens and evoking their most cunty dreams, playing dirty old man to the little girl in them.

"And then there's muscle brain," Eliot said to himself as he stepped out of the tub. He had met Martin five or six times and finally it became painfully obvious to both of them as well as to Julia that they would never manifest anything more friendly than a strong dislike for one another. Eliot grudgingly gave Martin full marks for his physique and took Julia's word that he could be a responsive lover, but nothing would ever convince the older man that the younger stud had anything but chopped beef where there should have been a brain. Now, however, he faced the unpleasant prospect of Martin's possibly finding out that he had fucked Julia, and in all of her openings, and in Martin's very bed.

What would he do? Eliot wondered, having no illusions as to how long he would last should the gym instructor decide to beat him to a pulp.

"Well," he sighed, drying himself, wrapping a dry towel around his waist, and putting his hand on the doorknob, "it's the lady or the tiger all over again." Then suddenly, unaccountably, he felt very young, very rakish and devil-may-care. He was up to his eyes in trouble, and it made his heart light to know that he was still capable of causing havoc with sex. One woman loved him; another was slightly foolish for his cock; and he faced the possibility of a jealous husband. Thus, when he opened the door and stepped into the living room, he was smiling. But Gail, whose anger had largely abated, was expecting the same slightly frightened and contrite man who had gone into the bathroom. When she saw Eliot emerge, washed, powdered, calmed, and smirking in smug self-satisfaction, her rage erupted once more.

He saw his error in timing a split second before the cocktail glass came hurtling at him, and had just enough time to duck as it smashed into the wall in back of him, the vodka, olive, toothpick, and lemon slice splashing in random disarray behind it. He straightened up and faced the reality, the fact that all the trouble he had been fantasizing was here, real, and would require that he invest time and patience in dealing with it. He would not be allowed the pleasant tingle of transition from one woman's asshole to another woman's cunt.

"I was worried sick!" she said, throwing the words at him with as much force as she had used on the glass.

"Now, now," he said, his hands raised in front of him in a gesture of placation, padding toward her steadily and warily. He got a picture of himself that was quite unpleasant, a short, pudgy middle-aged man in a dingy apartment trying to make nice to his mistress because he'd kept her waiting a few hours. The fact that he was a powerfully weathy financier, and attractive and virile enough to have a dozen of the world's most beautiful women ready to lie at his feet, made his present situation all the more ludicrous.

What is it with her? he thought looking at Gail as she stood facing him, her face slightly puffy from tears and worry, and wearing a goofy housedress which totally obscured her body. *She's a great lay, but so are most of the women I fuck. She's not any more intelligent, or interesting or amusing. What is it about her that can make me put up with this kind of scene?*

It was then that he saw the truth of his feelings. The thing that made Gail special was that he was, in his way, in love with her. It was a word that ordinary caused him to wrinkle his nose. He had seen too deeply into the human heart and known too clearly precisely what money could do even in relation to that supposedly most sublime of human feelings. Although, once, when he was in his early twenties, there had been a woman and he had laid his heart at her hands, surrendering himself to her, only to realize that it was to his own emotions that he was yielding, and that what she responded to in him was not what he gave her but the spectacle of a man vulnerable. At once he had frozen and retreated, not wanting to act the part of a freak in a circus sideshow. When he broke off the relationship, she wept. His final words to her had been, "You're crying for yourself. Please have the decency to do it in private."

Maybe I should just get dressed and tell Gail to fuck herself, he thought. *Instead of going through this whole tedious repentant husband routine.* But again, he stopped himself. He had acted badly, and he did feel guilty, and he looked forward to his punishment. If Gail had tied him to the bed and whipped him with a belt, he would have been the happiest man in the world. And she the most exultant woman. But they were not in touch with the authentic needs of the psychic organism; they did not even entertain the possibility of direct action, and so drifted off into the great arcane verbal substitute, the big waste of time.

"Don't give me that 'now, now' shit," she said, her voice already rising. "Where the fuck were you?"

"I was at a meeting," he said, checking his levels of truth and duplicity like a person testing the safety bar of the roller coaster car before it takes the first enormous dive.

"How was she?" Gail retorted. By this time she had forgotten that she was basically amused at his having had another woman.

Eliot executed a sharp military turn and shifted his direction away from her and toward the kitchen. He now needed the drink he had previously asked for as a ruse. Also, he was still enough in control to understand that the best way to deal with accurate accusations is to allow them to glance off one's mind. In that way, they are registered but don't have to be acknowledged. It was a trick he had learned in Hong Kong when he had stayed in the same hotel as Jesuit priest there on some obscure church business. Eliot and the priest had become drinking buddies and had exchanged secrets of each other's trade.

He moved into the kitchen and began fixing a second drink. His entire left side was tense, for he didn't know whether she would follow him. When he saw that he would be alone, he called out, "Would you like a martini?" There was a long, a very long pause. Then Gail replied, her voice a bare croak.

"Yes," she said.

Eliot smiled to himself. He had survived another round. He didn't know how many there would be altogether, but it was like a judo match. She would come at him or try to get him to go at her again and again until they were both exhausted or until a clear victory had been won. He was willing for her to win, and even wanted that, because she was in the right and because it would remove the resentment. But he didn't want to be battered or badly beaten, so he would fight as best he knew how. This could end in his attaining the final point, which would introduce a significantly weighty element into their relationship, something which might push them to a new level. For the first time that night Eliot considered the possibility that he and Gail might actually split up, and the insight was immediately followed by alternating waves of exhilaration and sadness.

When he finally turned and went back into the living room, holding the two glasses in front of him, he was a much more sober man than he had felt himself to be for quite some time. As so often is the case in life, one slips quite suddenly from the embrace of normality into the kiss of crisis without so much as a caress to mark the transition.

Again, Gail responded to his mood. As he mixed the drinks she at first sat on her couch, then sagged into it. Beneath the veneer of anger there lay a pit of corrosive exhaustion. She had a sour taste in her mouth and was looking forward to the clean cut of the vodka to scrape the fuzziness off her tongue. She too had shifted from the tactics of the immediate to the strategy of the structural, beginning to feel the edges of questions that had been put on the shelf since that night when Eliot had wanted to drink her piss. And when he came toward her a second time, now holding the drinks, she sensed the deepening of awareness in him, and let herself be washed over with the imminence of decision.

Eliot sat next to her. She took a glass. They clinked rims and smiled at each other the way two boxers touch gloves in the center of the ring before trying to beat each other into insensibility.

"Cheers," he said.

They sipped in silence for a few minutes. Outside a brigade of fire engines boomed down the street, klaxons blaring. Gail's cat strode into the room glanced at the humans, found them dull, and leap onto the window sill where she gazed down onto the street, pondering whatever it is that cats ponder when they sit with the rapt absorption and stillness that might make a zen monk envious.

"Where were you?" she said at last, calmly now, conversationally.

Eliot took a surreptitious breath. This was the first major

shift, the dangerous hurdle, the trap of reasonableness. Coming after the recent explosion, her peaceful sweetness threatened to melt something in him which might cause him to blurt out an explanation too close to the truth. His first impulse, for example, was to claim that Julia had been taken with a fit of hysteria because of the accumulating pressures of her breakup with Martin, and that he had taken her for a drink and talked her down from her suicide threats. And that in the process he had had no chance even to get to a phone. This would have caused Gail to capitulate at once, blaming herself for doubting him, for being angry. Then it would have been all peaches and blowjobs, as Gail outdid herself in making dinner for him and pleasing him erotically. Of course, as soon as she finished with him, she would be on the phone to Julia. Julia would then have to think very, very, very quickly indeed to piece together how the situation was moving.

That would be a test for my super-efficient little executive secretary, he thought, suppressing a smile.

But such a scheme, like nuclear warfare, was unthinkable.

"I . . ." he began, and then fell silent, staring at the rug. His mind was an absolute blank. He literally didn't know what sort of story to make up.

"I want to marry you," he said.

Her mouth fell open. His mind reached up a hand and slapped itself across the forehead. They were both flabergasted. Little chill thrills of delight ran up her spine. This was the last thing in the world she expected. Little thrill chills of fear ran down his spine. This was the last thing in the world he expected.

"I don't understand," she said.

"Neither do I," he replied, quite honestly. But now that he had the opening sentence, the rest of the paragraph was much less difficult. It was easier to be logical than to be original.

"It occurred to me this afternoon," he went on. "I was sitting at my desk, planning the Hartsville deal, thinking about seeing you tonight, hating the idea of coming to this place, remembering all the reasons why you want to remain financially independent." He took another sip of the martini. Everything he had just said was true. It was amazing. Once the initial lie was given and accepted as a premise, there was suddenly a space for the truth to rush in. It was much like the philosophical notion of as-if which takes as its first premise that any first premise must be a mental construct not having anything to do with the chaos of creation, but which will serve as a compass to see one through without having the boat prematurely sunk.

"And I got to thinking about our relationship. What is it now, fourteen months? And wondering what we do next. I mean, how long can we go on playing this game? So, I thought about splitting up, and that didn't feel good. And before I knew it, my mind was jumping in the opposite direction."

"I can't believe you're saying this," Gail said. She was gazing at him with open wonder.

"I can't either," Eliot replied, smiling openly this time, the inner and outer duplicities finally congruent. *Maybe that's what truth is,* he thought, *when you've finally got all your lies lined up like needles and you can pass a single thread through them all.*

Gail put down her drink and sat up and pushed herself toward him. She took his hands in hers. Everything had been abruptly and finally forgotten. Eliot saw the change, and mused that he had been utterly successful in extricating himself from his triple bind, for this move would absolve him with Julia and stave off any possible recriminations from Martin should he ever learn of the fact that Eliot had fucked his wife. On the other hand, it was a heavy price to pay for an indiscretion.

But then, what the hell, he thought, *maybe deep down I do want to get married.* And the moment he allowed himself to think that, the next words came spontaneously to his mouth.

"I've reached the age in life where I've done everything else," he said, returning the pressure of her hands. "The only thing left is to have a child. And I want to have a child with you."

Gail leaned forward and put her face against his chest. She began to weep. Eliot and the cat regarded one another quizzically. The cat, of course, couldn't understand the dialogue, but it knew that something rather significant was happening between the humans, and it had at least a rudimentary awareness that what affected them affected it. Eliot was taken, as many people are, by the fact that cats are simultaneously less intelligent and more conscious than monkeys, even of the talking kind, and in his state of abstraction was caught in the revolving door between the cat's organic and psychic levels. The confusion and intensity got too much for the cat also, and it leapt lithely to the floor and strode into the kitchen to see whether the remainder of the evening's meal hadn't congealed too badly to be nibbled at.

Gail pulled back and looked deeply into Eliot's eyes. Her soul was a well of questions.

"So when it came time to leave the office, I went for a drink. I figured that would make me a half hour late, but that's no big deal. But the more I drank, the more I realized that I was going to ask you tonight. And I couldn't get on the phone to tell you what was going on, or even just to make an excuse. You'd have picked up my agitation immediately, and perhaps been even more worried."

"But why did you get so upset? Is marrying me such a traumatic thing?"

Eliot turned his face away. The next line would be the most difficult he would ever have to deliver, and yet it was necessary.

"I was afraid you might say no," he told her, looking at the wall over his shoulder. The minute he spoke the words, the thought flashed into his mind. *Maybe she will say no.* Again, exhilaration and insecurity zipped through him, and he turned back quickly to look at her, actually curious as to how she would reply.

A thousand years of conditioning seized Gail at that instant, and when she felt the weight of his penetrating glance, she hid behind a faint blush and went all over coy. He had presented her with his heart and mind and testicles, now resting in the palm of her hand. The feeling of power was delicious, and she didn't want to relinquish it on the spot. It was not the man that she had power over, but the situation. The ball was in her court, and the nature of the game was such that she could take her time in returning it.

"I . . . don't know," she said, her voice clear and perfectly enunciated like that of a British actress on a small stage.

The relief that both of them felt was so palpable that the cat, disgusted at the crust that had formed over the meat in its plate, came back into the room, and sprang onto the couch between them, insinuating its body directly into the field of force generated by their mingled auras. They looked down at the animal and both smiled, their hands touching as they reached simultaneously to pet it. It was at once the ideal distraction and symbol, for in its presence they saw the child that would issue from their union.

"I've never been married," Gail said.

"Neither have I," Eliot told her.

"What does it mean?" she asked.

"I'm not sure. There's the license and all the legal business. And it's customary to live together. And then to have children."

"And aren't there fights, and infidelities, and all that?"

"I have friends who are married," Eliot said. "And they manage the situation in quite a civilized manner. As far as fights are concerned, this is the first we've had in over a year, and it wasn't much of a battle. Both of us are basically killers, so we aren't likely to get into scraps. Only clumsy and mediocre people squabble. As far as infidelities are concerned, I imagine we can both be relied upon to continue the discretion and tact we've been practicing. I don't know what you do with whom when I'm not with you, and I don't want to know. I only ask that you act intelligently. And that you return me the favor."

"We're talking as though it were already settled."

"It is in my mind," he said, and when he checked into his mind he found that indeed it was. The decision had come upon him by surprise, but then he had earned a fortune by making just such snap conclusions. He believed that the intuition worked behind the scenes of consciousness, and when it emerged to take a bow, a wise man let it steal the scene. Thought, the rational faculty, served its purpose by figuring out how best to carry out the dictates of the hunch. Also, he worked very quickly totting up the variables. It would be pleasant to be married, to have a home to return to, to be able to escort Gail around in a legitimate manner. Also, as his wife, she would quit her job, and be free to travel with him. It would be fun to show her the world. She'd never been further from New York than Philadelphia, a fact he still couldn't fully assimilate, having been in every country in the world except China. And on top of that, there would be the children. He already envisioned a son and a daughter. "And you?" he asked.

Gail stood up and walked to the window. It was a highly dramatic moment for her, and she surprised herself by feeling all the conventional emotions, going through all the stereotyped reactions. And then there was deep pulsation in her womb, where Eliot's seed would be planted. At the same time, part of her could not deny its lust for the lifestyle his wife would lead, the travel, the charge accounts, the apartments in the major cities of the world. The sheer prospect of it made her dizzy. And Eliot was fifty-four, twenty-six years older than she was. When he died, she would still be young, and very wealthy. She immediately drove the thought away as unworthy of her, but it had made its point.

"I know this is going to sound adolescent," she said after a while, "but I need time to think about it." She watched his face map out his feelings, going from expectancy to disappointment, and she relented at once.

"Oh, that's not true. It's just that I want to savor it, to sip at it for a few days. And besides, if I say yes too quickly, you'll think I'm easy."

Eliot leaned back against the couch. The cat curled up in his lap. *It can't be bad,* he thought. *I don't really lose anything, and I gain an awful lot.*

But his self-congratulations were interrupted by Gail's exclaiming, "Oh, won't Julia be surprised!"

That called Eliot back to the trigger which had detonated this entire train of events, the fact that just a few hours earlier Julia had whipped her panties off and thrown herself face down on her bed and rasped, "Come on, you prick, give it to me. Give it to me dirty, the way only you know how."

At the memory, his cock stirred. The cat became uncomfortable with the development and moved away to the other side of the couch. Eliot looked at Gail. She was a very attractive woman. And under that robe she was naked. And now he had not only her pussy, but her womb itself.

He stood up.

"How about another drink?" he asked.

She glanced shyly at him. She knew exactly what he had in mind. Or so she thought. And so he thought. But it didn't matter whether they did or not. Not that night. For passion was ascendant, and for them passion ruled.

They burned the sheets until dawn, slept three hours, and then went off to their work, he to the office, she to the school. She called Julia and told her what had happened. "Let's get together tonight," she had gushed.

Julia hesitated before she agreed. Gail was perplexed. They made a date for seven o'clock to talk about their lives.

Robert and Martin ate at The Peacock, an Italianate Italian restaurant that featured home-cooked soup, pre-Raphaelite paintings, and a steady supply of Bach, Beethoven, Vivaldi, Mozart and Mendelssohn. It was a perfect afternoon restaurant for bookish cruising, the women generally self-contained and remote. A perceptive man, however, that is to say, a man on the *qui vive,* might notice that as the mousy librarian type in the corner hung over her coffee cup and peered into her Proust, her chest might heave with a most unladylike sigh, or her nostrils widen with a tremor of quaveringly suppressed passion. Further inspection might reveal trim ankles, delicate fingers, and, when she noticed him perusing her and looked up to cross glances, four hundred pages of brown eyes complete with an index.

But in the evenings it was taken over by couples. Single couples, couples of couples, tablesful of couples. Martin had gone there with Julia at least a dozen times and felt that mixture of resentment and reassurance that comes when we see ourselves so blatantly reflected in the social mirror. Each couple was precisely the same, down to the detail of viewing themselves as unique. Martin remembered one dinner hour spent gestalting each woman in the room and reminding himself that only the most outlandish quirks of fate resulted in his being with the woman he was with, that his feelings of love, desire, and even friendship were innate and might be attached to any object. Once that object had been chosen, however, there was a tendency to turn it into a fetish, to make it a prized possession, a there-is-no-one-in-the-world-quite-like-you bit of sentimentality. And yet, when he did not look back at Julia, he realized that he did love her, cherish her, and not any of the others, thet they all existed in alternate or parallel universes. The sensation of being sealed off in a plastic bubble with Julia, forever cut off from the rest of the world, overwhelmed him with such a rush of claustrophobia that he had to go to the men's room and run cold water on his wrists.

Now he sat with Robert, at the table right next to the one at which he had been with Julia.

In a sense, Robert and I are a couple, he thought. *We came in together, we are focused on one another, we are excluding the rest of the room from this intimacy. And yet, I don't feel that sense of oppression, of being tied to a stake. There is no anxiety, no clutching, no undertow of echoes.*

"This place all right?" Robert said.

"It brings back a few memories."

"You came here with your wife?"

Martin nodded.

"Do you miss her?"

"Only when I'm horny," Martin said, then laughed. He was silent a few seconds and added, "I don't mean that the way it sounds, and yet I do mean it in a way. There are times when I want to be with her, want to very badly. Sometimes it's to fuck. My very cells cry out for her. At other times, I may remember a word or a gesture, and be almost crushed with the desire to be near her, to smell her, to bury myself in her, not to fuck, but to get lost, to find living oblivion. But the most poignant times are in movie theaters. There are certain films that I know she would love, and just how she would love them. And when the picture is over, I turn and find the seat next to me empty, and then I almost cry out her name."

He finished his narrative with a tonal flurish, turning the self-revelation into a sally instead of a cul de sac. He felt, on one level, that he was revealing too much too quickly, and yet something in Robert made it so easy for him to spill these things out. And aside from a long talk with his mother and a fairly brief conversation with a friend, he hadn't talked about his feelings with anyone. The marriage, the breakup, and the two months since were all locked up inside him. To compensate for his trepidation, he put a lilt to his voice, keeping the mood light and conversational. He was afraid that if he entered the confessional too fully, he might begin to crack up.

"Have you been in touch with her?" Robert's questions were gentle, almost tender, but penetrating. It was not so much what he asked, but the quality of genuine curiosity which infused his words. He gave the impression that he really wanted to know, that the information was important, a means of getting to know a person better, something that seemed the most important concern in life.

The waitress shuffled up. It was the sixth hour of her shift and she began to look like a soldier who was nearing the end of a thirty-mile hike. The image of soaking her feet in hot water and Epsom salt hung over her head like a balloon in a cartoon strip. She flipped two menus onto the table as though they were the first cards being dealt in a hand of blackjack. Knives, spoons, forks, napkins followed. And the reflex action of whipping out the pad, pencil to the ready, a posture she must have assumed several hundred times that day, a proletarian mudra which, manifesting in materialistic society, was not awarded any special significance by those who saw it, even to the point of not accepting it as a signal that she was ready to write down an order.

"Something to drink before you order?" she rasped.

"Milk," Martin said.

"Tea," Robert told her.

The men settled into their chairs and studied their menus. The beverages came. They drank and gave orders for food. Then they sat back again, and watched each other in silence for a while. Martin noticed that Robert had blue eyes, something that he must have registered as a fact of perception. But this was the first time he realized that Robert's eyes were highly appealing, crisp, intelligent, alive with an inner light.

It must be all that yoga, he thought.

"Have you seen her since the breakup?" Robert repeated his question.

"Oh! I'm sorry," Martin replied. "I forgot you'd asked me that before. No, not really. A few letters. One phone call. But there is a strong tacit agreement that we leave one another alone."

"A cooling off period?"

"In a sense. But I don't have any notion that we'll get back together. Aside from those times when I miss her, frankly, it's such a goddamned great relief to be alone, that I have trouble imagining putting my neck back into that noose. Living like a teenager again. Home every night right after work. Tied to one another's schedules and moods. Resenting the way she cuts in on my liberty, and even hating the way I cut in on hers. And there's nothing to do about it. All that emotional baggage, the fear, the jealousy, the insecurity. Taking two adults and reducing them, through a process of pressure that would make a prisoner-of-war camp seem like a playground, to nagging, sulking, seething monsters who are unable to feel the slightest impulse toward unstructured pleasure without having to swallow a bellyful of guilt."

"My Lord, but you sound bitter," Robert interjected. "But then, so did I after I broke up with Norman."

"Norman?" Martin repeated, his eyes opaque with sudden stupidity.

"We lived together for five years, and it was the same thing. For the first three years we thought it was sex, because we were both so possessive. But then we got over that, and each of us could go out tricking whenever we wanted without any hassle on that score. Sometimes we even brought our good fortune home to share. But beyond sex lay the problem of unstructured time, which isn't all mapped out by the unrelenting presence of another person in your life, night and day, forever. Oh God, what a nightmare that was! And the worst part was that we still loved each other. But there wasn't anything we could do. So he finally left, didn't tell me he was leaving, did it in classic style with a note on my pillow—*tear-stained* pillow, I might add. I didn't think I would take it so bad, because we both knew it was coming. So I went out, and partied and did this and that, but I was miserable. And maybe even ready to do myself in. And that's when I met Babba."

"I didn't realize you were homosexual," Martin said. "I'm sorry."

"Oh, no need to be sorry," Robert told him. "My mother has quite accepted it."

The transposition of keys went by a bit too quickly for Martin to grasp, so he let the implications flutter by and went on with his train of thought. "I mean, I'm sorry if I led you on. I was just being friendly, accepting this invitation, and didn't want to give you the wrong idea."

Robert looked at him with wry affection. *What a dumb hunk,* he thought. *The Lord sure had a sense of humor when he put that conditioning in that body.*

Martin squirmed about in his chair as though he were about to stand up and leave.

"Well, you can relax," Robert drawled. "I promise not to fling myself at your knees and beg to wail on your dangling wang. My intention was also friendly. If there was any ulterior motive it's that I've been sensing that you are troubled, and I wanted to talk to you, to get you to talk, to see if it would make you any clearer about whatever it is. And I wanted to bring you to Babba. He saved my life, as melodramatic as that sounds. And I thought that, if he was in a good mood tonight, he just might save yours."

Robert's rapid switches from sincerity to sarcasm left Martin a bit breathless in the mind, but that was a sensation he found highly exhilarating, much like skiing down a very fast slope and coming upon rock outcroppings all of sudden, and having to swivel, pole, kick, and shoot past in a single fluid motion without a trace of hesitation for in that would come immediate disaster. He was never that quick cerebrally, but because he was an adept on the physical plane, he could recognize mastery in others on other planes.

"I guess I must sound a bit stereotyped," Martin finally admitted. "But that, uh, homosexuality, is about as familiar to me as workings inside the Kremlin. It just makes me nervous."

"It makes me nervous too," Robert said, and they both laughed, past the first hurdle, already having shared a moment's uncertainty, intimacy.

They fell silent again, each staring down at the tablecloth, fingers busy at twirling a bread stick or plucking at a string.

Martin glanced up surreptitiously and found Robert looking back at him. He looked back down immediately, and then laughed briefly, and returned the gaze. He was extremely embarrassed, at the level of a child who is afraid his parents will do something mortifying in public. His ears began to burn and a warm large ball began to glow in his stomach. As he examined his sensations, he realized that he was feeling the same sort of excitement that he used to feel before a football game during his college days. He recalled the stench of tension as he put on his uniform and drank in the brute power of fifty young men, all big and powerful. It wasn't something he would ever have assoicated with erotic feelings, even though the slight breathlessness and tingling were the same.

In the restaurant, two women sipped capucino and watched the two men. Robert, tall, thin, each movement quicksilver sparklings through the smoky air; Martin, compact, strong, drenched in all his boyish ingenuousness. The women caught each other staring, and made moues at one another. One lifted an eyebrow, questioning. The other wrinkled her nose.

"Gay," she mouthed, without sounding the word.

The second women looked back at the men, her expression halfway between puzzlement and dejection. She had been troubled for some time now over the fact that more and more attractive men seemed to be homosexual. In fact, it had become a rule of thumb that the more goodlooking a man was, the more relaxed, the greater the probability that he was gay.

"It's odd," Martin said after a while. "We've spent so much time together and never really got to know one another. And now I'm sharing things with you that I've never shared with another man." He paused, took a breath, frowned. "Is this what homosexuality is about?" he asked. "Just this kind of intimate talking?"

"Why give it a sexual twist? Why not call it friendship, or simply humanity?"

"Because this isn't anything I do with other men, even men I've known a long time."

Robert gazed at the wall over Martin's head for a few seconds and then replied, "I guess that the major advantage of homosexuality is that it tends to remove the fear of homosexuality. Two men who get close usually get frightened. Will he embrace me? Will he kiss me? Will he grab my cock? And all that. But when you've already done all that with a man, there is no fear. Then, so what if he does? The trouble with homosexuality is that it often tends to get fixated at that level, so that a gay man will often opt for a bit of flesh friction before he even exchanges names. I think I've pretty well cooled out both extremes, with Babba's help, so when I'm close to a man I don't necessarily want to fuck him, nor will I necessarily push him away if he wants to fuck me. I can just be with him, without innuendoes or undercurrents."

"And women," Martin asked. "What about women?" He was hungry for knowledge, and he did not know how to find it. With Robert, suddenly, he thought he had found a handle and he would pump it until the well produced the water of truth to slake his thirst.

"Women are a problem to men," Robert said simply. "Because we issue from the womb of a woman, we have a tendency to mistake the hole between her legs for the Source of All Creation. Mother Nature and all that. We wind up worshipping pussy instead of God. We turn cunt into a fetish. And the ladies, as you know, are very suggestible. If a man looks at one with moons in his eyes and tells her that she is the most important thing in the universe to him, she will have her head turned and believe him, never suspecting that it is his cock talking and using his mouth like a ventriloquist's dummy. Then, when his desire is slaked, which takes anywhere from one night to one year, depending on how much charge differential there is between them, he begins to see the stretch marks, and finds her asshole less than marvelous, especially since she, from time to time, farts under the sheets. At this point, he usually turns on her, and blames her for not being perfect, which is what God ought to be. She accuses him of being unfair. He flexes his muscles. She has an affair. Etc. etc. etc."

During the entire discourse, Martin nodded his head, again and again, more and more forcefully as Robert detailed the graph of modern relationship. At the end he took a deep breath and let it out with a sigh.

"Oh, don't you know it," he said.

"The foolish worship of women is counterbalanced by an equally absurd phobia. The monthly blood, the hideous emotionalism, the inability to think coherently, the essential whorishness, and all the rest of that trip. It's the same in the gay world, from the usual refusal to even touch a woman to the Judy Garland cult. And beneath all that, somewhere, is a creature that is of the same stuff as us, in fact, of the same stuff as all creation. Women are just one more manifestation of God, although a very thorny one. Not nearly as easy to deal with as, for example, trees."

The waitress arrived with a circular black tray nearly three feet in diameter. She put it down on the adjoining table and transferred the various bowls and plates to the space in front of the two men. She had heard the last two sentences of Robert's talk, and it might have fascinated her under other circumstances, but at that moment the insistent ache in her arches took dominance over the most airy and delicately articulated metaphysics. She had an hour and forty minutes to go. It would be a long stretch.

Outside, on Greenwich Avenue, thousands of people swept by, strolling, rushing, prancing, shuffling, cruising, shopping. Most of them were fixed on a goal, a destination, oblivious of automobiles, dog shit, and the setting sun. They operated on automatic pilots, their bodies mere vehicles to get them from one psychic melodrama to another. A few paused every now and then to wonder at the wonder of it all. Occasionally a street crazy ambled by, talking out loud, gesticulating to an invisible audience. It was a circus of conditioned anarchists, choreographed by an industrial afterthought.

"Have you ever been . . . involved with a woman?" Martin asked, wondering whether he might be transgressing the bounds of civility.

"Oh, a few," Robert said. "I'm even a father. Had an affair with a girl in California when I was nineteen, I left for New York shortly thereafter, and received a letter from her telling me she was pregnant. I sent a telegram telling her I would pay for an abortion, but she wanted the baby. She later married a Navy Lieutenant stationed in San Diego. And then there was Anita, who broke my heart. And a hooker who got to be my friend and used to drop by to talk and have coffee and give me free fucks. I think I've done most of the basic scenes that a man can do with women."

"Will there be anything else?" the waitress said. She had been standing at their table since putting the food in front of them, waiting for them to notice that she had indeed served them. Martin glanced up sheepishly.

"No, no, thank you," he said, and made a note to himself to give her an extra large tip. She grimaced and walked off. Her ploy of anguished intimidation made her approximately fifteen dollars a day more in tips than she might have ordinarily accumulated.

The two men picked up utensils and spent the next several minutes concentrating on their food. They were both slightly ravenous and ate rapidly, Martin taking large bites and swallowing almost at once while Robert chewed each mouthful exactly twenty times. It was only after they had consumed half the volume of stuff on their plates that Martin went on.

"I really don't mean to pry . . ." He stopped and checked himself. "I'm sorry, that's foolish. I do mean to pry. I'm very curious, and everything you've said so far is opening up my thinking tremendously. What I don't understand is why you . . ." He let the sentence trail.

"Why did I become a homosexual?" Robert finished. "Is that what you want to know?"

Martin nodded.

"Well, it was summertime, and we were cruising the Caribbean. There was a moon, and the music from the lower deck, and . . . well, I know it was a mad, mad thing to do, but Dirk was so handsome, so irresistible, that when he took me in his arms I . . ." Robert had undergone a complete transformation. The pleasant, soft-spoken man of a few moments earlier had turned into Holly Woodlawn. He talked in a throaty falsetto and waved his arms about, his hands fluttering like spastic moths. For an instant Martin could see the invisible shawl he flourished in the air. But in the middle of his monologue he stopped, froze, and stared Martin in the eye. It was another of those sudden shifts which left Martin stunned and totally at a loss as to what to say. Robert saw the other's consternation and smiled.

"I hope it doesn't upset you when I dash off like that. It's just that you get so serious sometimes I can't help myself."

Martin blinked. "It's all right," he said, clearing his throat, "it's something like watching a frog turn into a prince before my eyes. But I suppose one can get used to anything after a while." He watched Robert watching him for a few moments then went on, "But seriously, why did you . . .?"

Halfway through the sentence, however, he heard his own voice and the incongruity of what he was saying and how he was saying it struck him. "But seriously, why did you become a homosexual?" was the full question and in such a form could give rise to nothing but laughter, which it did. The two of them sat in their chairs and laughed, long and loud, Martin ending in a high-pitched giggle and Robert in a low chuckle. All through it Martin thought, *I'm laughing, I'm really laughing, I must be having a good time.*

They settled down after a while and resumed their meal. The other people in the restaurant withdrew the covert glances they had cast in lieu of open and friendly attention. The two women who had looked them over earlier now exchanged expressions of smug certification, a harmonic I-told-you-so humming between them like a bridge across which an army is marching in locked step.

Somewhat abashed, the two men finished their food, and watched the table be cleared and fruit brought for dessert before they went on talking.

"Homosexuality is one of the simplest and most complicated of all human syndromes," Robert said at last. "I mean, what could be more natural than two people's liking one another, showing affection to each other in a physical way? But then you can go to the libraries and bookstores and find literally thousands of volumes written on the subject, analyzing a kiss or a lick between men to such murky roots of motivation that it makes your head spin. For me the choice was very simple once I realized that being gay was no more or less peculiar than being, say, a gasoline truck or an avocado. I'd had a child, I'd had an affair of the heart with a woman, I'd had hard-edged hooker fucking, and that just seemed enough of that. I decided to go with men because it was more pleasant, more friendly, healthier. I know that may sound weird, but it's the truth. All of the married couples I knew were busy strangling one another, playing *Woman in the Dunes* on one level or another. But the gay world gave me support, understanding, a way of life that was expansive, not continually contracting."

"But what about sex itself?" Martin broke in. "Is it as pleasurable with a man as with a woman?"

"I miss cunt sometimes," Robert admitted. "But I just look upon it as a drug I once enjoyed and have given up."

Martin's mind was swarming with fragments of photographs. He tried to picture Robert with another man. What did they do? Did they embrace and kiss and hold hands? Who fucked whom? Did Robert suck cock? The images proliferated and filled his mind with pressure which could only be relieved by his asking more questions. And yet he was loath to say such blatant things, afraid he might be offending or embarrassing his newfound friend. The result was that a fierce excitement began to build in him, a need to explode which came close to having him squirm in his seat. Robert watched the man go through his changes, and had he been a bit less sophisticated he might have thought that Martin was getting in touch with a strain of repressed homosexuality. But Robert had for a couple of years resigned himself to the knowledge that Martin probably had no closet to come out of along those lines. The man sitting in front of him needed to be awakened, to be liberated, to be shown the reality of God. If, in the process, Robert could wrap his lips around the other's sizable cock, that would be a bonus in a good cause. But it was unlikely to the point of impossibility.

"I almost wish I could be that blithe about it," Martin said. "I've been without a woman for two months now." He leaned forward and added in a lower voice, "Well, I did stop in at a massage parlor three weeks ago and got blown but I hardly count that. I mean, the girl didn't even undress. For all the contact I got, she might as well have been . . ."

Again he was forced to stop before completing a sentence. Talking to Robert elicited more references along the lines of homosexuality than he had ever known in a conversation, yet each was decidedly difficult.

Robert had caught on to the intended last word and rescued Martin from his momentary dilemma. "One of the idiocies of the conventional condemnation of homosexuality is that we engage in unnatural acts, like assfucking and cocksucking. Yet no man thinks a woman unnatural for going down on a man. And as far as I can tell, a mouth or an asshole doesn't have any gender."

"That's the way it felt," Martin admitted. "It could have been a man. And it wasn't enough just to come. I wanted to touch her and taste her and smell her. You know, get down between her thighs where it's hairy and wet."

"Ah yes," Robert sighed. "Pure nostalgia. Let's take a walk down memory lane, there where the pussy willows grow."

"Then there are times when it all seems like a dream," Martin continued. "I look at women on the street and they might as well be mannequins. I try and try but I just can't remember what the cunt even looks like. All I have is an impression of a mat of hair and some movement underneath. I think of myself lying on a woman, my cock inside her, moving around, grunting grabbing, pumping, and then the sperm scalding my tubes, and it doesn't feel anything like me. I know I used to do that, and I know I'll do it again, but right now I'm outside the pale."

"One of my big revelations," Robert said, "was looking through a men's magazine. They had photos of some woman lying across a bed, you know, with her fingers in her bush and her tits flopping to either side and this look on her face that said, 'Ain't I the most beautiful thing you have ever seen?' And I really studied that picture until I found out the hidden message, which is that she is supposed to be a kind of mindless pit of pleasure, and a man proves himself by giving her orgasms. I was right back at the old worship syndrome where women are regarded as some kind of rare object."

Martin was leaning back in his chair, his eyes unfocused, his chest rising and falling with his breath. For an instant Robert was concerned. "Anything wrong?" he said.

"Oh? No, nothing, nothing really."

"You look pale."

"I was thinking of Julia, that's all."

"That strong, huh?"

"I loved her very much. Well, I still love her, whatever that means. I don't know, when I get to feeling cynical, it seems like loving is just another kind of addiction. And missing her is nothing more romantic than going cold turkey on heroin."

"Do you believe that?"

"Oh, I don't know. I realize that I'm saying that a lot, but it feels good to admit it. One of the horrors of my marriage was that I always had to know, always had to be on top of things, always had to make sense."

"That's one of the horrors of civilization. We need to use our knowledge to earn a living and yet the way to God is by daily discarding what we know, cleaning out the mental attic of old informational shoes and dusty bits of data so that Divine Grace can pour in."

"Excuse me," Martin put in, "but I still kind of wince when anyone talks about God."

"So did I," Robert said. "And probably because my early training was so ridiculous, picturing God as an old man on a throne. Later, after my atheistic phase, I got to think of God as a concept, the Supreme Idea. But when I met Babba, the bottom fell out of all that. God is the basic, eternal reality. God is what scientists are chasing when they search for ultimate particles or origins. It is what philosophers seek in their quest for meaning. It is what poets and lovers find in the embrace of their muse, the kiss of their beloved. It is what the conventional man seeks in his marriage and his work and his children. It is what the homosexual cries out for as he sinks to his knees before a throbbing erection. God isn't to be found apart from any experience, any manifestation. But God isn't these things."

"I'm a bit confused," Martin said.

"There are two basic errors that human beings make. The first is to deny that anything exists except what they can experience. These are what might be called materialists. For them, if it can't be registered by the senses or by instruments which are extensions of the senses, it doesn't exist. It's an attitude so provincial, so limited, so stupid that one wonders anyone can entertain it for more than a second. And yet, entire nations are ruled by such thinking. The other mistake is thinking that what we experience is only an illusion, that there is some kind of ultimate reality of which this palpable universe is merely reflection. These are the idealists, the ones who hate life, who despise the fact that we are transitory, fragile, fated to live under the conditions of mortality. They are weary of earth, so they conjure up a heaven in which there is no pain, no separation, no death. And to rule over this place, they invent an idealized version of themselves and call it God. Any adolescent with a trace of intelligence is capable of seeing through this nonsense, and, unfortunately having no alternative in the culture, shucks the whole question. Thus people grow up vapid. And as they get older, they thrash about, trapped in the inevitability of their demise, grasping for some of consolation. Some get so bitter and frustrated they burst out in violence, or sink into debauchery, or run for president. Anything to keep from facing their ingrown mediocrity. That was the place I was at when I met Babba. And he just looked at me, and saw into my soul, and the next thing I knew I was in tears, prostrating myself at his feet."

Martin looked at the man across the way, this relative stranger with whom he'd spent more hours over the past three years with anyone else except his wife, and with whom he had seldom exchanged a personal remark. Robert was glowing, his skin pink, his eyes flickering with an inner strobe, his hair shimmering gold in the soft light of the restaurant. Martin had heard words like that before, notably from what he considered fanatics on the street trying to give away free tickets to listen to some Korean munitions manufacturer who claimed he was the Messiah, here to complete the job Jesus never got finished. He'd picked up the same fervid tone watching Billy Graham on television one night. He was well read enough to know about the power of blind faith, the way in which the mind, when concentrated by a powerful belief, could accomplish extraordinary feats including curing disease, and totally transforming a person's lifestyle. He even knew a couple back in Michigan. The man had been an Associate Professor of English Literature. He was a Ph.D., an urbane, witty, well-balanced man. One weekend he and his wife had gone to see a preacher who had come to town with his particular brand of Christian revival, and the couple just went around the bend. The man began telling his students that they had to put their trust in Jesus, that this was the only thing in life that mattered. His wife gave sermons at bridge parties. The incident was treated with civilized embarrassment, most people figuring that everyone was allowed at least one flip-out, that the couple would soon be over it and everyone would be able, before too long, to laugh at the entire affair. But when it persisted for more than three months, action had to be taken. The man was dismissed, and shortly thereafter the two of them left town, presumably to join the preacher's caravan. Martin hadn't even pretended to understand the dynamics of conversion, but then he didn't understand the roots of schizophrenia either, and he dismissed the incident as just one of those peculiar things that happen from time to time.

"I don't really know what to say," Martin said. "You act and sound like you'd inherited a million dollars, and I can only be happy for you. But it's no money in my pocket, and then, for all I know, you may be hallucinating and projecting like crazy."

"I wouldn't expect any other response," Robert replied at once. "If someone had come on to me that way three years ago, I would have reacted in exactly the same way. And maybe not even as gently as you are doing."

"Is it ever possible to upset you?" Martin said abruptly.

"If you can find a me in me, I guess you can upset it," the other man shot back. And then smiled shyly. "That's a bit of a boast," he went on. "That's the ego claiming that there is no ego. If I were to say something like that in Babba's presence, he'd whack me with his stick."

"What about his ego?"

"Babba is a perfect and authentic manifestation of Divine Consciousness in human form," Robert told him. And then, seeing the look that crossed Martin's face, added, "But unless you are touched by his Grace, those words will only put you off." He glanced down at his wristwatch. "We have a half hour. Why don't we walk over? We're meeting at a devotee's loft tonight, on Chambers Street down near the World Trade Center."

Again, Martin felt a tug of hesitation, and when he examined it saw that it was a conditioned reflex from his days of living with Julia when he was continually subliminally on schedule, when they called each other to say they'd be a half hour late, when they had no liberty of movement. Now he saw that was as much a security as a fetter, for while he had been denied the freedom of exploration of time and space he was also protected from wild and ragged influences. As he paid his half of the bill, and the two men walked out into the spring evening, he was taken by an unreasoning excitement, a sense of high adventure out of all proportion to merely walking twenty blocks to see an Indian holy man.

It must be an indication of the degree to which I've been leading a sheltered life, he thought.

"I'll follow you," he said to Robert, and the tall man turned right, heading southwest toward the river.

They walked down Greenwich to Seventh Avenue and then headed for Sheridan Square. They didn't talk for a while, enjoying the kinesthetics of their stroll. Martin strode with an almost military precision, his arms swinging widely in exact counterpoint to the movement of his legs. Dressed in loose slacks and a sports shirt, all in dark blue, he might have been on parade. Robert wore his customary white—baggy yoga pants and a loose madras shirt. He moved more like a robot on skates, his feet sliding forward while his legs followed unbending and his torso glided without torque. They drew more than the average number of glances for the attractiveness of each was compounded by the presence of the other. For most of the way, it was Martin's erotic turf, for the warm night had flushed thousands of scantily dressed women onto the streets, and they now minced, pranced, strode, strolled, marched, and ambled past, in skirts, jeans, shorts, and dresses. Martin could not control his eyes. The lurch of breasts, the sway of buttocks, the bulge of cunts rubbed images against his brain like the eardrum-raping klaxons of fire engines blasting their way through traffic. His cock stirred and grew stiff enough to provide an embarrassment and he forced himself to stare at the sidewalk until the tingling tumescence had been strangled at its psychic root and starved into submission to social reality.

But when they turned onto Christopher Street, the number of women on the sidewalks dropped to practically zero. The change was so abrupt that one might expect it to be more noticeable to a casual passerby, in the same way that the shift from concrete to grass at the edge of a park impresses itself upon the attention. But Martin had already retracted his sensors, and so remained oblivious of the shift of gender.

Now it was Robert's turn to run the gauntlet. This was the most notorious homosexual neighborhood in the country, the place where the historic Stonewall riot had lit the torch which flamed into the movement known as gay liberation. Here, to be heterosexual was to be out of place. Every half block a bar spilled its particular variation on the subculture into the streets, so that one passed clusters of men dressed in levis, or in leather, or as cowboys, or others whose clothes suggested those of women. Bookstores offering homosexual literature and movies and backrooms where orgies took place served as beacons of identity. Men held hands openly, and late at night it was not uncommon to find men necking in hallways, sucking one another in parked cars, or screwing each other behind the trucks parked near the river.

Robert's eyes were magnetic mirrors, attracting and reflecting glances all up and down the narrow boulevard. He was well known here, and within a few minutes had acknowledged looks from five men he'd had sex with during the past month. But such was the attraction of the strip that hundreds of new faces appeared each week, from other neighborhoods, from New Jersey and Connecticut, from Europe and California. This was the support that Robert had spoken of earlier when he explained why he had decided on the gay life. A man arriving in a strange city usually ended in a sterile hotel room without company or knowing where to find conversation, food, sex, or relaxation. But a gay man had all that prepared for him. The bars, the baths, the special neighborhoods, all guaranteed that unless he were very old or very ugly or very contankerous, he would be able to find all the necessities and a few of the luxuries within a few hours of arrival.

By the time they reached Hudson Street and began walking

south toward the twin towers whose lights had begun to blaze in the polluted gloom of twilight, Robert was more than a bit nonplussed, his nerve endings twanging deliciously. Martin, unconscious of the ambience he had just passed through but no less affected by it, asked, "What does Babba say about sex? I thought that people who became spiritual had to be celibate. Or at least monogamous."

Robert smiled. "See that church over there?" He pointed to a small, neat stone structure next to a large garden. "Every Thursday night about a thousand people gather to listen to a wacky old woman cackle about God. She talks like Archie Bunker's wife and claims she's having an astral love affair with Pericles. Thirty years ago she and a friend took a few hundred dollars and went to India on a sort of lark. She came back strange and holy and wild. But she has a real power, and she is building a strong following. Anyway her leaning is toward celibacy. Shooting the juice up the spine instead of out the lower plumbing. And that's valid for those who are in sympathy with her. What I'm trying to say is that there is no one way to God, since God is all there is. Only God exists. Everything we know is just one or another modification of that eternal consciousness, that infinite energy. To know God you only have to become yourself totally. And that, as you know, can take a dazzling variety of forms."

"So you can kind of do whatever you like?" Martin asked.

"Sure," Robert replied, "so long as you know who *you* are. If you think that you are this individual named Martin Gordis, so tall, so many pounds, then whatever you do is a product of delusion. But when you know, not just intellectually, but throughout your entire being, that you are the universe and all that it sustains, then you are free. Because at that point total freedom and total lawfulness are one and the same."

"More paradoxes," Martin muttered.

"Nothing but," Robert said.

"So are you at that stage?" Martin asked. "Is that why you can be homosexual?"

"Not at all," Robert laughed, as though it were the most amusing thing he'd heard all day. "Although there is no discrepancy between enlightenment and being gay. Babba says that when you are clear, there is no fixed form that you must take. But until you are clear, you should enjoy the form you are in, understanding it, rendering it harmless to others, while the deeper process of understanding works inside you. When you attain realization, then you may continue in that way or not." Robert laughed again. "When I went to Babba with my homosexuality, I was ready to give it up, you know, to make a big sacrifice in order to be saintly. But all he did was to wrinkle his nose. Then he leaned forward and said, 'You find pleasure in the hole where the shit comes out?' Well! That coming from this holy man, in a thick accent yet! I almost fell over. But he repeated the question and stared at me until I nodded my head. He looked around at the others in the room, mock consternation on his face, and then launched into a long story about a monk who had a binding passion for mangoes."

The two men walked along in silence for half a block before Martin realized that Robert had finished the tale. "That's it?" he asked.

"It was enough," Robert replied. "It put the whole thing right in its proper perspective."

"And you had to do all this in front of a room filled with people?"

"But don't you see," Robert said quickly, "that he took the thing I was hugging to my chest as my own private problem and put it in such a humorous and wide context that the thing just fell away. What Babba was saying was that sticking your cock in another man's ass is a rather bizarre bit of behavior, but no more or less remarkable than someone's having a passion for a certain kind of tropical fruit. It isn't the fruit or the asshole which provides the impediment, but one's attachment to the thing, to the sensation, to the need. And when it was exposed to all the others in the room, everyone had a chance to examine his or her own pet problem, whether it be drugs or booze or romantic love or money or fear."

"So he gave you permission to do whatever you wanted sexually?"

"No, he let me know that he wasn't going to take the responsibility for my choices. He's not a leader or a teacher in the conventional sense. He's a guru, which means that he does nothing but show us the living reality of God in human form. When you see that, then your life begins to change, even though it might appear on the outside that you are doing exactly the same things. He rarely gives an order, or even makes a suggestion. So, when that pressure was removed, I stopped assuming any postures in relation to being gay, and just began to be it. And when that happened, I did begin to change. I stopped using grass and poppers. I had also been on the road to getting into a heavy S & M trip, and that stopped. I extricated myself from the more kinky loops of the gay belt. I stopped hurting myself in such gross and obvious ways. And it was then that I discovered yoga, and became a vegetarian. And Babba didn't tell me to do any of this. He just gave me his Grace, and a certain kind of light began to flow through me."

"It sounds quite beautiful," Martin said, a bit sourly. He had reached the point where the effulgence of another person starts to cramp one's own basic dissatisfaction. They walked for another block in silence as Martin's mood grew heavier.

"Why don't we cut over to the river?" Robert said. "We have a few minutes. We can sit down and watch the last bit of sunset over the Jersey slums."

"You're the guide," Martin said, but the change in direction and topic halted the movement of his funk, and he regained a sense of curiosity and excitement as they came in view of the water.

The space immediately in front of them was a huge construction site where nearly five thousand acres of river had been corraled and was being filled to provide the ground for Battery City, a complex of high-rises, parking lots, shopping centers, and parks. Behind them rose Liberty Village, five forty-story buildings with as much élan as a Moscow suburb, drab brick structures which managed, despite their newness and height, to appear gray and squat. The whole area was dominated by the twin towers of the World Trade Center, latter-day pyramids erected as monuments to a dead civilization. This was old New York, the first portion of Manhattan to be settled, then forgotten as the action moved uptown, leaving behind Wall Street, the Fulton Fish Market, and block upon block of warehouses. Now the turf was being reclaimed. As usual, the artists had arrived first, moving into deserted lofts, turning sooty and abandoned spaces into airy studios. The developers followed suit, blotting out the sky with expensive projects. And after them, pots and pans clanging on the sides of their buckboards, the merchants. Finally, to give the kiss of completion, the former owner of Max's Kansas City chose Chambers Street as the site to open his new bar-discotheque-restaurant, and with that came the progression of self-conscious scenicruisers, to be followed, ultimately, by teenagers from Queens anxious to discover the in crowd.

Martin and Robert sat on a thirty-foot length of rusty pipe large enough to hold a Great Dane. The sky was the color of cement. Cars and trucks thudded by under the closed-down West Side Highway. Two drunks sat in front of a deserted pier building and waxed philosophical over a pint of burbon that they passed back and forth like lovers swapping spit.

"Julia's probably taking a bath," Martin said. Robert continued to stare ahead. His mood had suddenly turned pensive. But Martin was speaking more to himself than to the other man and so Robert's inattention made no difference.

"She used to complain that I came home too early every night and spoiled her favorite hour. She said that she looked forward to that hour of solitude all day. I began going home an hour later but that didn't work either. There was no way to hide the fact that I was an intrusion into her space no matter when I arrived." He balled up both his hands into fists. His face had become hard, tight. Old angers licked at his mind.

"Maybe I should have been more forceful. A few times I found her lying on the couch wrapped in a towel and I took her right there, thrusting into her mood with as much strength as I plunged into her body. And it was glorious, to transform her in that way. But when it was finished, the lassitude returned. We would make dinner and drift toward night, but I was no closer to her for having made love to her."

"It sounds more like fucking than lovemaking," Robert said, suddenly returning to the conversation.

"Well, what else can you do when the person you're with

doesn't respond except physically? Yes, you're right. It was fucking. And for the brief time I was driving her to orgasm, she was alive to me, like a corpse being prodded with electric current. And her very distance drove me mad. All her beauty was there in my arms, her mouth sucking on mine, her fingers digging into my shoulders. And all the signs of passion appeared, the wetness, the sounds, the tremors down the spine. Her legs were like arms, supple and vital around my waist, my back, even reaching around my neck. You know? She held nothing back, but it meant nothing. Because the moment we finished, she drifted off into her reverie, her endless self-absorption."

"It's difficult for me to comment," Robert said. "I take what you're saying at face value, but I'm hearing only one-third of the story."

"A third? Don't you mean a half?"

"No, in any relationship there are three people. Him, her, and us. To understand it all I'd also have to hear her out, and then see what patterns the two of you act out that neither of you as individuals are aware of."

"I suppose you're right. And I guess it doesn't matter anymore."

"Except that whoever you get involved with next will present you with an opportunity to face these questions again, and not so academically as you are now doing with me. Unless you're going to become gay or celibate, you are going to go through the same mill again."

"You mean I'll pick someone like Julia again?"

"Not necessarily. But any woman you live with will provide you with the force of her being, and that presence will flush out all your tendencies, negativities, weaknesses, patterns of withdrawal, power games. Ultimately, it is yourself you have to deal with. This is what any discipline does, it forces you to face your intrinsic waywardness. But when the source of that discipline is someone emotionally involved with you, the issues get confused, which is why it's better to make that kind of primary relationship with a guru, who remains stable and doesn't get petulant."

"But you can't fuck a guru."

"Fucking's not the issue. I'm sure you've fucked quite a few women. But none of them put you through these kinds of changes, did they? I think that the problem comes from the way in which we transfer the sort of interpenetration we experience in sex to other areas of our lives. When someone's giving you head you cry out, 'don't stop.' But when you wind up living with that person, you need to cry out, 'Please stop.' The hardest thing in the world is to find the proper distance on the morning after the intimacies of the night before, and to do that as an ongoing process, day after day. I'm trying to do that with Babba, who's a master of that game, and we're not having sex. And with all that, it's terribly difficult. For a man and woman to try it, in the pressure-cooker of a marriage, without a teacher to help them, is practically suicidal."

"I reached that point," Martin said, riding the crest of the other's verbal wave. "I used to sit in my office at the club and toy with the .38 that's kept in the desk for protection, taking the bullets out and pointing the barrel at my temple and pulling the trigger. One night, and it makes me almost piss in my pants just to remember this, I actually played a game of Russian Roulette. I kept one bullet in the barrel, spun it, and took the chance."

Robert turned his head and looked at Martin with a kind of curious respect. He did not for a fraction of a second doubt that Martin was telling the truth, and the idea that this very conventional man, almost obsessed with health and physical perfection, should take such a risk was exhilarating.

"I take it that the bullet didn't go off," he said. "You must have been in quite a state."

"There was barely a me to be in a state," Martin replied. "That was a good part of the trouble. I got so involved in her, in us, that I lost touch with myself. By the time I started playing with the gun, I was a walking catatonic. I went through the paces, but everything had lost its flavor. I even stopped looking into the women's locker room on the closed circuit t.v."

"I didn't know . . ." Robert began.

Martin glanced quickly at the other man, looking both sheepish and proud of himself. "It's a deal I made with the company who installed the security system in the lobby. Three firms were bidding for the contract, but the salesman from one of them offered me a bribe. He set up a hidden camera in the woman's dressing rooms and ran the line to my office." He held up one hand toward Robert. "But you musn't breathe a word. If anyone found out, every woman who belongs to the club would sue us silly. And I'd probably end up in jail."

"Will you let me come peek?"

"I thought you didn't like women?"

"I'll just look at their asses," Robert said. He smiled at Martin. "I assume you're feeling better now and using the thing again."

"Well, now I have the opposite problem. Looking at those wet naked bodies drives me crazy. I'm not a sex-saturated married man anymore."

"If you'll pardon my indelicacy, just what's keeping you from getting laid? I know there are at least ten of the ladies who come to the club who would like nothing better than to drain you of your excess sperm."

"I suppose," Martin replied, "that I'm still hung up on my wife. I haven't had another woman for five years, not counting that little episode in the massage parlor, which was so peripheral I barely felt it. I think I'd be embarrassed with another woman. I wouldn't know how to hold her or kiss her or talk to her in that sexy way."

"Nonsense," Robert exclaimed. "It's like swimming or riding a bicycle. The body remembers, even if the personality doesn't."

"Well, perhaps," Martin said, but his tone was not convincing.

Robert looked at Martin for a long time, seeing the slope of shoulder, the tension in the brow. He was struck by the contrast between his friend's powerful physique and weak self-esteem. He was convinced that Martin had no idea how beautiful he was, for in the world of maleness he inhabited the only acceptable word to use would be "handsome." If he were a bit younger, more impressionable, more given to impossible passions, Robert would have been quite smitten by the other man. But he was able to be somewhat objective, viewing him in part through the eyes that had been trained to see by Babba. More and more he looked at other people and saw their hidden suffering, beneath all their entertainments and smiles. He would have loved to embrace Martin, to hold him and urge him to cry, but he knew that such a gesture would be utterly misconstrued. Instead, he caressed Martin with his voice, trying to reach inside him to touch the core of sorrow.

"Tell me about her," he said. "Not the problems you had, or the things she did. But about her. Her soul, her heart, her mind, her cunt."

"I was just wondering whether she's with someone now," Martin said after a long while.

"Not that," Robert urged with intense gentleness. "You loved her. You still love her. Tell me about that love."

The sky was almost black. A tugboat chugged by on the wide river. On the other shore, lights signaled the existence of an entire world. Homes, offices, factories. Hundreds of thousands of people were finishing dinner, going out for an evening's pleasure, or settling in front of their television sets. It was all so distant, and yet so immediate. Each light signified a life, and all those lives had their stories. Love, marriage, divorce, children, death, ambition, empires which extended across vast oil refineries or no further than an intimidated spouse. In the face of all that, one man's tale could only seem trivial, but then, from the viewpoint of God, the whole human story, the entire history of earth, the solar system, the galaxy, the very manifest universe, was equally frivolous. Robert smiled to himself. He felt the glow of Babba's Grace in his chest. Soon he would be in his physical presence. And maybe the guru would be able to reach out and touch Martin's heart.

"She was the only person who ever made me unhappy," Martin began. "I know that sounds wicked, but I mean it in a very loving way. I've always been a pretty simple person, cheerful and dumb, not too concerned with mysteries. For me, a spring day, a cold beer, a playful woman, summed up everything a man might need to experience in life. But behind that lurked the suspicion that I was missing out on something meaningful. I often felt like the person who had missed the point of the joke and was wondering what everyone else was laughing at. I never understood poetry, for example. Oh, I could enjoy a good description, but I had no idea what sent people into raptures. I once dated a girl who accused me of being shallow, and I felt the sting of that for a long time, I guess that deep down I believed it was true. After all, I was just a jock.

"But Julia changed all that. She made me feel pain and excitement. She made me think about my life. And about having children. I guess she forced me into maturity."

"Which you consider unhappiness?"

"I was much better off when I was ignorant and naive."

"But you can't stay a child forever. You have to pass through the stage of knowledge, of knowing that you know. And then it is possible to find a new level of innocence." Robert spoke with animation. He was beginning to see Martin's life unfold in terms of the basic structures of the spiritual search. He had suffered the same torment. "So she was a kind of teacher to you."

"Once, when we were in Italy," Martin said, "we came to the edge of a high cliff. We had been irritated with one another all morning and it was good to find a place where there was so much emptiness and silence. I sat at the edge and fell into a reverie and Julia wandered off a bit behind me. I guess fifteen or twenty minutes passed, when suddenly I heard a tremendous sound. Something had fallen from the cliff and crashed into the forest below. For a split second I experienced nothing more than a startle response, and then I thought, 'Julia!' I rushed over to where I had heard the sound come from, calling her name. She didn't answer. I grew frantic, running back and forth along the edge, until I saw her jacket and handbag piled in a neat bundle under a tree. A shudder of relief went through me, for I realized at once that she must have gone for a walk and gone further than expected. But when I got to the spot where her things lay, I found a note pinned to her sleeve. It said, 'Goodbye. Remember me. Julia.' I must have gone mad. I began wailing like an animal over the body of its dead mate. I was seized by pictures of her hurling herself from the precipice, her body smashing to pieces below. It was a three-hundred-foot drop. It was impossible she could have survived. But more hideous than any of that were the unmistakable flashes of relief that flushed through me. For all my anguish, for all my grief, a little voice danced in my brain, shouting, 'We're free, we're free!' And then I heard her laugh. I whirled around and she was standing there, at the edge of the woods. She was naked except for her boots and hat. I exploded into a ball of fury and leaped on her. I slapped her and threw her to the ground and kicked her and then threw myself on her and fucked her brains loose. Afterwards, we slept and when we got up I was nauseous and stiff, and had to spend the next four days in bed with a fever. Julia suffered a black eye and bruises on her legs."

Robert clucked his tongue against the roof of his mouth. "Was there a moment when it occurred to you that you might actually throw her off the cliff yourself? I mean, you had the note. You were in a strange country. You probably could have gotten away with it. Poetic justice."

"No, you don't understand. I was furious at her, ready to kill her, but at the same time totally enthralled. I had never known anything remotely like that in my life. There was so much *feeling*. I've never taken drugs, but I imagine it must be the same. The sensation is so strong, so convincing, that one has to go back to it. Except that Julia wasn't a powder or a weed, she was a human being consciously moulding my mind." He paused, a certain parallel suddenly dawning on him. "I guess it was something like your guru does."

"With all the difference in the world. Babba doesn't want anything from anyone. It sounds to me like Julia is a sponge for attention."

"Yes, there's the spoiled child in her. But I suppose that's what made her so irresistible. Sometimes she'd pout, just like a six-year-old girl. And I would take her on my lap and try to cheer her up. Her mood was real, so I'd get lost in the game, and pretend that she was my daughter. Until I felt her squirming on my thighs, and my cock would stir. She'd put her arms around my neck and talk baby-talk, pressing her breasts against me, her cunt hot through her panties and skirt, through my pants and shorts. She got like a fire sometimes, and it drove me mad. Some nights I would have fantasies of her fucking a dozen men at once. I had no doubt but that she could handle it and walk away swaggering. The extremes in her strung me out, the little girl and the pornographic nymphomaniac all in one.

"Then, when we got down to it, I sank into her like a stone in mud. I wasn't anything near being a virgin when we met. I'd had my share of women, ranging from nice girls next door to Mexican whores. But Julia was something else. There was a quality in her eyes, a kind of hurt pleading that used to rise up like mist from a swamp and totally engulf me so that I couldn't see anything but that strange burning in her brain. And all the while she did shameless things with her body, her cunt sucking at me like a gaping toothless mouth, slurping, drooling. Time stopped and space disappeared. At times I felt like I was dying, because the world had become an emptiness, and I was being sucked into the whirlpool, a blazing comet doing a swan dive into a black hole from which there could be no return or escape, ever.

"Then she'd start to talk dirty. 'Fuck me,' she said over and over again. 'Come on you humpy jock, you big juicy hunk of meat, do your dirt all over me.' I'd get scared and look at her to see if she had flipped out, and there was no recognition in her eyes. She had become a mindless moaning cunt leaching at me as though she wanted my very blood."

"Wow," Robert said under his breath. "Wild."

"And it went on for hours. You know that I'm in pretty good shape. And I know how to hold my come. Sometimes we'd start after dinner and by the time I got up it would be three in the morning."

"I'm impressed," Robert said. "If you make me your agent I could make you a fortune. Of course, you'd have to break this prejudice you have concerning the gender of your sex objects."

"She wasn't impressed," Martin said. "After a bout like that, she'd get up, smoke a cigarette, and start chattering about how she had to get up early for work, and then go off to pee and make coffee and pick at her face in the mirror for a half hour before she came back to bed, gave me a friendly kiss, and rolled over, shoving her ass into my crotch as though I were some pet teddy bear she kept for comfort. The worst part was she wouldn't even ask me whether I wanted any coffee or not."

"Tell me, what did you do when you weren't mounting these erotic melodramas?"

"I don't remember."

"What?"

"It's all a blur. Somehow we passed a lot of time. I don't know. We went out, to movies, plays, that sort of thing. We had friends, I guess. But the more I think of it the more I realize that they were just acquaintances, not people I cared about or who cared about me in any deep sense. We watched television, read, took care of the household chores. Each year we took a vacation. Two weeks in the sun."

"So you vacillated between boredom and a kind of terrified ecstasy."

"That's pretty much it. But that doesn't get to the heart of the matter. Which can't be described. Which is what you asked me about. Which is love."

"Yeah," Robert breathed, and in that single syllable encapsulated a lifetime of searching.

"That was the air we breathed. It was the stage that all this happened on. Whether we fought or laughed. Whether we fucked with desperation or made love with joy. Whether we flew through Europe or languished in boredom in New York City. Through and below and above all that was the love we had for one another. And I don't know what to say about that. Sometimes we sat in the living room paying no attention to one another, me reading and she listening to music, when a light would fill the space, a radiance that was an unspeakable bliss, and I'd look up at the same time she would, and her eyes had turned to angel's eyes. Or we'd be walking down a street in a hurry to get somewhere, dodging traffic and swimming upstream through the heavy vibrations of the thousands of others rushing about, and she'd stop abruptly, and touch my arm, and when I turned to her she'd look at me as though she had never really seen me before and say, 'I love you.' Or in the middle of the night she'd wake up from a nightmare and be sobbing, remembering her mother, and burrow into my arms and cling to me in a way that I don't think any woman ever will again.

"And even these don't capture it. Now, I get along. I earn a good salary, I'm in the process of finding a new apartment, and I feel free. I don't think I could go back to living with Julia the way we were. It would only destroy us both again. Yet, at odd times during the day, when I haven't thought of her for several days and am beginning to think of which of the ladies at the club I'm going to grace with my marathon cock, I'll see her face in the air, and my heart will stop. Not figuratively, but actually. Stop. And for a few seconds, I know I am dead."

Martin's words hung in the air for a long time after he finished speaking. By now the sky was black and a slight chill had entered the air. The two men sat side by side and watched the sluggish polluted river. The far shore was ablaze with lights and the rim of industrial civilization was reflected in the oily water. They were silent for many minutes. Several times Robert had to check an impulse to put his arm around Martin's shoulders. He could not trust that the other man would understand the meaning of the gesture.

But then, do I understand my own motivation? he thought. The images unleashed by Martin's narrative surged through his mind like waves over a stormy sea. The raw eroticism, the sweat, the grunting exorcism of the devil of lust, all sang in his bloodstream. But in the movies of his imagination, it was not Julia that spread herself beneath the athletic warrior of the sheets. It was himself. Yes, he lay face down and bereft of all context as Martin ranged over him, moving in hot, tight circles, both of them silent and deep, deep into that realm where each breath, each thought, each atom of awareness hummed in a sea of infinite emptiness. It was something that he could never reach with a woman, for what woman could ever penetrate him, take him, enter him, make him moan with surrender? And it had never been enough, for it was temporary, a thing of a few minutes or even hours. And it gave him an insatiable yearning for eternity, for that was what it was. When all the fear of homosexuality and all its false chic had been seen through, what it was was the endlessness of the self knowing the self as the self. And the body alone was not sufficient vehicle for such a realization, for the body was transient, limited. No, the truth of homosexuality was the truth of knowing the gods, and once one had sported among the gods, it became necessary to know God. And so he had met Babba, who had inspired in him that same surrender, before whom it was a joy to kneel and touch one's head to the floor. Yet, he was still tempted by the sensations of the flesh, forgetting that they were not truth but only the messengers of truth. Babba was patient, and allowed him his lingering love affairs with those messengers, but warned that with each encounter Robert risked losing sight of ultimate reality, forsaking the infinite forest for a single phallic tree.

Now, with Martin, he felt the tearing along his metaphysical seams. He knew that the man needed to see Babba and to know what the guru meant. But at the same time he intuited that Martin would blossom in an entirely different way if he could simply slip through the grid of his heterosexual conditioning and fall gently into the arms of a man who might love him.

"Well," Robert said at last, "I wouldn't worry about it. After all, death is nothing more than a commercial for God. It's his way of making sure that we don't forget him."

Martin, climbing slowly out of his reverie of Julia, was perplexed. He couldn't filter out the meaning from the humor in Robert's remark.

"I mean," Robert went on, "if we were immortal, we could play at life with much more aplomb, couldn't we?"

"I suppose . . ." Martin began, uncertain as to where this was leading.

"Your problem with Julia," Robert continued, now a bit reckless, "man's problem with woman. That's at the core of it, don't you see? Without them, we can maintain the illusion of immortality. Even as we die, we live forever. But a woman denies all that by her very existence. She reminds us that we are nothing more than the detritus of her bloody hole, and every time we gaze into her eyes, we see the grave. Which is why she holds such a fascination for us. And why some of us have fled her. But you are bound by the horrible beauty of her reality. For you, on a very deep level, Julia is your last defense against God, and your last defense against accepting yourself as a man, a creature who must find his own salvation."

A huge ocean liner sailed past, heading for New York Bay

and the ocean beyond. Robert stood up. He grabbed Martin under one arm and helped him to his feet. The gesture was so straightforward, so brusque, so conventional, that not a whisper of homosexuality was there to gossip about the contact between them.

"This is getting too murky," Robert said. "Let's go see Babba and have some light thrown on the matter."

They turned their backs on the river and walked east, to the loft where Robert's guru was holding sat-sang with all those who had been drawn to him.

Two

When the doorbell rang, Julia's long evening of preparation fell apart. Gail's arrival, interesting to deal with from the vantage point of silence and solitude in a warm bath, hit like a large rock in a shallow pool. The impact of what had happened the previous night, how it would be resolved now, caught her up breathless.

When she'd felt the impulse to fuck Eliot the night before, all the considerations which might have stopped her were quickly and easily swept away into the hollow tube of erotic tunnel vision. She dismissed the problem of Martin. They were separated, and anyway, he would never find out. Besides, she had already cheated on him with Eliot a year earlier.

Dealing with the question of her relationship to Gail was a bit more tricky. Eliot slept with many other women; Julia knew that. So it wasn't as though she were taking a faithful husband away for a rare fuck. Also, Eliot wasn't Gail's husband and probably would never be. Gail hadn't spoken too much about their affair, but Julia got the impression that her friend, while deeply involved, had not let herself fully fall in love. At least, Julia had never heard Gail say the word. All in all, she had been ready to have her brief fuck with Eliot and then drop the incident into the garbage bin of history, to pretend that it never happened.

Then the roof had come crashing in. First Gail's call while Eliot was still there, naked and contented. His hurried dressing and leaving while she had to go through a universe of changes in order to talk to her friend. The idea that Eliot would have stood Gail up in order to be with her was fraught with almost too much madness. Eliot was ten kinds of bastard in his way, but he was not a careless or thoughtless man. Such a thing was practically inconceivable, not because of any tenderheartedness on his part, but because he was always such a meticulous planner. The long long conversation with Gail which had to go on until Eliot reached her place was pure hell, including the paranoiac undertones of wondering whether Gail suspected that Eliot had been there.

Julia began the next morning, this morning, ready to tear Eliot's head off, but the only trace of him was a message left with his office secretary that he would be out of town for two days, whereabouts unknown. Her morning coffee, a cigarette, and the *Times* had been the next order of business. She was to see Gail in the evening and wanted to be totally together, the previous evening utterly erased. That small hope was shattered by the first phonecall of the day, Gail calling to tell her that Eliot had proposed, that she was going to accept, that she realized that perhaps she had loved him all along.

The day had been spent nursing a dull headache, and while it shied back somewhat when treated with aspirin, the way a vampire is supposed to flinch at the smell of garlic, the pain settled in for a long visit. The obviousness of its cause was not a factor in its cure. Julia had one of two very unpleasant roads to travel: telling the truth or telling a lie. And each time she swung from one to the other, her head hurt a bit more. She considered canceling the date for the evening, but she knew she would have no rest until she'd seen Gail, talked to her, and either found a new way to relate or else lose the friendship altogether.

Thus, after work, she plunged herself into hot water and grass, hoping to find some rest from the dilemma, so that when the moment of confrontation arrived, she might at least act spontaneously. The spell of relaxation had removed her headache, but had not indicated what her decision ought to be.

Julia sighed, walked to the door, and opened it. Gail rushed in, threw her arms around her, and hugged her, dancing up and down. Julia remained rigid in the embrace, her body unyielding.

"Isn't it fantastic!" Gail almost shouted.

Julia looked at her through lidded eyes and didn't say a word.

She was so silent, so stem, so set in her posture of withdrawal that the mood cut through even Gail's reckless mirth. Gail's mouth went in and out of a smile half a dozen times. Her eyes were like birds on a beach just before a storm, electric, sharp.

"Something's wrong, isn't it?" Gail said at last in an exaggerated drawl which embraced the worst that a little child could possibly be experiencing and letting it know that whatever the problem was it could be fixed up in a minute. It was an attempt at humor, that quality which is born halfway between abandon and concern. Even her expression was like that of the schoolteacher she played to children each day.

Then she looked into Julia's eyes. Then she knew that whatever it was, it was bad, very bad.

"Should we sit down?" Gail said. Her first thought was for her friend, guessing that something had happened to Julia, perhaps in relation to Martin. Or maybe it was the death of a relative or friend. Or grim news from a doctor. Gail was ready to drop all of her excitement and go to the aid of her friend.

Julia saw that, knew the depth of Gail's friendship, knew that she herself would have acted the same in reverse positions. The brief bit of limited passion the night before now loomed as such a terrible mistake and Julia wondered how she could have rationalized it even for a second.

It didn't seem like much at the time, she thought. *I didn't know he had a date with her. I didn't know he was going to propose to her.*

Gail took Julia's hand and began to lead her to the couch. "Should I put some coffee on?" she asked.

But Julia stopped. She knew it was then or never. The longer she stayed in Gail's presence, the more difficult it would become to tell her. It would be impossible. And then she would have to live with it. She would be asked to be Maid of Honor at the wedding. And afterwards, how could she spend time in the same office with Eliot? She now swung as wildly into the direction of blame as she had gone in the direction of nonchalance the night before. She was taken with the worst symptom of panic—not knowing that one is in a panic. She turned halfway around to face Gail who was a step ahead of her on the way to the sofa. The room seemed carved out of flawed crystal. Everything stood out with stark precision, and yet nothing was whole.

"He was here," Julia blurted out. "When you called last night. Eliot was here. When you called . . . he had just finished fucking me in the ass."

Perhaps a society is possible in which the simple communication of mundane sexual activity might be noted and accepted with as much flurry as is given to, say, a listing of what one had for breakfast or dinner. Had Julia said, "When you called last night. Eliot was here. When you called . . . he had just finished eating an onion bagel with cream cheese and Nova Scotia salmon," no one would have made much of it. The terrible contraction which the species had developed in relation to its erotic activity, however, propels people to rank melodramas of the most turgid variety, sometimes to physical violence and even murder. It is possible to envision a society in which an announcement such as Julia's might be made with utter ease and received with some simple, offhanded remark? A "how droll" perhaps, or even "how icky."

But the two women, intelligent, perceptive, experienced, and friendly to each other, could not, in light of all their conditioning, do anything but take the steps they did. Gail sucked her breath in sharply. Julia reached toward her. Gail drew back. Julia turned her head away. Gail looked out at Julia with eyes that signaled warmth through an iron grid of pain. In short, they did the dance of heavy news, taking an intrinsically neutral event and straining it, through the cheese cloth of social dilemma, into a cause célèbre, a scandal which eclipsed famine in Africa and earthquakes in Italy. It, in short, really gave them something to talk about.

"If you tell me you hate me and turn around and walk out and never speak to me again, I'll understand," Julia said.

Gail weighed the offer. Calculations ran through her mind like sand through an hourglass. But since all manifestations of everything which exists in the universe can be reduced to the result of three forces, even the seemingly complex rush of emotions that ransacked Gail's wardrobe of rationalizations resolved itself into three factors: herself, Julia, and Eliot. Eliot was out of town for two days. He had left her apartment at eight in the morning and told her he wouldn't be back until Thursday. Now she understood the real reason for his leaving. She wouldn't be able to deal with him until he returned. His surprise would be a strong one for he couldn't have imagined that Julia would tell.

"Don't be absurd," Gail replied. "I'm too much in shock right now to know whether I'm more angry or hurt. And in any case, it's done. If I walked out now, in ten minutes I'd be crazy wanting to talk to you about it. So. Let's talk."

"I'd make some coffee?" Julia suggested.

"Wine would be more like it," Gail said.

"Well," Julia said, the word almost a sigh. "Why don't you have a seat? Make yourself comfortable."

The sudden stilted structure of the distance between them was as noticeable as an elephant in a rose garden. Each woman was filled with a score of tiny impulses to do something to break the tension. But there was no quick route to relaxation. A lot of words had to be spoken, many feelings had to be exchanged, certain understandings had to be reached. It would be a long evening.

Gail shrugged, indicating that she saw as well as Julia did how awkward the situation was and yet how thin the pane of glass that separated them. Julia nodded, and then turned to go to the kitchen. In a few seconds she could be heard in a dialogue with glasses, bottles, ice trays. Gail looked around the large space. Her glance fell on the bed at the far side of the room.

It must have been there, she thought.

Now that she had a brief moment to sort herself out, she realized at once that whatever she felt, it wasn't jealousy. Relieved, she was able to toss that label out of the box of rubber stamps she used for cataloguing her experience. She knew that Eliot fucked other women, and even as she considered marrying him she was aware that fidelity was out of the question. She had never asked that of him; all she wanted was discretion, consideration, tact. The fact that one of the women he fucked was Julia, however, brought her up short. How long had they been making it? Should she consider herself betrayed? After all, until the night before, she had no special claim on Eliot. She was just one of his cunts. Probably his number one, but that carried no status which anyone, including Julia, had to respect. But as a friend, shouldn't Julia have told her? On the other hand, how did they define friendship? And perhaps this was the only time, and if so, then Julia was honest because she did tell. And what of Eliot? Gail was forced to smile when she thought of his performance the night before. No wonder he was so flustered. If he had made it with just any other woman, he wouldn't have been so completely thrown. Then what about the proposal? Was that just a panicked coverup? Yet he did have deep feelings for her. It was all very interesting, very subtle.

I'm the injured party, and with that insight her mood shifted. She could afford to wait, to let the others do the explaining and apologizing. But even as she felt that, she was ashamed. Eliot and Julia must be suffering quite a bit. And they weren't villains.

She sat on the rug in front of the couch just as Julia came back into the room with a tray of wine and crackers and cheese.

"It was supposed to have been dinner," Julia said. She sat down on the floor, putting the tray down next to her. "I was going to make veal, but . . ." She couldn't finish the sentence. Unaccountably, she began to cry. Her shoulders shook, tears wet her cheeks, she covered her face with her hands. She made no sound. She wept like an actress in a silent film.

Gail watched her for a few minutes, coldly at first, detached from the other's sorrow. But then something stirred in her breast, a sympathetic warmth, a tiny flickering like that of a candle name. Julia's feelings flooded the air, and Gail breathed them in with every breath. She saw that Julia was not weeping only for herself, but for all of them. For Eliot with his super-controlled life, in which each encounter ran on as strict a schedule as German trams. For her, for Gail, a nobody schoolteacher being kept by a wealthy man, finally having her bondage made respectable by a marriage license. And for all the poor people on the planet, trapped in their pitiful limitations, in their paltry possessiveness, in their rancid identities.

Not surprisingly, Gail felt her own eyes go moist, and without thinking she reached out and put her arms around Julia's shoulders. Julia stiffened, then let go, and in a second the two women were embracing one another tightly, sobbing fully, letting themselves be overwhelmed by the cataract of rushing feeling, the sweet release that even pain provides when it is expressed, given the full range of fecundating power.

They cried for a long time, while a world spun on, unconcerned. In the same building, a score of other dramas unfolded. A man and wife entered the ninth hour of a fight. They had reached the point where they were dredging up little tender secrets they'd told each other a year earlier, things they'd whispered late at night after making love, and had now shaped the truths into sharp barbs, dipped in the venom of anger and meanness, and were hurling them into each other's heart, purposely, viciously, wanting to hurt, to tear, to destroy, like outer-directed scorpions doing a dance of destruction. An eighty-five year old woman lay on her bed and felt her body protest each time she took a breath. "*It* wants to die," she said out loud to the empty room, "but *I* don't." And for the hundredth time that day she dozed and strolled down the long lane of memory to see if she could remember who "I' was, knowing that death would come that way, surreptitiously, as she bent over to smell a flower that had bloomed before the century was born. On the roof a young boy had attained the goal he'd worked on for almost a month. A thin, pouty girl had consented, after much attention, false promises, and concentrated mauling, to pull down her jeans and let the youth roam inside her sticky cunt with the middle finger of his right hand while she rubbed the bulge in his pants with the palm of her left hand.

Beyond that multi-leveled stage, the city throbbed its night song. Millions of bulbs burned with indifferent heat upon the full range of human behavior. A surgeon in the emergency room of a city hospital stitched up a split scalp; a mugger stepped out from behind a truck and waved a gun at an elderly man; a hundred thousand people lifted glasses to their mouths in an effort to get drunk; a scholar discovered a nuance in an ancient Hebrew text; a priest put on street clothes and walked up and down Eighth Avenue until a hooker caught his eye; a mother hummed a lullaby as her two-day-old infant sucked at her nipple.

The darkness spread, east and west, north and south,

deepening over the face of the globe until it began to meet the light, and twilight and dawn, evening and morning, night and day, striped the earth with perfect symmetry. Green and blue and white and black, the earth spun slowly on its axis, sang its circle about the sun, which followed its prescribed course in the galaxy, joining a billion billion galaxies in a vast and seemingly endless expansion into realms so far beyond human comprehension that only our fantasies suffice to give any solace to our minds.

Gail and Julia wept until their tears were done, and then they pulled back from each other. For a while they busied themselves with handkerchiefs, dabbings, blowings, and sniffings. Then, that out of the way, they had no alternative but to look at one another. They both smiled shyly, a bit embarrassed.

"I must look a mess," Julia said, her hand going to her hair in a reflex gesture.

"You're so very beautiful," Gail said. "I mean, not just your looks. I've always known that you were attractive in that way. But I feel that this is the first time I'm really seeing you. I mean, what's inside." She pressed her lips together. "Oh, am I making any sense at all? I feel like I'm talking inside a big paper bag."

"How about some wine?" Julia asked. "That should clear both our heads."

She poured, and they lifted their glasses, made a silent toast, and drank. The alcohol was a solvent cutting through the glue of self-consciousness. It bit the tongue, flushed the throat, warmed the chest, and hit the belly like a felt hammer on a bronze gong. It was a very good wine, and they finished the first round, poured a second, and were halfway into that before either spoke.

"It seems we have a lot to talk about, and yet, suddenly, I can't remember what was so important," Gail said. "I came over to tell you that Eliot had proposed. And then you told me that you made it with him last night. And I suppose I'm supposed to be outraged or vindictive, but right now I don't feel anything but comfortable. Do you mind if I take my shoes off?"

"Take off whatever you like," Julia said. The sentence echoed off the wall and bounced back on her, causing her to tilt her head slightly, but she dismissed the perception.

"How long have we known each other now?" Gail continued.

"I don't know. Must be three years."

"It's funny. When I think of you, I always say to myself, 'Julia my best friend,' like that, all in one breath, 'Julia-my-best-friend.' And now that we're sitting here, I realize I barely know you at all. That's peculiar, isn't it? After all this time, I realize I've never seen you cry, or cried with you. And there are some things we've never talked about."

"I guess we've just enjoyed each other's company and never felt the need . . ." Julia began to say. Then she shook her head. "No, that's bullshit. There have been a lot of things I suppressed. I guess I was trying to be polite."

"You know I had a crush on Martin, don't you?"

Julia kicked off her own shoes, and cut a piece of cheese. She popped it into her mouth. "No, I didn't know."

"I kind of fell for him when I used to go to the health club. It was a blow when I learned he was married But I tucked my pussy away and switched the vibration to one of pleasantness. Then he introduced us that night, remember? And I liked you so much all at once, and I thought, 'Well, maybe I've lost a stud but I may have found a friend,' which is so much rarer."

"I liked you a lot too," Julia said. "Meeting you was so good for me. I was beginning to feel the first letdown after our Europe trip. And I had just begun working for Eliot and I got onto a kind of speed trip. So I was simultaneously depressed and strung out. And being with you was like the first breath I had taken in ages."

At hearing Julia say "Eliot," Gail gnawed at her lower lip, and her eyes threatened to fill again. Julia didn't see the reaction until she'd gone on past his name, and when she noticed Gail's unhappiness, she hung her head.

"Oh Gail, I'm so sorry," she said. "I wouldn't hurt you for anything in the world. I don't know what got into me. I was just so horny. I haven't fucked in almost two months. And I guess you don't know this, but Eliot and I had had a very brief affair, just before you met him. We're together all the time. You know? I mean, we're very intimate."

She looked up to see how Gail was taking all that she was

saying. Her friend had an expression that seemed to hover between pain and hatred. There was nothing for Julia to do but accept it, to absorb the feeling and transform it within herself. This was part of her dues.

"Shall I go on?" she asked.

"Yes," Gail said, her lips tight. "I want to hear. Please."

"Well, I know things about Eliot that could send him to jail for ten years. He's a lot of things to me. A father figure, a boss, a teacher, a confidant. When I began to go through really big trouble with Martin, Eliot listened to me for weeks and weeks."

"But during all that time you hardly told me what was going on."

"I suppose I have a natural instinct to go to a man when I need help."

"I know what you mean," Gail replied, her bitterness hanging out.

"Anyway, there was something in the air all day yesterday. Both Eliot and I felt it. And when quitting time came, it was just obvious that we both wanted to fuck. And I worried about Martin and I worried about you, but somehow it didn't seem to involve anyone else. After all, we were consenting adults. We were both free. And it never occurred to me that Eliot had a date with you. You know his style. His appointment book is immaculate. He even schedules a precise amount of time between appointments, enough for transportation, enough to think about the next person he's going to meet; he even leaves himself time to piss, for Christ's sake."

"I know," Gail said, and a shadow of a smile fell across her lips.

The two women stole glances at one another. A subtle checkpoint had been passed.

"So I thought we'd just *do it*. You know. Get the panties off, get the pants down. Cock hard, hole all greased up. Huff and puff, move the old ass around, rub my fingers on my clit, and get my fucking rocks off."

Gail's eyes opened wide. She had never heard Julia speak like this before. In fact, she'd never heard any woman speak like this before. She had thoughts which used those words and those images, but they were fleeting, formless things which never got translated into sound, much less communicated.

"Are you shocked?" Julia said, seeing Gail's expression. "Well, I'd choose more fancy language, but that's exactly the way I was thinking. I knew there wouldn't be any gooey stuff between Eliot and me, and no traces the following day. We could both do the thing and draw a curtain over it and act like it never happened. He's a very attractive man in his brutal way, as you well know, and a certain charge builds up over time. So we discharged the charge. And nothing would have come of it if he hadn't proposed to you. If he hadn't stood you up to come over here." She poured more wine into both their glasses. "I wonder why he did it?"

"Maybe he wanted something to happen. Maybe it was his way of blowing the lid off." Gail picked up her glass and sipped at the wine.

"What do you mean?"

"Well, look at what's happened. Eliot wound up proposing. And you and I are having probably the first real conversation of our entire friendship."

"It seems a hell of a roundabout way to get at things."

"Life is funny," Gail said.

"Life is a soap opera," Julia amended.

The two women looked at a spot on the floor between them. The pattern of their talk for the evening had been set. It would be a series of spirals ending in resolution at each level, with a pause before going to the next plateau. The movement was endless and could carry them for the rest of their lives, defining the meaning of relationship, A melting was taking place, a process they both felt, and the unexpected blow which had hurled them together so violently was indeed proving a form of caress.

"What about . . . Eliot?" Julia asked. "Are you going to tell him that you know?"

"I'd have to, if I was going to have anything more to do with him."

"Are you?"

Gail looked up sharply. "Julia," she said, "do you mind if I ask something personal?"

Julia smiled broadly. "Well, what could be personal now?"

"What was there between you and Martin? I mean, really. Without any bullshit."

Julia stirred and changed her position. She unfolded her legs and sat with her back against the couch. The white terrycloth robe fell open and revealed her thighs far up past her knees. Gail found herself glimpsing the expanse of white skin. Julia's hair hung loose about her shoulders. Her breasts were half exposed. Her face was open, easy, intelligent. Gail caught her breath. She was caught by a brief, intense desire to put her arms around Julia's waist and bury her head in the other woman's soft belly.

"I guess at first it was the challenge of getting married. You know. We've all been handed the story from the time we could understand English. That's *the* big one, right? And then there was the physical part, of course. Martin is such a stud. Hung like a horse, and practically tireless. He used to screw me so long and so hard sometimes that I couldn't close my legs for an hour afterward." Julia looked about her almost absent-mindedly. "Do you have any cigarettes?" she asked.

"No," Gail replied, "but I brought some grass. Would you like a joint?"

"I'm already a bit stoned, but why not?"

Gail reached into her bag and pulled out a tiny cigarette case from which she extracted a thin, hand-rolled marijuana cigarette. "This is a present from Eliot," she said. "Just in from Thailand. A hundred and seventy-five dollars an ounce."

Julia made a whistling gesture with her lips, which jolted Gail with its suggestion of kissing.

Gail lit up, inhaled, ballooned the smoke in her lungs, and passed the joint to Julia. The next few minutes were given up to the ritual of the grass high, letting the weed work its subtle alchemy, setting up temporary headquarters in the brain, rearranging the pattern and intensity of signals. It was an extraordinarily powerful strain, and by the time they were down to a roach, holding the ember with the tips of long fingernails, they both found it difficult to focus on anything but the waterfall of sensations exploding in their bodies.

"Whew," Gail said. She leaned back against the sofa, her head on a pillow. She unbuttoned the waist of her skirt and pulled the bottom of her blouse out. She slid down until she was three-quarters reclining on the floor.

"Why don't I put on some music?" Julia said.

She got up and went over to the stereo and stacked six records on the spindle. She listened only to slow music, and her collection reflected only the most mellow of whatever genre she choose. In popular, it was, for example, Donovan, not the Stones; in classical, it was Debussy and some of Satie, not Wagner; in Indian, it was Ali Akhbar Khan, not Ravi Shankar, So it didn't matter which records she chose; they would all reflect the same mood.

When she returned, Gail was largely disheveled, her skirt hiked up past her knees, the top four buttons of her blouse undone. She was gazing at the ceiling, her eyes somewhat glazed.

"Where were we?" Julia said as she lay down.

"Martin was hung like a horse and you couldn't close your legs after he fucked you," Gail replied, her voice drowsy.

Julia sighed and sank back into her story. "Right. After that, there was the prospect of Europe. He wouldn't have gone in a million years, but I was able to move him out of that dreary little town and that absurd job and for almost a year we lived like rich people. Moving all the time. Then there was domesticity, which lasted about three months before I got bored with living a twenty-four-hour schedule. It was like having two jobs: Eliot from nine to five and Martin from five until nine the next morning. And when I looked deep into my heart, I knew that if I had to make a choice, I'd prefer giving up the job with Martin. It wasn't as exciting, and I didn't get paid. After that, it was just a matter of time."

"What about him?"

"Who knows? He's not the world's most articulate man. But I suppose if it takes two to make a marriage, it takes two to make a divorce. I assume he got as bored for his reasons as I did for mine. Anyway, the last few months before we split up were practically unbearable. We used to lie around all night and silently hate one another."

"I didn't realize," Gail said. She rolled over on her side and looked at Julia who still lay on her back. The grass had imparted a softness to her aura, and Gail suffered a momentary loss of erotic indentity. For an instant she looked at Julia the way a man might, seeing the lush. unconscious invitation of the almost perfect body, the pose of utter lassitude. When she snapped back into herself, however, the feeling did not leave. And she found herself thinking. *This is desire. What I'm feeling is desire.*

"That was the worst part, getting caught up in that terrible trap of the closed pair. You know, the bond between a man and a woman is so strong, so total in a way, that it shuts everything else out. There were a hundred times I wanted to call you, to talk to you. But I had this idea that I owed Martin one hundred percent loyalty, that I couldn't be really real with anybody else. You know, I was less upset over my sexual infidelity than over talking to somebody else about my marriage."

Julia turned her head to look at Gail. Her eyes widened and then narrowed when she saw her friend looking at her. Gail's face was a pool of such clear water that the bottom could be seen, magnified, clarified. And the feelings that lay at the core of Gail's person at that instant were so sharply defined already that Julia couldn't mistake them. Except that she did, for she had not made that leap across gender lines, and any erotic component to the mood of the moment could not be registered. What Julia perceived was concern.

"Gail, what's the matter?" she said.

"I guess I'm mixed up," Gail replied. "Suddenly it seems like there's a lot of people in the room."

"I'm sorry. I didn't mean to get so depressing."

"No, it's all right. I wanted to hear about it. I guess I want to know whether I should marry Eliot. Every marriage tale I've heard sounds pretty much the same, and I guess when anyone gets married they think, 'Mine will be different,' and then it never is. I've been consoling myself with the idea that money will make the difference. We can even afford to maintain separate apartments, and Eliot travels a lot so I won't even be seeing him a lot of the time." She reached over and put her hand on Julia's arm. "Am I being too cold, calculating it all like this?"

Julia took her friend's hand and held it. "No, baby, not at all. You'd be a fool if you didn't. The only thing is, you never really know until you do it. Once that piece of paper is signed, it's like living in a foreign country. I don't know how to explain it, but it's like hearing a door slam behind you."

"Isn't there anyway out? Does it have to be like that?"

They slowly disengaged. Gail's hand was on fire where Julia had held it. Julia's heart was beating rapidly. Both women were breathing hard. They fell back as though exhausted, the extremely powerful marijuana amplifying each nuance of feeling a hundred times. Julia's reality crashed in upon her. Time telescoped and psychological space turned in upon itself. Telling the story of her relationship with Martin had impacted that experience so that she felt his presence very strongly in the room. Superimposed upon that was the hangover from the fucking she'd received from Eliot the night before. And now there was this abrupt and titanic breakthrough with Gail. And she had no resting place in the rapid flow of events within which to integrate, to allow it all to be absorbed into the wider stream of awareness that was her life. She felt flushed, undone. She slid forward even more and lay completely on the floor. She heard Gail do the same. The woman next to her had become a mixture of threat and consolation. Gail's presence was filling her entirely, and at the same time crowding something in her, some wall of privacy that rarely got approached, much less climbed. Not even Martin had touched spots that were, madly, surrendering themselves to Gail's vibrations. Julia had a wild impulse to tear her robe off. She sighed, arched her back, and tried to melt into the floor. The first record dropped and she realized she had not heard a note. With the second, the strains of Judy Collins filled the room. She was singing about clouds and life and somehow coming to understand that it is impossible to understand. She stretched. Her left hand touched something. It was Gail's hand. She began to pull back with the unquestioned reflex of social nicety, but Gail's fingers closed over her own. For an instant Julia panicked, not knowing why, but suddenly afraid. And then she took a deep breath, and relaxed. The contact was made, accepted.

Gail could barely contain herself. Insights galloped through her mind like steeplechase horses before the pack has thinned itself out. Thundering hooves pounded the turf of her consciousness, and then tons of muscle and bone lifted itself in the air to fly giddily over the hurdle of an ancient resistance, to come thudding down on the other side, pursuing the race. Every now and then, one didn't make it, and horse and rider went sprawling crazily across the earth. The images in Gail's mind were now too sharp, too vivid, to be denied. There was no hazy distance across which she needed to peer to discover what she wanted. She was hungry for Julia in a most direct, physical way. She wanted her friend in her arms, their breasts mingling, their thighs pressing tight. She wanted Julia's kisses, her ripe mouth and tender tongue. She wanted to smell the pungent heat between Julia's thighs, to savor the tart taste, the viscous musk of slow excitement.

This is insane, she thought. *I have to get a grip on myself.* But even as she forced herself down against the rug, biting the inside of her lip, Julia's hand found her own. It was a moment of such electrifying intensity that Gail's scalp crawled. It took superhuman effort to keep from rolling over violently and flinging herself on to Julia, raping her vulnerability. She felt Julia begin to pull away, and her heart dropped at the idea that she would lose even that little precious contact. So all her life's conditioning to the contrary, she seized her friend's hand.

And then, all at once, it was easy. They were lying side by side, relaxed, breathing fully, holding hands.

All that just to reach something so simple, Gail thought, and allowed herself an inner sigh of relief. *I almost made a fool of myself.* The actual, full, direct physical contact had skimmed the cream off the top of the tension that had built between them. And with that, they both subsided into a long, deep dreaminess, striking into the music, enjoying the soma that spiced their mundane physiology. They drifted along the edge of wakefulness, flirting with sleep, at the thin edge of hypnogogic ecstasy, the most exquisite jewel on the spectrum of consciousness. Around and between them, a subtle energy flowed. The full release of waking structures liberated the electricity of expression. And since they were totally inert on the gross level, the energy was free to dance like transparent flame over their bodies. Their fingers loosened and their palms became conductor plates through which flowed the essence of their selves. They entered a union so profound that it was attached to no experience whatsoever.

In time as measured by the clock, a half hour passed. In time as measured by the music, months passed. In time as measured by the depth of the women's breathing, eternities had come and gone. When Julia finally stirred, moved a finger, opened her eyes, she experienced what she imagined an infant must feel, that chaotic sense of wonder at color and shape. When she went to move her left hand, she found that it was glued to Gail's hand. Disengaging was not a mechanical process, but had become a radical alteration in the nature of her relationship to the world. As she began to pull away, Gail moaned softly and her eyelids fluttered.

"Wow, where were we?" Gail said at last.

"Another universe," Julia replied.

"I've done that alone, but I never went there with anyone else before."

"Me neither. In fact, I usually can't space out that much. When I'm alone my thinking usually takes over. But with you—I don't know. It's like you took the place of my thoughts."

"Did you feel my presence?" Gail asked.

Julia pulled herself up a bit, rested her shoulders against the couch. "Yes. There was a place when everything turned violet."

Gail also sat up, excited. "Right. It was a kind of mist, with mountains barely showing through."

"Right," Julia chimed in, "and something that looked like a huge lake in the distance—it was a deeper purple."

Gail opened her eyes wide in astonishment. "That's *exactly* what I saw," she exclaimed. "We *were* there together."

"Telepathy!" Julia said, awestruck. "It's real. And it's not like reading somebody's thoughts. It's going to where thoughts go, only in your mind with someone. Oh, I'm not saying this right."

Gail smiled, reached out and held Julia's hand again. "You don't have to. Don't you see? We shared it together. We don't need the words."

"We . . . don't . . . need . . . the . . . words . . ." Julia repeated, the full impact of the words hitting her with methodical repetition, like the left jabs of a master boxer slamming into an already groggy opponent. Julia shivered, a chill shaking her so violently that her entire torso shuddered.

"Oh dear," Gail said and spontaneously moved forward and put her arms around Julia, holding her tightly. Julia shook in her friend's embrace for almost a minute, the energy exploding playfully up and down the nerve nodes of her spine. Not having any knowledge of the relationship between astral events and physical reactions, never having been introduced to the concepts of kundalini and chakras, both women experienced the phenomenon in ignorance, which meant that they tasted more fear than they might otherwise have, but at the same time appreciated the occurrence more nakedly, without a superstructure of rationalizations.

Finally, Julia calmed down and Gail's embrace became looser, warmer. Soon, there was no need for Gail to be holding her at all, and yet neither woman made a move to pull back. Julia's arms moved up slowly, tentatively, and made their way around Gail's waist. When the contact was made, the moment and its implications accepted, they fell further into each other's arms, holding on with all the ardor of lovers.

As sensitive to each other as they were, each minute aspect of the embrace hummed its separate song. The most immediate, the most obvious, was the pressure of their breasts as they brought their chests together. Neither of them had ever hugged another woman before in quite that way, so intimately, so long. The brief embraces of social convenience with relatives and acquaintances never reached the point at which they could feel the details of the other's body. Julia's robe was open and her breasts bare. Gail wore only a thin blouse, two-thirds unbuttoned. The heat where valley met valley climbed to troubling temperatures.

And yet, it was not quite erotic, for neither was prepared for such a reality. It seems like such a small step, to go from an embrace to a kiss, from a kiss to a caress, from a caress to a penetration. Yet there is a point at which quantitative change become qualitative, and then one is in another realm entirely. Such is the realm of eroticism. At a time when the casual fuck is the official insignia of the culture, when its only rival is the sanctified fuck of marriage, the notion of fucking as a branding of the soul, an alchemical transfusion from essence to essence, has fallen into disuse. Even the cross-cultural borrowing from tantric buddhism has not quite made the point, for those who study its methods and metaphysics tend to see merely technique or discipline or transcendence or union. And in relation to what fucking really is, these qualities are unspeakably petty, although from the point of view of the common person, they are held up as surpassing goals.

We all know this instinctively, and yet we forget, we have it trained out of us, along with all the other wisdom which is our birthright as children. And we go through all the dreary stages along the path of erotic development so-called, from shy romance to hard-edged debauchery, until we are caught in some mechanical routine, which may be garlanded with flowers of the most subtle sensuality, but remains essentially lacking in meaning.

Gail and Julia understood, inchoately, dumbly, that under no matter which rubric they might take their clothes off and plunge into the arms of Eros together, they would be transgressing the bounds of social safety, that they would become, on the spot, bound to one another. And even if they casually parted the following morning and treated the incident as a marijuana excess, the mark of erotic love would have been burned into their souls, and there would be no going back from that, for to be born again is as ineluctable in its implications as being born. For each time one is born again, one must die again.

They disengaged and pulled back slowly. When they were no longer touching, they looked into each other's eyes.

"Gail," Julia said. "I love you."

Gail's eyes were moist. "All this time. Three years. We've been in love for so long and never known it."

"When we met, there was that sparkle, that joy, that sense of adventure. If you had been a man, I would have recognized it at once."

Gail nodded. "What was it? The sex? Is it that we were afraid of sex and so we couldn't accept love?"

"There's no love without sex," Julia said. "You know that. Not love the way I'm feeling it now."

Gail closed her eyes in agreement, and when she opened them she looked out with the trembling ingenuousness of a teenage girl feeling herself turn into a woman for the first time.

"Do you want to have sex?" Gail asked.

"I feel it," Julia replied. "You do too, don't you? But actually doing it. I don't know. What would it mean? Where would it lead?" She paused a moment and then her face broke open in a laugh.

Gail watched her and did not change expression. Julia subsided into a smile. "I just got a picture of Martin and Eliot as we called them in for a conference and then announced the news that you and I had become lovers."

Julia grinned and looked at Gail, expecting a smile of corroboration. But Gail was stonefaced. "What is it?" Julia asked finally. "It's not a cheap joke," Gail said evenly. Julia's eyes widened. "Oh Gail, I didn't mean . . . Hey, don't be so serious."

"Why shouldn't I be serious?" Gail snapped. Julia was silent for several seconds. "Now I do need a cigarette," she said. "I think I may have some next to the bed."

She got up and pulled her housedress about her, cinching the cord at the waist, then walked over to the far end of the large room She staggered slightly, a bit more affected by the wine and grass and heavy run of emotions than she had realized. She rummaged in a drawer of the night table, found a wrinkled Pall Mall, smoothed it out, lit it, and inhaled with intense concentration, then let the smoke out with an almost exaggerated sigh of relief. She ran her hand over her face, made several gestures which might, if she were an actress on stage, indicate to the audience that she was clearing her head, and turned to go back to the couch. She stopped halfway there. She couldn't see Gail, but was able to sense her. Some strange and unsettling emanation came from the area behind the couch. A premonition of dread chilled her heart and she rushed forward suddenly, hair flying.

"Gail?" she called out. She couldn't see Gail on the floor, and for a wild millisecond surmised that her friend had vanished, utterly disappeared. She turned the corner around the back of the couch, and found Gail lying on its pillows, stark naked.

Julia's breath caught in her chest. In her confusion, in the low light, she thought she was looking down at herself. Her experience with nude female bodies was extremely limited. Several times, at the health club, a woman had come into the steam room without a towel around her, but that had been so formal, so public, so in keeping with the context, that Julia could view it the way she might look at photos in a nudist magazine. Before that, she couldn't remember the last time she'd seen another woman without clothes on. The only naked female body she was familiar with was her own, and that was precisely the image which her mind hastily conjured to throw over Gail in the same way that a passerby might cover an accident victim with a coat.

Julia didn't know what to do. To look or to look away; both were perplexing. Meanwhile, Gail's figure pulsated almost imperceptibly, and Julia was drawn by its vibration. She lay with her right arm crooked up and over her, the forearm serving as a pillow for her head. Her left arm was by her side, relaxed. Gail's right leg was raised, bent at the knee so that the angle between it and the left leg, stretched out flat and long at the edge of the couch, was enough to cause Gail's cunt to appear as the merest hint of black and pink beneath the thatch of thick, curly pubic hair. Gail's breasts fell, as large breasts do when a woman is lying down, to either side of her chest. Julia's glance returned more often to Gail's nipples than to anywhere else, for they were perfectly smooth purple discs, the tips long thin stems now drooping slightly. Gail was breathing deeply, her mouth was open and her eyes, hot mirrors, showed Julia the image of herself.

"Gail," Julie said, her voice breaking.

"Why shouldn't we be naked with one another?" Gail said.

"Gail . . ." Julia repeated.

"Why shouldn't we love each other, and fuck each other, and tell each other what's in our hearts? Is that something that only a man and woman can do together? Who said that, Julia? Who made that law?" Gail smiled abruptly. "Have a seat, sweetheart. Make yourself at home."

Julia's eyes focused sharply and the lines of her face went straight. Something like anger flared. She brought the cigarette to her lips, sucked in the harsh smoke, and blew it out again almost at once. With her free hand she pulled the top lapels of her housecoat tightly together, all at once a prim matron putting a young man in his place.

"I don't know that I want to continue this," she snapped.

Gail leapt from the couch, her movement so quick, so unexpected, so seemingly opposed to the law of gravity, that Julia almost fell over backwards.

"Well, how shall I do it?" Gail shouted. "Do you want to be taken by force? Is that the way a man would do it for you?" Gail pulled the cigarette from Julia's fingers and flung it into the fireplace.

"What's so precious under here?" Gail grabbed the edges of the housedress and yanked so violently that Julia's fingers were pulled loose from their grasp. Gail tugged and pushed, stripping the robe from Julia's shoulders, and then, in a single sweeping gesture, peeled it off entirely, dropping to her knees to complete the movement.

Then Julia was also naked. Her eyes flashed fire but her lower lip trembled. She pressed her thighs together but her arms remained at her sides, the hands doubled into fists so that the pectoral muscles flexed and pulled her breasts taut. The two woman froze in those postures of defiance and revolt, of tender violence, stunned that they had come so far.

The presence of clothing is so fully conditioned an aspect of our lives that its simple removal is enough to be considered a major shift in identity. Whether it is done conventionally, as among nudists; or aggressively, as with stripteasers; or casually, as among people who have lived together for a long time; or radically, as with streakers; no matter what the mood or approach, the event is significant. Because it reveals what are called the private parts, the parts that shit and piss, the parts that fuck and fart, the parts that bleed and ejaculate. So deeply ingrained is our involvement with clothing that a multi-billion dollar business has sprung up based on nothing more extraordinary than photographs of women examining their vaginas as though they had suddenly chanced upon a totally unique discovery. A human being is not free to walk the face of the earth naked, and that is all the comment that need be made upon the entire human condition.

Julia relaxed by degrees, and in a few moments she was standing there with something approaching naturalness. Gail shook her head, amazed at her temerity. She rose slowly to her feet.

"All right," Julia said, smiling suddenly, "we're naked. Now what?"

"Now we can take it easy and enjoy the rest of the evening," Gail replied. "We don't have to do anything special. This is interesting enough, so far."

"Well, if we're going to actually hang around in our birthday suits, then I suppose I'd better make a fire," Julia said.

"Fine," Gail told her. "And I'll make us some proper drinks and roll another joint." She glanced at the stereo. "Jesus, I wish you had some music with a bit of beat to it. This is like having marshmallows poured in my ear."

"You never criticized my taste in music before," Julia said.

The two woman looked at one another wonderingly. Gail snorted, a huff of gruff merriment. "We haven't even been to bed together yet." She frowned. "Maybe sex does open the door to disrespect."

"But there's the radio," Julia added quickly. "You might find a nighttime FM station with some rock." Julia smiled. "Don't worry about it," she added. "Martin didn't like my taste in music either, but he never had the balls to say so. I don't mind if you lean on me a little bit. In fact, it feels good to have somebody really relating to me and reacting to me and not afraid to shake me up a little bit."

"OK," Gail said. She went over to the console, turned off the stereo and switched on the radio. She spun the dial to 102.7 and at once a smooth, raucous guitar, backed by a throbbing base and sinuous drum, slid out of the speakers, changing the mood of the room. The place became darker, more vital, filled with nuances the way a wood is alive with sounds and sharp hidden eyes at night. Julia had turned to begin the makings of a fire, but when the music came on, she glanced over at Gail. Her friend was standing in front of the amplifier, her back to her. She was swaying slightly, doing a tiny dance to the sounds. Julia's eyes were drawn to Gail's ass, a tight, soft, vibrant organism that had sprung into life, and was signaling in a language of basic gesture and primitive meaning. Julia could feel the unmistakable urge to go across the room and put her hand on the dark inviting cleft that now shifted and spoke like the shadow of a stick on the sandy bottom of a shallow stream.

But Gail spun to one side and moved off into the kitchen, her voice trailing behind her. "Vodka tonic all right with you?" she called out.

"Fine," Julia shouted, her own voice snapping her out of her reverie.

She bent down and built the basic structure of the fire carefully. Rolled up copies of the *Times,* strips of cardboard, thin splinters of wood. She lit it in four places and in seconds it was blazing easily. She put thicker pieces of wood on top, and when flames had begun to curl around their edges, laid on three thick logs. She scooted back, and sat with her shoulders against the couch, feeling the warmth of the fire begin to caress her skin. It was fairly obvious that she and Gail would make love. It had happened suddenly, without warning. Nothing in her life had prepared her for it. And yet there it was. She thought she could guess what it would be like, reasoning that one didn't have to drink to have a notion of what drunkenness was. She was curious, a bit turned on. But this was already at a level once removed from Gail's immediate presence. And some arcane voice inside her, one which rarely spoke because it had not been listened to since Julia was five or six years old, before she had had her sense of magic destroyed, now tried to whisper that what was about to happen was enough to rock the very foundations of civilization as it had been practiced for more than ten thousand years. Julia had no political consciousness as such, and women's liberation was something she vaguely associated with articles in *Cosmopolitan.* In that sense, she was on a par with countless lesbians for whom the act of physical intimacy between women is a perfectly private affair. The radical middle, that group who understood that the issue is not having sex, but the *freedom* which having sex implies, would have smiled on Gail and Julia that night. Yet neither of the women had any inkling of the historical ramifications of what they were doing, that this night was both a product of and a movement in the growing awareness that the heterosexual bond, unqualified by homosexual love, and resulting in the rigid, terse, tense form known as the couple, was a relatively rare manifestation, and ought to occur only in those instances when it is consciously chosen by mature individuals who find it organically congenial to their needs, temperaments, and values. To have such a thing imposed ruthlessly upon an entire people is a kind of cultural fascism so profound that those who point it out are inevitably seen as some kind of crank. Among the Indian tribes on the continent, all forms of social erotic forms existed. The European wiped all that out and forced monogamy upon everyone, including such gentle rustics as the Mormons, thus crippling not only those whose inclinations might be toward other paths, but even the true monogamists themselves who had to bear the guilt born of association with the dictatorial decree.

For Julia, now, however, there was only the warmth of the flames, the insinuating insistence of the music that the pelvis must be moved, the mind must be shaken loose, the heart must expand. And in a few minutes there was Gail, beautiful, young, smiling with a universe of friendliness and warmth. Gail carrying a tray with two chilled glasses and their transparent bellyfuls of cheer, a tray with another marijuana cigarette with its ticket to realms of telepathy and sensual fulfillment.

Gail sat down. Julia watched her the way a cat looks at shadows. It was extraordinary to look at the hundred common gestures that a person makes, and to see them without the protective coloration of clothing. *I really haven't seen anyone in my whole life,* Julia thought. *I've just seen their clothing.* She watched the slight jiggle of Gail's breasts, the folds at the tops of her thighs as she bent over, and always, the hypnotic center, the living cunt.

They each picked up a glass. "Here's to . . . what?" Gail said.

"To now," Julia replied without thinking.

"And then," Gail added.

Both women hovered around the edge of a smile and sipped at their drinks. The liquor did its job of instant loosening as the alcohol was absorbed into the bloodstream and made its way to the brain. Gail put her glass down, and lifted the joint up, her eyes questioning. Julia nodded, her expression that of a mischievous smile.

"Will we regret this in the morning?" Julia asked.

Gail lit the joint, inhaled, passed it to her friend. And once again the ritual was re-enacted, the formal decision to sail on a carpet of sensation into an other-wordly realm in which the concerns of chronological reality lost all substance. The solid world of the morning newspapers, of men in terrible machines killing other men, of a species run amok with its technological toys, of dreary routines in offices five days a week, of small pleasures, of absurd ambitions, of anxiety, of telephone calls from parents wondering why you haven't been in touch. They would flee all that, even for a brief time, escape into their minds, find an infinitude of curlecues with which to distract themselves.

Gail took a lungful of smoke, leaned forward, put her lips on Julia's open mouth, and exhaled, forcing the breath and grass into Julia's body. It was done so deftly, so effortlessly, that the transfer had taken place before Julia realized that the movement was actually a kiss. Her chest exploded with heat, with the totally unfamiliar sensation of having someone else's breath in her lungs. Her lips began to tingle almost at once. Gail's eyes smiled into her own.

Julia took a toke, and then Gail, who repeated the mouth-to-mouth resusciation. But this time their mouths stayed together longer, their lips clung, and when they parted it was with deep sighs.

"I don't know," Gail said, replying to Julia's question. "I won't regret this. This is the most beautiful moment in my life. If I were a man I'd ask you to marry me."

"I'm already married," Julia said.

"And I'm engaged," Gail added.

"I guess it's hopeless, then," Julia said.

The joint was finished.

"What about them?" Julia continued after Gail dropped the

tiny roach into the ashtray. Her head was already beginning to swim. But it was with precisely that kind of disorientation that she wanted to talk about her situation, to know it from the point of view of unreasonable perspectives. "What about the men?"

"Martin's your problem. As far as Eliot is concerned, I'm going to tell him that I know about you two. And I'm going to tell him about tonight. And I'm going to make him understand that my relationship with you won't take second place to my relationship with him."

"Will you marry him?"

"If we can keep out separate places," Gail said with sudden conviction. "I like my apartment, I like my life. I don't want to have to change who I am because I get married. And I want to be free to see you, to spend nights with you." She glanced at Julia, a sudden flicker of fear in her eyes. "Unless I'm presuming too much. Unless this isn't as important to you as it is to me. I can't tell you what this means. But it's like I've only been seeing out of one eye. And now I've taken one of my blinkers off. Do you understand? I've loved you for three years. And now you're here, naked, lovely, and we're free. Free! Do you think I would ever give that up? Would you?"

Julia shook her head slowly from side to side like a small child denying that it had done the naughty thing it was accused of. "No," she drawled. "Anything or anyone that told me I wasn't free to love you totally would have to be evil."

"I'd like to marry Eliot," Gail continued. "I would like his child. I would like to travel the world with him. I would like to pass the years knowing him. But not at the price of my liberty, my individuality."

"Maybe we could do threesomes," Julia said, and the minute she said it she put her hand over her mouth as though she had just belched. "Oh dear," she said. "Did I say that? I usually don't talk when I'm stoned. I can begin to see why. The words just bubbled up."

"Well, maybe we could," Gail replied. "Right now I feel like anything's possible. What the hell. We're free, aren't we? The earth is our home, isn't it? Nobody gets born a ruler over anybody else. Why the fuck shouldn't we do whatever we want to? Who's stopping us?" She had raised her voice, slipping into a kind of parlor oratory. She was voicing the question asked by every radical human being ever born, the question that cuts at the very heart of the senile dictator called civilization.

"I guess nobody's stopping us but us," Julia answered. She sat down on her heels and picked up her glass and began to sip slowly. Her expression was disconsolate, her posture sagged.

"Hey, what's wrong?" Gail said when she saw the change. "Why so sad?"

"I don't know. I guess I just got a quick snapshot of what a waste my life has been, the way I've boxed myself in. And for a few seconds, while you were making your speech, everything got light and very very wide. It was as though I had been living in a cave and suddenly somebody came along and lifted the whole mountain off my head. And then I thought of you and me, and wondered if this was some kind of wild fantasy. And I thought of Martin, and how he would shrivel if I ever told him these things. And I thought of going into the office and dealing with Eliot. And with my whole stupid career. I got such an ugly picture of myself, hustling and wheeling and dealing and using people like machines just to get ahead, to make a bundle. Forcing myself to be ruthless, insensitive. Waiting for the day when I could take everything I'd learned from Eliot and step out on my own." She turned wide, moist soulful eyes on Gail. "Oh, I don't know. I just don't know anything anymore. And I miss him. As dumb and exasperating as he is, I love him, and I miss him. I didn't want to throw him out of my life altogether. I just wanted him to back off a little bit, that's all."

"It's so fucking hard, isn't it?" Gail said.

"And the worst part is that I've never even been able to talk about it. Not like this."

"Maybe you have to get naked before you can get naked," Gail said.

Julia smiled just as the first tears were beginning to fall. "And what about us?" she said. "What's going to happen with us? You're talking brave now, but what happens when you get alone with Eliot and he dismisses all this as little-girl shit? I can just hear his tone of voice, and see his expression. What if all this seems childish to you when you're in his duplex or on his boat or in his private airplane?"

"And Martin?" Gail countered. "When you see him, and you will, can you tell him this? You said it would shrivel him. Would you take that chance? Or will you just let him fuck you again and slide all this under the table, like you were going to do with your thing with Eliot last night? Will you tell him about that? Are you going to be honest with him? How can you accuse him of being dumb if you lie to him?"

They turned away from one another. Julia gazed into the flames. Gail stared at the floor. The rush of words and feelings had momentarily emptied them, and they breathed heavily like boxers after a skirmish. Julia sat like a stone, still, drenched in millions of years of time, having watched entire forests rise and fall. Gail rocked back and forth, a thin reed in a gentle breeze. For Julia, sight had captured her entire attention. The dance of the fire mesmerized her utterly. For Gail, it was the kinesthetic rapture of drifting back and forth over her own center of balance. What they had just experienced was not an argument or fight in any of the accepted uses of those terms. Rather, it was a clash of conflicting aspects of the single will they had become, even if only for the duration of the influence of the marijuana upon their subtle bodies. It was one more adjustment to be made in the accomplishment of their union. And from a biological perspective, it was the exuberant explosion of a mating dance.

"I'm afraid," Julia said, speaking not to Gail, not to herself, but to the silence which surrounded them. "I can see so much now, so clearly. And one of the things I can see is that I am weak. I may betray this truth. I may betray you, betray us." She looked up sharply. "Do you understand?"

"Yes," Gail said. "I feel the same way. Maybe I'm talking braver than you right now, but I have the same fear."

"What can we do?" Julia asked.

Gail roused herself from her somatic weaving, the tracing of arcane patterns in the air. She took a deep breath. She fixed her gaze and bracketed Julia with her look.

"We can promise to be faithful to one another," Gail said at last.

Julia blinked. "Faithful?" she repeated.

"Yes," Gail replied. "Not sexually, because we both want men. And not sexually because we're not sure how much that will be a part of who we are together. But on a different level altogether. On a . . . a . . ." she groped for the word. "On the level of commitment involving our very lives."

"You mean, like marriage?"

"Like marriage, but not that," Gail said. "Like . . . I don't know how to put it." She ransacked her entire library of cultural references for a term which would describe this new concept, this primitive, powerful feeling. "Like people in a revolution who would rather be tortured and shot before they would betray their comrades, their friends, their lovers."

"Gail!" Julia said, her voice rising with inflection, expression surprise, wonder, awe.

"Yes," Gail said simply, "like that. A promise that we keep this sacred. This night on which we became telepathic and climbed purple mountains together. This night on which we discovered that we loved one another, as much as either of us has ever loved a man. This night on which we saw that if we stay together, we can give each other the strength not to get pulled back into the horror where a woman must turn her back on other women in order to love a man."

"Can we really do that?" Julia said, her eyes wide.

"You got married, didn't you? Why can't you make a sacred promise with me?"

"My marriage is on the rocks, Gail," Julia said. "That may not be the best analogy in the world."

"Well, it's the only one I've got right now," Gail said waspishly. "It'll just have to do." She shot Julia a glance of smiling exasperation. Julia mirrored the expression, except on her it came out as frowning amusement. They locked into mutual imitation until they could no longer maintain the thrust of seriousness which had begun to propel them, and they broke up, snorting and guffawing.

They laughed until the riff ran down and were once again silent, sober. They were being sucked gently into that mood of smoldering attention which is the ground in which the flowers of eroticism grow best. It combines the gravity of the serious mood with the seductive directions of pointed humor. Those who get stuck at either extreme of that spectrum, becoming ponderous or silly, are continually attracting one another across the full range of subtle gradient possibilities in between and go at their sex either like blacksmiths at the anvil or nuns at their knitting. Gail and Julia had been fluttering back and forth throughout the entire evening, adding dollops of anger and dashes of insight to give the inevitable a proper context. But each time they passed through another series of reactions, their relationship to the center became stronger. Sooner or later they would have experienced all the ways in which they manipulated the fact of simple and powerful presence, of nakedness, of confrontation, of love.

"Well," Julia said, "do you want to spend the night?"

Gail began to say something, but the words refused to come. She blinked, turned slightly to one side, drew her knees up to her chest, and leaned forward over the triangles formed by her legs and the floor, her breasts against her thighs, her arms folded over her shins. She took a deep breath, and then let go, her whole torso melting into the support of her legs. She closed her eyes, and leaned her cheek on one forearm. She did not move for several minutes. Julia watched her, her attention wavering between her friend and the unfamiliar trembling in her belly. It was a feeling that was poignantly familiar, but she had no memory to hang it on. Flutters and ripples, shiftings, tremors.

All at once it came to her. Sixteen years old. A date with a twenty-year-old college student who owned his own car and had a reputation for really knowing how to get a girl to do what he wanted. Elaborate cover stories to be used by her girlfriend in case her parents should call. For the whole week before the date playing over the conversation she'd had with another girlfriend who'd experienced the fabled boy first hand. She had had her bare breast fondled, and her crotch cupped from under her skirt although over her panties. She'd also mingled tongues and allowed him to press against her ass and rub until he had an ejaculation. The tale had made Julia delirious with anticipation and she'd had her friend hint to the boy that Julia might like to have a date with him. It had been arranged, and she was, all of a sudden, actually there, sitting on the vinyl covers of the back seat of his car, waiting for "it" to start. Her stomach had become a madhouse of moths.

She had begun to tremble then, and at first the boy took it as a sign of titillating anxiousness. But the symptoms had become so bad that he began to worry that something was seriously wrong with her. Her teeth rattled, her fists clenched, her ears turned red. She began to hyperventilate, although neither of them could describe the condition so precisely. Finally he took her home where she was at once put into a hot tub by her mother and made to stay in bed for two days until the "flu" had passed.

"How are you feeling?" she asked Gail.

"As nervous as a teenage girl on a first date," Gail replied.

"Oh my God," Julia exclaimed.

"The flutters in my belly got so bad I had to wrap myself up around myself to keep from flying apart." She smiled at Julia. "And you?"

"Like a teenage girl on a first date," Julia told her.

"I guess we're still doing it," Gail said. "Real life telepathy."

Then there was no margin left, and each of the women uncoiled, Gail from her posture, Julia from her tension. Gail rose up, arms opening as Julia sagged forward. Julia buried her head in Gail's belly, her arms going around Gail's waist. Julia hugged her tightly, so hard her back began to hurt. She put her hands on top of Julia's shoulders, as though to push her off. Then she saw the meaning of the movement, and she arched her spine, her stomach pressing hard into Julia's face.

Julia began to work her way down, burrowing like a gopher trying to escape a hawk. Gail could feel the first delicate, tentative flickers of Julia's tongue around her navel, the tiny strokes against her smooth skin. For a second she was about to give in, to let Julia do it this way, finding her way to the cunt in this blind, groping fashion. Yet almost at once she saw she couldn't allow it to happen like that.

She waited until Julia had worked her way down, until her mouth was just at the edges of her pubic hair, and then she grabbed Julia's ears and pulled back, forcing the spasmodic mouth up and away. She kept pulling until Julia's face was totally visible, and Gail could look into her eyes.

Julia wanted to look away, to do the thing alone, unobserved even by herself. But Gail would not let her turn her head and after a minute, Julia stopped trying. She held Gail's stare. They locked eyes.

"It's too important," she said. "I want to feel it coming."

Julia bit her lower lip and whimpered.

"Oh, I'm so afraid," she said. "I want to do it and I'm afraid I'll hate myself for doing it. And maybe it will change me. What if . . . what if I become a lesbian?" Her voice was so filled with histrionic misery that it caught the attention of both of them. Once again, they swung back from ultra-seriousness toward humor, feeling the pull of the black hole of erotic finality as they passed dead center.

"Then I'll become one too, and keep you company," Gail smiled. She leaned forward, and brought her lips down to touch Gail's mouth. Gail opened her lips slightly, with fragile wonder. They kissed, and then kissed again, and the third time their souls and hearts and minds and breath and spit and blood and tears and piss and farts and thoughts and all the longing of the single thing to be rejoined into the totality of all that is lived in their mouths and sang.

Finally, they pulled apart. Gail disengaged. She leaned back and lay on the floor. She opened her legs wide and lifted her knees, planting her feet on the rug. At the center lay her cunt, now a smear of hair resting on the split between her flattened buttocks.

Julia stared. It was so real. Even to the small pimples and blemishes on the smooth white skin. Julia brought her hands forward. She grasped the very edges of the outer lips and pulled them apart slowly, like drapes across a stage. The inside of Gail's cunt sighed and visibly relaxed. The pink was exposed. The spongy ring around the very hole itself, the now minute opening at the core of all the elaborate structure surrounding it, the folds and fancies and curls of hair, glistened in the dying light of the fire. Still Julia stared. Gail let out a low moan and the insides of her thighs trembled.

Julia's breath came heavy in her chest. The flutters in her belly had stopped to be replaced by a dull heat, as though a warm lead ball were sitting behind her navel. Her cunt was already wet. Her nipples hard. But more than anything, her mouth watered, hungered, thirsted, yearned for the slime that was at this moment beginning to slide out of Gail's pussy.

Julia's tongue slid out from between her lips and curled upward. She leaned toward the slick, aromatic pouch.

"The promise," Gail sighed.

"Yes," Julia whispered, her mouth already touching the sensitive, still, wet lips of Gail's vagina.

When she made the first tingling contact, it was more than flesh meeting flesh. The meaning of everything they had said and felt and done exploded in that instant and they gave themselves to one another totally. Julia opened her mouth wide and stretched her lips as far as they would go, engulfing the pumping cunt and pulling it into the vacuum she created by emptying her lungs through her nostrils. Gail's cunt lips surged into Julia's mouth. She let out a sharp gasp as the sensation of blood flooding the gender membranes inflamed her imagination and she put her hands on the back of Julia's head to push her face more fully between her thighs. She flexed the inner muscles of her pussy and filled Julia's mouth with the soft, mucous mounds of the inside of the deepest part of her cunt. Julia was seized by a fierce flurry of gulping, licking loss of control. All the lifetime associations she had with cunt flourished in her consciousness. The piss hole, the gash, the bleeding wound, the stink pit, the sticky slit . . . all the terms and feeling of negativity governed the instant of her awareness that she was really lying on her belly digging her tongue into another woman's hole.

Julia slid her hands under Gail's buttocks and pried the soft globes apart, slipping one finger into the already loosened and lubricated asshole. Gail let out a whimper and flexed her pelvis, impaling herself more deeply on the abrasive intruder. She spread her legs even more and let herself be had. Julia lost herself entirely. The only thought in her mind was, *So this is what it's like. This is why men are so hungry to lick us between the legs.* The notion that she was eating a cunt left altogether after a while, drowned in the waves of taste and smell and constant motion. Gail's cunt was capable of the most subtle and voluptuous expressions of her personality, and the organ was mute.

When Gail began to climax, Julia went mad. She had never been with or seen or heard another woman have an orgasm. In a way, what was happening seemed unreal, or hyper-real. She had the uncanny sense that it was she herself that was coming. The way Gail tensed her ass, the way her cunt hit a rhythm of thrusting which grew looser and faster. The sounds of abandonment, and the bringing up of her hands to caress her own nipples. The trembling in the thighs. The tautness in the belly.

Without being consciously aware of it, Julia began pumping her hips also, pushing her cunt into the fabric of the rug. From a third point in the room, it was clear that the two women were being drawn into one pulsation of excitement, Gail on her back grinding her wet pussy into Julia's mouth, and Julia on her stomach thrusting her pubic bone into the floor. Julia held Gail's ass and pushed her finger more and more deeply into the now clutching asshole. She licked and sucked and slobbered like a hungry animal.

Gail whipped her head from side to side, her cries of pleasure now loud and intense. She was very very close to climax. Julia dug into her cunt with her lips with even more fierce intensity and pushed Gail over the edge.

"Oh my God!" Gail yelled as she came, bucking, twisting, twitching, spurting secretions and urine into Julia's wide sucking mouth. The tart taste of the lubrication that was oozing deep from Gail's cunt and the sharp tang of piss that exploded uncontrollably from the burning hole right under the shrieking clitoris, sent Julia into a frenzy and she fucked the floor wildly until, seconds after Gail's orgasm, she experienced her own, thrashing about on the rug with total abandon.

They lay still for a long time, waiting for their breath to return to normal, and when they had regained the borders of their egos, Gail pulled herself along the rug until she was turned a hundred and eighty degrees around.

"Now me," she whispered, and slid her hands between Julia's moist thighs, parting them, revealing the already dripping cunt.

She brought her mouth up close to Julia's juicy mound and licked the very edge of her cunt lips lightly. Julia stirred as though from a dream, feeling the warmth starting to spread between her legs. She opened her eyes and found that Gail's cunt was still inches from her face.

"Oh," she sighed, and the two women moved simultaneously, burying their faces in each other's crotch, where they lost themselves for hours, driving one another to peak after peak of wild explosion, until they were exhausted, spent, fully satisfied, and reeking of the body's most pungent smells. They finally crawled into bed where they wrapped their arms around one another and fell asleep kissing.

As Martin and Robert walked south on Chambers Street, they were met by a counterpoint of music styles that alternately blended and fought, producing a sine wave of cacophony and strange harmony. From a bar came the thudding intricacy of rock, while from wide windows of a loft directly across the street spilled the undulating cadences of an ancient chant. The contrast was so precise that Martin stopped to wonder at it.

"That's the Lower Manhattan Ocean Club," Robert said. "It's owned by the guy who used to have Max's Kansas City."

"I've been there," Martin said, as though he'd just learned that a man he used to play cards with was the Duke of Buckingham.

Robert arched one eyebrow. *"Everybody's* been there," he drawled. "Once it became a celebrity hangout, the slide downhill to long lines on the sidewalk with teenyboppers from New Jersey trying to get a glimpse of Mick Jagger was inevitable. So the owner sold out, lay low for a few years, and now opened this place. In the meantime he started two other places, two of the most popular restaurants and bars in the city. He's a genius of bars. He makes bars the way Brancusi makes sculptures, trim, elegant, perfect." He tilted his chin to the canopied entrance on the other side of the street. "It's only been open three weeks and already the old crowd has started to hang out there. This used to be a deserted street after six o'clock at night, but now it's buzzing with cabs, drunks, thrillseekers, and all the other scavengers that descend whenever the decadence gets thick."

"You sound bitter," Martin said.

"You might say that. I've lived in this neighborhood for three years. It was one of the finest places in the city. It's a twenty minute walk to Wall Street, or to Chinatown, or to the Village. City Hall is just down the street, and the river is two blocks away. During the day there's all the shopping and noise and marketplace liveliness you could want, and at night and on Sundays it was absolutely quiet, and safe. Then those goddamned towers opened up, the World Trade Center, Rockefeller's pyramids. And that was the beginning of the end. The developers moved in and tore down lovely old buildings and built thirty-storey monstrosities. Bars began to flourish, and restaurants. Pretty soon we'll begin to have robberies, and all the misery that goes with affluence and high profile. And for what? Just so a few scummy bastards can get rich."

Martin had never seen the other man so agitated before, nor so angry. Robert spun around and continued to walk toward their destination, a building that looked as though it had seen its best days at the turn of the century. It looked abandoned, and had he been alone, Martin wouldn't have even glanced at it, much less considered going inside. When they reached the front door, the war of the world was felt and heard most sharply. The sound of chanting fell from the windows above and cascaded down the stairway inside the front door. The rock music blasted directly from a large jukebox situated right behind the glass that separated bar from street. Martin could see the people inside. He got a fleeting impression of beards, glasses, cigarettes, women posturing and laughing, and a low swell of animal heat.

"I guess it's a good place to go to pick up women," Martin said as they entered the building.

For a moment, Robert didn't know which place he was referring to, the bar or the loft. Then he spotted the confusion, stopped for a second, smiled, put his hand on Martin's shoulder, and said, "Wherever you go, it's the women who pick you up. Your only job is to keep from getting in the way."

They climbed the stairs, David Bowie hooting at them as they went, his voice growing dimmer as the booming chant grew louder. Martin could now make out a drum, a stringed instrument of some kind, and snatches of the lyrics, which were not English.

"Hana hana mooloo jeebee, hana hana mooloo jeebee," the song seemed to say.

To Martin, whose tastes in music were formed in the 1950's, the foreign sounds made no less sense than the lyrics of most of the rock music that had erupted since the Beatles. He followed Robert up two flights of wooden stairs in the poorly lit hallway, halfway between curiosity and annoyance at himself. Like millions of Americans, he had read about gurus and meditation in newspapers and magazines, and he was excited to be finally seeing the thing firsthand. At the same time, part of him was still in the bar across the street. A cold beer in his hand and a hot woman on the hook seemed to offer all the enlightenment that any man might ever want.

Robert threw open the door of the loft. He stepped aside, put his arm around Martin's shoulders, and eased him in.

For a moment, Martin couldn't make out details. He was struck first by color. It seemed that orange predominated.

He didn't know that there were so many shades of orange, from the screaming red end of the spectrum to the diffident yellow. He looked down on a carpet of orange shirts and robes. Everyone was sitting on the floor, all facing in one direction. The air was thick with incense. And the space was thick with the chant, the very atmosphere of the scene. People swayed, their eyes closed, clapped their hands, rocked their bodies gently from side to side, and sang the words over and over again. Martin glanced from one end of the loft to the other, a distance of nearly a hundred feet long by thirty feet wide. And nearly every square inch was filled.

There must be five hundred people here! Martin thought.

Robert took his arm by the elbow and led him inside toward what had to be the front of the loft, the place where everyone was facing. Martin balked inwardly at what he took to be a bit of impoliteness, but he trusted that Robert knew what he was doing. They went almost to the front wall and sat down no more than inches from a tiny wooden platform raised a few feet above the floor. It was covered with an orange rug, and held a cushion, vases with flowers, and a few artifacts and implements which were totally unfamiliar. The two men did not cause a ripple in the crowd; no one so much as glanced at them.

"He'll be here shortly," Robert whispered after they had settled themselves and merged into the mood of the place. Then he turned away, closed his eyes, and began to clap his hands and chant in unison with the others, his voice rising high and clear, adding a fresh input of energy to the common effort. His entrance stimulated a number of people around him and Martin could feel the chant growing in intensity and volume, spreading out from Robert's chest. Martin felt the strategic embarrassment of not knowing how to behave. Joining in the song was clearly out of the question; he didn't know the words nor the purpose in singing them; he couldn't pretend to be in the spirit of the thing. On the other hand, he felt awkward and wondered whether he might be considered snobbish. He glanced around surreptitiously to see if anyone was watching him.

It was as though he were in an opium den. Everyone in the room, without exception, was wrapped in some private world, communicating to everyone else by means of a fixed ritual. It was a form of fascist anarchy whereby the individual could feel or think whatever he or she pleased so long as his or her behavior was absolutely uniform with everyone else's. Martin couldn't help but contrast it to the bar where there was a wider latitude of behavior but a more rigid focus in terms of interior life.

Unused to sitting cross-legged on the floor, Martin pushed back a foot or so until his back was against a wall. He now looked more openly around him, the fear of being the object of hostile curiosity having disappeared. The space was curiously bare. One corner held a kitchen, stove, refrigerator, sink, table and chairs, and shelves with dishes and foods. Nearby was a door which clearly led to the bathroom. At the very far opposite end, a sleeping loft had been built, with a staircase leading to it. Under it was a desk, chairs, small library. And that was all. Martin leaned his head against the wall, closed his eyes, and let himself be drawn into the monotonous rhythm of the chant. It was quite soothing, and his thoughts made little curlecues, like paper airplanes thrown off a cliff. He speculated on who lived

there, and what all these people were looking for, and before he
realized that he was falling asleep, he was asleep.

And then was awakened by a sound he had never in his life
heard before. He was awakened by the thunder of silence.

Martin opened his eyes to find a different world from the one
in which he had gone to sleep. The loft was still there, and the
people were still there. But it seemed that someone had turned
a great many lights on. The place was much brighter. And the
people were absolutely still, sitting upright, spines erect, their
hands in their laps. It was as though they had been a group of
green recruits sloppily lurching across a field and then, by some
miraculous transformation, instantaneously changed into crack
troops, doing a precision march across an asphalt drill field.

Martin pushed himself away from the wall very slowly,
almost afraid to stir. Robert was next to him, sitting cross-legged,
his gaze distant. Martin followed the direction of his eyes to
the small stage. It was no longer empty. Sitting there, wearing
nothing but a tiny loincloth, waving a palm leaf fan in front
of him, was a plump brown man of indeterminate age, smiling
vaguely into space.

The first impression we receive always reveals the essence
of the meaning a person is to have for us. We may have to
work our way through the personality, the history, and all our
projections, needs, and deeper perception to understand what it
was we saw, but when we have reached through to the end of the
entire string of egoic manifestations, the prize is nothing more
than affirmation of what we'd known all along. When Martin
first looked at Babba, the guru's body was superimposed over a
memory Martin had of watching Joe DiMaggio pivot and move
toward left center field at precisely the instant he heard the crack
of the bat against ball. Martin never forgot the spooky feeling of
uncanny processes at work whereby a man could gauge exactly
where a ball would land just from hearing how it sounded when
it was hit with a piece of wood. That spontaneity, that accuracy,
that power, that perfection of instinct, was the first thing that
Martin saw in Babba, and it was that perception which rendered
him acquiescent in what followed.

What he couldn't know was that each person saw in Babba

that quality which he or she most admired. Some saw a towering intellect, others a selfless saint, yet others a magician and healer. He was felt as father, leader, teacher. And when written about, he was called the very embodiment of God, the living consciousness of That from which everything arises, and which is indistinguishable from everything that exists. To all such appellations, Babba replied with a modest denial.

"I am the lowest of God's creations," was his favorite phrase. "I am no larger than an ant." And would add, "If you wish to know God, you must become that small, so small that you go through the world unnoticed. Only then will you be free to see what is here, the splendor of God's power."

The silence was thick, alive, intelligent. Through it Martin could hear the faint strains of traffic from the street and the echoes of rock music from the bar. But even those familiar sounds were rendered exotic by the quality of silence in the room. It was as though the loft had been transported all at once to a mountaintop in India and the noise of the western world relegated to a quaint memory of a peculiar time.

All the attention was on Babba and it was impossible for Martin not to add his own curious gaze to that of the others. Babba sat, nonplussed and utterly at ease, as though he were alone by a river watching clouds turn crimson in the sunset. From a purely theatrical viewpoint alone, the performance was admirable and extraordinary. Martin had never seen anyone on a stage reflect such calm. People on stage either gave speeches or acted or sang or danced or projected a presence. But Babba did none of these. He merely sat, and the simple act was so powerful, so breathtaking in its simplicity, that it commanded attention.

Given that implacable stillness as a ground, the slightest hint of movement erupted with the violence of a lightning flash. So when Babba suddenly sharpened his glance and sent it sailing into the middle distance, it was as obvious as if he had hurled a bright red beachball into the crowd. The recipient of the glance stiffened as though stuck with a pin, flushed pink with embarrassment, and then smiled in confusion. It was a woman in her late thirties, with all the plainness of a dime-store saleslady on a Saturday night just before closing after a day of frenzied shoppers. She wore a white blouse and a black skirt, and carried her mousey hair behind her skull in a tight bun. She was totally unexceptional, and Martin would not have noticed her if a thousand like her had passed him marching in goosestep down Fifth Avenue. But now, for a few seconds, she was a radiant star, singled out. Her eyes shone with joy and a pixie spirit danced above her head. For a few seconds, she was beautiful.

Martin looked quickly back to Babba. The man had not so much as flexed a muscle. Whatever it was that had flowed out of him couldn't be measured very easily in units of physical strength. Then, as Martin watched, Babba's eyes shifted again and did some extraordinary dance, seeming to whirl around, each eyeball in an opposite direction, come together, vibrate like yoyos at the edge of their strings. The heads of the people in the audience turned from Babba to the woman and back again, and everyone laughed, as though an irresistibly funny story had just been told. The woman blushed even more, half-hid her face in her hands, and sank into the general laughter.

Martin was confused. He had understood the earlier bit of flattery, subtle as it was, but this escaped him. He turned to Robert for a clue, but his friend was caught up in the general mood of merriment. Martin waited for the hubbub to subside and then turned back to Babba to see what could happen next. But the guru had escaped to vapidity; his attention had turned inward, it seemed. A long time passed. Martin's legs began to ache. As supple as he was, the unfamiliar posture was stretching muscles that were almost never used in this manner. He shifted his weight surreptitiously, and as he did Babba's eyes turned and fixed him on the spot, catching him unaware and off balance. Worse, the eyes of everyone in the room followed the guru's gaze to see what he was focusing on now. Martin suddenly found himself the object of attention of some five hundred people.

He half-turned to Robert for protection. He was experiencing the first wave of a very strong panic. He had never felt so exposed in his entire life. But Robert was only looking at him with a kind of rapt imbecilic smile, and in his newfound friend's face he saw no recognition at all. It was a moment of madness.

Then, as quickly as it had come on, it stopped. Babba flicked his eyes elsewhere, and the concentrated energy of the room spun toward a different direction. Martin was seized by a spasm of intense relief, followed immediately by a dull throb of disappointment. For no matter how unpleasant the moment had been, it had also been fantastically explosive, a shock of impacted light, a shaft of iridescent vitality such as Martin only felt as the peak of his form atop the parallel bars when every system in his body was attuned to the complex adjustments necessary to maintain such a strenuous balance. Martin found himself straining forward slightly, as though by his posture he could lure Babba to turn back, to fix those magic eyes on him once more. Without any self-consciousness, without any word having been spoken, without a thought having crossed his mind, he had blended into the awareness of the hundreds who sat at Babba's feet. If the Martin of a half hour earlier could have seen himself at that instant, he would have scoffed in disbelief; for this Martin had that same look of blind yearning which marked the follower of any charismatic figure. His eyes were a bit moist, his cheeks slightly pink, his mouth teasing the dawn of a smile.

Then, without warning, Babba turned his head again, like a searchlight sweeping a prison yard. He went past Martin, whose heart ducked a beat, and stopped with Robert, who took the attention with perfect ease by leaning his tall torso forward until he touched the floor with his forehead. He remained in that posture, prostrate, for several seconds, and then righted himself to smile at his guru.

"This is your friend?" Babba said in a voice that barely escaped the metallic twang which afflicts those wise men whose native language is one of the Dravidic dialects.

Robert nodded. "Yes," he said.

Babba inclined his head and then glanced up at Martin. Once again Martin braced himself. The previous look had been humorous, gentle, but this time the guru's eyes were hard, harsh, almost cruel.

"Why have you come?" he asked.

Martin's first reaction was social outrage. After having done Robert the favor of accompanying him, he had not only been singled out for public notice but was now being asked a rude question in terribly blunt terms. Yet he could not escape answering; everyone was waiting for his reply. He simultaneously rationalized Babba's crudity by ascribing to him a lack of knowledge of American customs and tried to formulate some answer that would be, somehow, satisfactory. But his brain had turned to porridge.

"Robert asked me," he said finally, his voice almost cracking and not carrying very far.

Babba frowned and shook his head from side to side a dozen times, all the while keeping Martin's eyes fixed with his.

Robert leaned over and whispered to Martin. "He wants to know the real reason. He wants to know what your problem is."

"I have no problem," Martin said in a low voice.

"What does he say?" Babba boomed.

"He says he has no problem," Robert said in a loud voice.

"See here, you have no right . . ." Martin started to say but his voice was drowned out by the laughter that erupted in the room. Babba was rocking from side to side, holding his ribs with his hands, his arms crossed in front of his chest, in perfect imitation of a chimpanzee that had caught its finger's in a printing press.

"Old fart thinks he's funny," Martin said to himself, chagrined at being the object of ridicule. And yet, he reasoned, he deserved it. Stating that he had no problems was a colossal lie. It would be a lie for any human being to say such a thing. Even if one had no personal problems, which would be extremely rare, there are still the problems of pain and suffering and hunger in the world, the problem of death, the problem of ultimate meaning. And such planetary and cosmic concerns aside, Martin was neck deep in emotional difficulties. He didn't give Babba any great credit for knowing that. From his position of power in the room and with his vast experience with people, it would be practically a reflex act to mock anyone who claimed he had no problems.

The laughter subsided, however, and Babba dropped his pantomime and resumed his posture of simple sitting. His eyes rested lightly on Martin. Martin's gaze was caught. Not only by the guru's glance but by the fact that everyone in the room was watching their confrontation.

"What does he want of me?" Martin said to himself.

Yet, even as he watched, he began to understand. Babba's eyes ceased being two black dots in a white round pill set in a sculpture of flesh called a face. They underwent a series of astounding transformations which escalated so far beyond anything explainable by physiology or psychology that Martin was swept up into the changes and taken on the strangest ride of his life. As he sat and looked into Babba's eyes he saw his father, then his mother. He saw himself as a child, riding his first tricycle in front of his house. He saw the expression of death on his grandmother's features as she lay in her coffin. Then, the word *seeing* itself was no longer adequate, for he lost all sense of himself as a separate entity. It was not that he sat in a place and Babba in another place and some peculiar activity known as sight took place between them, but more as though they were the space itself, aware of itself, alive, pregnant with infinite possibility. Martin fell out of time and place altogether. There was only that awareness, that emptiness, that space, which began to glow, to vibrate. It was like climbing on a car in an amusement park funhouse and suddenly being plummeted into a world of dazzling surprises. But at the very point when it seemed that the experience would sprout its most bizarre leaves, everything was ripped away and Martin was back in the loft on Chambers Street, sitting on the floor, while Babba looked down at him from his platform, and a thousand eyes peeked in on the drama.

Now he was vulnerable, for the veneer of these dimensional illusion had been temporarily removed and Martin had accepted the alternate reality, presented so deftly and ingenuously by the guru. The weight of Babba's question increased a hundredfold. Why had he come? Babba's eyes had become drops of molten lava, rock subjected to such intense heat that it actually melted. The fierce fires of endless sorrow burned in Babba's heart and turned the world to ashes. As Martin's gaze was drawn more deeply into the guru's mind, a lifetime of loneliness and sadness welled up inside him. Now he not only saw the facts of his past, his parents, his childhood, the death of loved ones, the disappointments, but he felt all the emotions that he had denied himself because little boys, when he was a little boy, were not supposed to cry.

Babba's question swelled in scope until it encompassed the

entire world. Martin knew he was being asked not only why he had come to the meeting, but why he had come into the world. From what mysterious source had he originated, and what was his purpose in being here. And the question was addressed not only to Martin, but to everyone in the room, everyone and everything in creation. Why was any of it here? And if there was a God to answer that question for everyone else, then how did God answer when He asked it of Himself?

All the people, all the trappings of the space, all that he had been up until the instant that Babba looked into his eyes, dropped away, and Martin was left with the sheer nakedness of the moment. And then, the most peculiar thing of all happened. Somehow, without his knowing how or when, it seemed that he was sitting on the platform looking down at himself. Only he had now become Babba. They had exchanged identities. And he saw that there was no difference between them, that one was the other, that the guarded and lauded thing called the self was just a momentary viewpoint. Martin began to laugh, only it was Babba laughing. He was caught in the confusion.

His ears popped, and he was back inside his ordinary awareness again. He was Martin Gordis, age thirty-one, a physical education instructor, recently separated from his wife, living in New York City. He was in a strange loft with several hundred people to see a man from India who Robert said had changed his life. This information was all very interesting to him, but whose body was that rocking back and forth on the floor?

He felt Robert's hand on his arm. His friend's eyes regarded him with warmth and gentle concern. He looked up at Babba. The guru had assumed yet a different mask, as though he had aged fifty years. He seemed to peer down from a mountain top. Martin wondered how he could ever have felt that the two of them were one thing, interchangeable parts of some unspeakable whole.

"There is sorrow," Babba said.

Martin nodded, but already he was retreating inwardly. He felt he had exposed too much of his feelings, and wanted to cover himself up. Also, he was translating his withdrawal into a judgment on Babba.

Sure there's sorrow, he thought, *the hokiest gypsy fortune teller can tell you that.*

"You are unhappy," Babba went on. "Why have you come?"

There was a buzzing in the crowd. Robert was leaning close. "This is very unusual," his friend was saying. "Babba almost never talks to people the first time they come. And even when he does, he never insists the way he's doing now."

Martin realized that he had dropped his head and was staring at the floor, refusing to look at the guru, and that Robert's explanation was by way of telling him that he was being given an extraordinary and rare opportunity. How could he continue to behave like a sulky child? And yet he did not want to give anything to Babba. He did not trust the man. His feeling was so strong that it surprised him, for Babba had not really *done* anything, and on what basis could Martin form a judgment of trust or distrust?

Slowly, Martin raised his eyes. Babba had not removed his gaze. Now he looked like a standard picture of a wise man. The white robes, the white hair, the cross-legged posture, the piercing glance, the air of composure. Martin took a deep breath and straightened his back. He looked back at Babba, waiting for another round of hallucinatory pyrotechnics to be shot off. But Babba became very still, and his image did not flicker as much as a candle flame in a windless room.

Then, in a clear, full, distinct voice, he said, "Divorce is death."

The words hit Martin like a fist across the temple. The calculating portion of the brain advanced and rejected a dozen hypotheses about what the words meant, all within a fraction of a second. The successful interpretation, the one that registered, manifested in the form of behavior, however, not thought. Martin turned to Robert and, without hesitation, said, "You told him about my marriage problems."

But Robert was wide-eyed before Martin even spoke, and even as he spoke Martin knew that the other man was innocent of the charge. There was no way he could have reached Babba with information he'd only received that evening. The only alternative was that the guru had taken a wild shot, and scored a lucky hit. But the look in Babba's eyes discounted that theory also. Somehow, Martin realized, Babba *knew* everything that was going on inside him.

Babba turned his head and looked out over the audience of devotees and the curious. And when he spoke, it was to everyone in the room. "Marriage is the most difficult yoga for a man and a woman in this age. Once, when it was clear what it is to be human, then marriage was very simple. Now we no longer know what it is to be human, so we cannot understand why we marry. Marriage does not seem necessary. Even to have children, we don't need marriage. And we can have more fun if we are single." The last sentence was delivered with that delicate intimation of a pause which the professional comedian uses to trip his listeners into laughter. It was successful. People laughed.

"Marriage now is like a prison. Husband and wife keep each other in their seats. They watch each other like thieves. Sometimes marriage is like a party. Husband and wife have sex with other husbands and wives. The best marriage now is like a school. It is a place to learn. It is a yoga. But this is still not the way it was."

He paused and gazed out into space. His face began to glow, and his eyes shone, like a child watching a Disney film. Babba gazed into the Golden Age, the first period after the creation, and his heart was full with the joy of what he saw. The vision almost shimmered above the heads of those sitting in front of him. Martin saw it too. It wasn't anything specific, not a picture. What he saw was more of a feeling, a time when he and Julia had lain in each other's arms and faced the inevitability of each other's death. Martin remembered the impact of the realization that one day he would exist in the world without her, or she without him. And it was as impossible to grasp as the fact of his own extinction. They had talked about it, and too overwhelmed with the brute reality of the truth that thundered in their souls, they had begun to joke about how they would end, and made a pact that if either of them were about to die, the two of them would jump off a cliff together, like lovers in the old Japanese romances.

"But they actually did that," Julia had said. "I mean, it's a historical fact. Lovers who weren't allowed to marry sometimes committed suicide together to make their love eternal."

"Would you really do that with me?" Martin had asked.

"Would you? With me?" she replied.

And for a while they had not spoken, staring into space, trying to imagine what it would be like to grasp one another in a final embrace and then leap from a cliff . . . the dizzying rapturous fall through space, the last kiss, the ultimate look into one another's eyes, and then the plunge into the arms of death, the consummate union of their love.

Each person in the room looked into the space where Babba's eyes were drawing a vision out of the ether, and each saw a different image, a different feeling, a different memory. And yet, all were united through him.

Babba suddenly withdrew his gaze from the air and whirled back to Martin who was caught totally unprepared for the lances of insight that shot into his mind. He was still tasting that moment with Julia when Babba leapt into his soul with both feet.

"Julia," Babba said.

Martin gasped.

"It is dark," Babba said. "You cannot see her. She cannot see you."

Martin's senses jammed. The floor tilted under him.

"There is sorrow," Babba said, repeating his earlier judgment. "There is much sorrow. You cannot see her. She cannot see you."

Martin heard the sound of sobbing. He felt tears on cheeks and hands. He was in touch with a deep ache going from throat to chest. And it took several minutes before he realized that all that was happening to him, and that it was all part of a single action.

I'm crying, he thought.

He had slid to the floor and was now curled up on his side, his face buried in his hands, sobbing uncontrollably. He wept from his belly to his brain. The tears of a lifetime were waiting to be shed, the sadness of a world waiting to be recognized. All the transiencies of his life swept before him, the lovely things doomed to perish. His parents, his friends, himself at all the stages of his growth. And finally, Julia. Julia, who had become a burr of anger, a wall of resistance, a symbol of continual discomfort. He understood how long it had been since he had even seen her, known the texture, the grain and smell and cut of her. She had become some grim thing on the periphery of his sensations, an annoyance whose name he knew. And through that sudden realization, there gushed the tenderness of the early days, the pure union of the first years. Memories like galaxies exploded in his mind. Words, fragments of glances, touches, silent subtle agreements, a shared destiny.

And it was lost, lost as fully as though she were dead. She had died to him, and he had not been there to leap off the cliff with her. Rather, he had helped push her from the precipice, as she had tried to push him. Babba's words burned in his heart, and each time it seemed he would stop weeping, a new layer of sorrow was uncovered, and he started to sob again.

Martin cried for almost a quarter of an hour. After the first few minutes Babba looked away, as did all the others in the room. He began to chant, a low, liquid sound, and it was taken up by the crowd. Within seconds, Martin's sounds were drowned in a great waterfall of voices, a mighty AUM which swelled and grew and lifted every thought and feeling and identity of all those under its sway, lifted them all to a space in which the eternal and infinite and ever-present source and beginning of all manifest creation flexed its unfathomable power to cause the countless universes to dance.

That single sound, the distillation of all sound, held by ancient sages to be the primal sound of creation, existing before light, before energy, before matter, before life, moved with the force of elemental consciousness to lift the people in the loft beyond all concerns of daily details, of earthly bother, of solar influence, and even of galactic programs. Sitting erect, eyes closed, Babba and his followers soared through the empyrean with all the ease and sweet grace of gulls skimming over water. The *A* began as a murmur in the belly and progressed to a rumble in the chest; the *U* opened the throat, the *M* vibrated through the skull, combing the tangled neuron patterns of the brain.

Martin knew none of this. All he could feel was the dam

bursting in his heart. For the first time in his adult life he could wail and sob and cry his anguish to the skies, bury his tears in the earth. The wall of sound which towered over him allowed him to lose all self-consciousness, and absorbed even his most powerful cries.

Gradually, he wound down. His moans were interspersed with seconds of silence during which he coughed and tried to catch his breath. After a while, even the constriction in his diaphragm let go, and he gulped air down into his belly, that flat, muscled plane which had been tucked in and plastered over with exercise since he was fifteen years old and formed a military concept of posture. Finally, he was at rest, curled up on his side in the fetal position, both hands over his face, fingers in his mouth, his nose running, his eyes red, sighing.

Who am I? was the first formed thought in his mind.

As the swelling and sediment subside in a river which has been engorged by melting snow, returning to its prior contours and rates of flow, so Martin's ego, shattered and blown out of all recognizable proportion, started to crystallize once more. Yet some other force was awake in him, that edge of panic, perhaps of greed or insecurity, that thing called evil or devil or ignorance, which cannot allow things to take their course; that curse of human beings who are aware of their own death and build civilizations as monuments to fear. It would not let him lie there, simply, like a child. Had that been possible, he would have emerged refreshed, reborn as it were, cleansed of tensions and alive to areas that had long been anesthetized. But the jagged rim of anxiety cut at him as a can improperly opened will snag the unwary finger, opening flesh and bringing blood.

What am I doing here? was Martin's second coherent thought.

He opened his eyes.

Oh, my God. What will they think of me? completed the catalogue of his conditioned attitudes.

Babba was looking down at him. The guru had undergone yet another transformation, it seemed. Now he was like Martin's grandmother as he remembered her. An old woman with a wrinkled face, lips that trembled slightly just before she began to speak, and fingers that knew how to grab him in just those spots which were ticklish or tender. His central memories of her were fat lemon gumdrops she gave him when she was pleased, and the brutally intimate pinches and squeezes she administered when she wasn't.

Martin shifted his gaze. Every other person in the room that he could see was also looking at him. Robert was gazing at him too, his expression like that of a parent whose child has said its first word. Martin slowly pulled himself erect. He reached into his pocket and took out his handkerchief. Sheepishly, he blew his nose. The action produced a loud, wet honk, like a goose with a head cold nagging its mate. The sound made a number of people laugh, and Martin glanced out over the white pyramid formed by his fingers inside the cloth grasping his nose. At once he realized how silly he looked, and the apprehension in his chest loosened, and he found himself smiling inside the tiny tent.

He wiped his eyes, folded his legs under him, put his handkerchief away, and waited to see what would happen next. He was already piecing together the event as rapidly as his reforming sense of identity would allow. The pure experience, already and instantly a memory, began to fade in intensity and focus, and the machinery of analysis started to grind out interpretations. These proceeded along the lines of a reverse ontology, beginning with Martin's highest level of comprehension and sliding down the scale from there. Having no education or inclination to allow a notion of the Absolute, or even the cosmic, Martin's first awareness was psychological. He understood that he had suppressed a good deal of feeling in relation to his breakup with Julia, and that the guru's extraordinary and unexpected line about divorce and death had unplugged a dam of emotion. He was even able to link that with the lifelong repression he had been suffering as a result of his childhood experience, given the culture he was raised in. But he did not, at that moment, grasp the wider implications, the notion that this was a lesson in the history of a people, or a process in group dynamics. He had no way of seeing just then that his tears had been everyone's tears, that he had cried for all the people in the room. It would be a long long time before Martin would be able to disentangle himself from the notion that his limited self, his idiosyncratic viewpoint, was utterly transparent, transient and unimportant; that it was merely a reflection of the true Self from which all manifestations arise and to which all manifestations return.

Babba knew this about Martin. So did Robert. And yet, a man had to start somewhere. And Martin had at least felt something other than his habitual gesture, his unconscious awareness of the world as a vast theatre built for no other reason than to hold his personal drama. Paradoxically, however, as he returned from that liberating experience, his first reaction was to re-affirm his basic attitude, hyping it with the energy derived from his momentary and fragmentary liberation.

From Babba's eyes, the incident was unremarkable, as were all phenomena in the created universe. Babba had attained a permanent state of consciousness, a state generally called "enlightenment" in America, but for which each culture has a name. God realization, being at-one with the Tao, bhava samadhi, satori, maturity, and so forth. He had been raised in a sanctimonious household, his father a minor priest in a local temple dedicated to Hanuman, the monkey god, his mother aggressively self-effacing in her effort to project a more abject humility than all the other wives of all the other minor priests in the area. At age eight, he suddenly saw through the stultifying hypocrisy of his parents, a feat shared by most children who are not absolute cretins. But with his insight he had felt a rare compassion. That is, he not only saw the stupidity of his parents, but he felt the sorrow against which their rigidity was a defense. He began to weep, and cried continuously for seventeen days. He lost thirty pounds and came close to dying. But in a land so riddled with religiosity, the event was not brought to the attention of a doctor, but to that of a holy man who had retired to a cave fifteen miles outside the village. The holy man, not stirring from his seat, had simply said, "Throw him into the river and then bring him here."

When Babba, then known by his given name of Rammurti, was flung into the water of the river, he began to splutter, thrash about, and drown, and he had to be pulled out by two men who dove in from the shore. The act, however, did accomplish one thing: the boy was no longer crying. The hermit told the parents that the child was obviously marked for special spiritual development, and told them to leave him in the cave. They would not have dreamed of protesting.

Babba then underwent a fairly standard training, although bizarre by the standards of human convention. He once went five years without seeing another human being besides the hermit. For two years he had to pluck all the hair out of his beard one strand at a time to teach him disregard for pain. At one point he lived on nothing but water and sunlight for three months. The hermit eventually sent him on to another teacher, and this continued until he was thirty, at which point, sitting with his current master, the entire complex of tensions and attitudes and habits which define the human being dissolved all at once, and he became himself truly. There was no longer a platform or vantage point from which he observed himself or the world. He had lost all sense of identification with specific manifestations of pure, unformed consciousness, and so was able to watch the manifest universes rise and fall with as much concern as he watched the rising and falling of his own breath. He was no longer in the world, nor was he out of the world. He was the world itself.

He and his master exchanged a silent blink of understanding, and Rammurti walked out of the temple and into the forest. He wandered for five years, carrying nothing but the blanket on his back and an eating bowl. He walked more than thirty thousand miles barefoot, begging his way from village to village. When he arrived at the edge of a village, he would simply sit under a tree, and within hours his presence would be felt and by that night most of the people of the village would be sitting before him. He would speak, or sit silently; sometimes he healed or gave practical advice on the affairs of life. And then one night he would slip away, leaving a legend behind, and perhaps a small shrine that the villagers would build to mark the spot where he had been. Finally, he just drifted off into the woods and stayed there for more than twenty years, totally naked, simply one more animal on the face of the earth. He had attained ultimate simplicity.

One day he was found by a group of government engineers surveying that part of the jungle. He was sitting on a tree limb. Surrounding him were a group of monkeys. Some of the people in that party say that Babba was speaking in grunts and gestures to the monkeys and that they all seemed to be laughing and having a good time. The men were startled, but the power of four thousand years of tradition wiped out the thin veneer of westernized technological prejudice which had passed for education in the British universities they had attended, and they stopped to acknowledge that a rare being was sitting before them, naked, bearded to his belly, talking to monkeys.

As might be expected, word got out, and before long people were making pilgrimages to that spot in the forest, and shortly after that Rammurti was prevailed upon to return to the world of people to give suffering civilization the benefit of his wisdom. Only those so steeped in the darkness of their tunnel vision that they can't see beyond the propaganda of progress will fail to understand what a sacrifice the man made in agreeing to leave the forest. Later on, when he had attained a following of tens of thousands in India, and twice as many in a dozen countries around the world, when he was accused of being on a large ego trip, only those who could see the man's soul and knew his history realized what a petty prize this adulation was in relation to what he had to give up: that absolute liberty, that soaring solitude, that mute oneness with unstructured life, that approximation to God.

When he returned to the world of manufactured things, he was given the name Babba by his first devotees. For him, from the first, everything he saw once he left the forest was some kind of absurd drama. He was amused by airplanes and television sets. He became addicted to cigarettes. He read a newspaper once, then rubbed it against his buttocks, saying "Toilet paper." He laughed a lot, and no one ever quite understood precisely why, although many rationalizations were given. The fact of the matter was that Babba had found vastly more intelligent, humorous, gentle and wise creatures amidst the bands of monkeys he had lived with than he ever found among the monkeys of the cities who wore clothing and spoke words and lived lives of such tortured tension and inflated self-importance that he could not believe they were of the same branch of animal life.

So when Martin appeared, his defenses bristling with the

obviousness of porcupine quills, and then collapsed into racking sobs. Babba was unimpressed. At the same time, he felt empathy with the condition, enough so that he moved the roomful of people into the rather theatrical chanting, something which had value merely as a soothing device, but which overemotional devotees tended to mistake for some form of occult teaching. Reality, plain and unadorned, was the heart of Babba's truth, and as all the scriptures have pointed out, there is no way to communicate it. Babba's techniques, tricks, talks all served but one purpose: to keep people around him long enough for them to catch on for themselves, to use him as a fixed point against which to view all the changes of state they passed through in their lives until they learn that enlightenment is little more than a posture, an attitude, a direction.

"You feel better?" Babba asked.

Martin nodded, and settled himself more comfortably. He had almost regained his former composure, that is to say, the subliminal guardedness which constituted his moment-to-moment presence in the world. With his psychological clothes back on, he was now ready to become discursive, to talk about what had happened, to discuss his thoughts. The massive attention of all the people in the room, at first a threat, was now delight. Martin was beginning to feel the first rushes of what it is like to be a star.

Unfortunately, he was only the moon; Babba was the source of light. And upon receiving Martin's nod indicating that he was all right, Babba smiled, then turned his head, paused a fraction of a second, and then cast his gaze on someone else in the room, a pretty woman who looked to be in her early twenties, with very large breasts unhampered by a brassiere, the nipples of which poked with soft insolence through the thin cloth of her blouse. Babba made some kind of facial expression Martin couldn't see, but most of the others laughed, and the woman blushed and closed her eyes in seductive withdrawal.

Martin blinked several times, rapidly, as though clearing his head from a blow on the chin. All at once, he was a nonentity, just another body in the crowd. The emotions that coursed through him were shifting too rapidly for him to identify. Anger at being ditched like a high school girl on a blind date; shame at being exposed; jealousy that the guru's attention was going elsewhere. These feelings mixed, boiled, and gave rise to judgments. Babba was a fickle fraud, a cheap showman taking cheap shots; the meeting had all the spiritual value of a nightclub in the Catskills; Babba cared only for his own aggrandizement, he had no true concern for individuals. He might have dug himself more deeply into a fit of chagrin, except that Robert, sitting next to him, put a hand on his shoulder.

"I know what you're thinking and feeling," Robert said. "But try not to let any of it scar you. We can talk about it later."

Martin glanced up and was about to look away except that Robert held his gaze. The tall yoga instructor wouldn't let Martin look away until he had acknowledged with a slight lowering of his eyelids that the message had been received at the depth at which it was sent.

The rest of the evening was a small torture for Martin. There was some more of Babba's horsing around with people, and then a long shaggy soul story about a fish looking for water, and a disconnected ramble among reminiscences, references to Vedic texts, and homely homilies. When Babba finished talking, a bony woman in her late fifties stood up clutching a piece of paper and read off a number of announcements having to do with various functions concerning Babba's organization, The Twilight Stallion Confirmation. And when she sat down, someone struck a gong and the group launched into a half hour of chanting, during which Babba sneaked away.

Martin was aghast. His legs were on fire. His eyes burned and he had trouble staying awake. But he was determined to stick it through to the end. But when everyone was singing the monotonous tune with its repetitive words, their eyes closed and their attention elsewhere, and Babba just sort of backed away from the edge of the platform and seemed to fade into the darkness behind the screen, Martin became furious. Still, he gritted his teeth, clenched his hands into fists, and suffered it through.

Finally, the chanting wound down, the room fell into a quaking silence, there was a moment's pause, and then people began to gather themselves to leave. Martin almost sobbed out loud with relief. He tried to stand up but his right leg was completely asleep, so much so that it did not even tingle. It was like a dead fish, a piece of soft rubber. He rose up on his left leg, which did tingle, to the point of almost debilitating pain.

"My oh my," he said to himself, "that's going to hurt when it starts to wake up." And slapped the right leg once, experimentally. No sensation at all.

He felt a hand slip under his right arm and grab his armpit. He turned. It was Robert. He was smiling, goofy, loose. But his arm was like a steel bar.

"I thought you were in shape," Robert said.

"I am," Martin huffed.

They made their way through the thinning crowd to the section of the loft that was used as a kitchen. Martin reached a chair just as his right leg began to twitch with the first rushes of painful sensation. He sat down heavily and began kneading the thigh of the afflicted leg. Robert stood nearby, talking to the woman whose place it was. The two of them walked over.

"I hope you're all right," the woman said.

"Oh, no damage," Martin replied. His professional pride was stung.

The woman put a hand on his shoulder. "I do hope you'll come to see Babba again. It was very unusual for him to single you out on your first visit. And what you went through was very beautiful, perhaps painful, but something which will begin to work in you and change your life. That's the way it is with Babba. When he touches us, no matter how well we think we understand what's happening, the truth of the experiences keeps unfolding."

Martin's leg was now a bottle of angry buzzing mosquitoes, each biting with silent fury. He wanted to give it his entire attention, to nurse the limb back to normality, but male vanity was stronger than organic pain. He stood up and smiled.

"I certainly never had anything like that happen to me in my life before," he said. He tried to strike a note somewhere between honesty and graciousness. The woman was a plump, pleasant person in her early forties, attractive enough to sleep with but not so much so that one would automatically consider it. "I really don't know what to make of all this. Perhaps I'll be back, but the whole thing is very strange to me."

"I don't think there's a person here who didn't feel that at first." She began to detail her own experiences, but caught a cautionary glance from Robert, and understood that it would be best to leave the newcomer to him. She waved a hand in front of her and gushed, "Well, you must excuse me. The one thing I don't want to do is sound like a used consciousness salesman." She smiled again, an expression so warm and pervasive that Martin was taken in completely. "I do hope well see you again," she repeated, and turned to make her way to the far end of the loft where Babba was sitting on a rug, some eight or ten people around him.

"Ready?" Robert said. "What's going on back there?" Martin whispered.

"A business meeting. Making plans for Babba's stay in the country this summer. He's going up to a place near Grossinger's."

Martin's eyes opened wide. Robert laughed. "I know," he said. "On one level it's just like a new wave in the Catskills. The old Jewish stand-up comedians are being replaced by Hindu sit-down cosmologists."

The two men went out of the loft, down the stairs and into the street. The culture shock was like getting off a plane that had just arrived from Tibet. Cars thudded past. People slid by, angular, silent, guarded. The air was two-thirds exhaust and industrial waste. The bar across the street was even more crowded than it had been. Rock still crashed through the glass onto the sidewalks and shouted its raucous affirmation up to the rooftops of the converted factory buildings that were fast becoming a hive of busy artists.

"What's your mood?" Robert asked.

"This may sound blasphemous, but I'd love a beer."

"Nothing wrong with a beer. Want to try across the street?"

"Do you?"

"Sure. It'll make an interesting contrast."

They crossed the street and walked up to the double doors.

Up close, the bar looked like a murky goldfish bowl, the cigarette smoke turning the air gray, the people, slightly drunk, moving with the spasmodic lassitude of underwater creatures.

They went inside. The bar stretched thirty feet down the left side of the narrow room. The opposite wall was bare except for a long counter, belly-button high. Not an inch of wood showed along either space. Men and women in about equal numbers occupied every available stool, stood in front of every available inch of counter and bar. Four bartenders moved incessantly, supplying customers directly, while a fifth filled orders for a stream of waitresses who serviced the back room, a barnlike space five times the size of the bar proper, with tables, booths, and a small space for dancing.

Robert and Martin walked several feet into the space and halted, letting it wash over them. A dozen women shifted their eyes and ranked the two men with erotically computerized glances, checking hair, clothing, mouth, crotch bulge, height, and general body attitude. Most of them, with uncanny instinct, dismissed Robert as a homosexual. For several of them, however, that offered more intriguing possibilities than were available with most of the men in the bar, swaggering types too inhibited to swagger, leering from their one-dimensional fantasy plots. A homosexual, at least, was more likely to produce amusing conversation, and those who were prone to fucking women usually did it very well indeed. Martin presented a more complex problem to those probing eyes. He was physically superb, a veritable bull, a classic stud. But the cut of his pants, the style of his hair, and the opacity of his stare indicated a certain lack of nuance or subtlety of understanding. He was the sort of man one would want to marry. He would work hard, sincerely do his best to please, and keep the old vagina properly pounded. The difficulty would be the absolute necessity for having an affair, almost certainly with some rotter, an artist with dirty dishes in his sink, brilliant canvases on his wall, crumbs in his sheets, women constantly ringing his phone, and a pound of grass in a cookie jar on his bookshelf. The women at the bar looked at Martin and by and large decided that they couldn't stand the guilt.

The entire weigh-in took place in less than five seconds, during which time the two men tacitly agreed to move on to the back room.

"Dinner?" asked a short Oriental girl with a ponytail down past her waist. She was dressed in the waitresses' uniform, a short black skirt and halter with a white blouse.

"How about coffee and dessert?" Robert asked.

The girl glanced professionally about the room, gauging the number of empty tables with her estimate of how crowded they would be that night, balancing the actuality of a small order against the probability of a full dinner, and decided that they could be seated. That art of judgment had been taught to her by the owner of the place. His legendary successes in the bars and restaurants he'd already opened were based in part on the fact that the help had to be smart as well as good-looking.

They sat at a small round table and ordered coffee and pie with ice cream. For a few minutes they didn't speak, simply letting themselves become accustomed to the ambience, both more quiet and less intense than in the front room. The people here were mostly in groups of two or four, couples who had traded in the hungry excitement of the jungle for the well-fed regularity of the farm. It was not, however, that the current of erotic truth became nonexistent, but that it was insulated, not so naked. After all, when one is alone, the expressions one wears when assessing a strange piece of meat are of one's own concern only; but if there is a mate or date nearby, it is necessary to become guarded, discreet, sophisticated.

"So. How do you feel?"

Martin pulled his attention back from its global reconnaissance and directed it toward Robert.

"I don't know. I'd like to report some drastic change as a result of what happened. But I don't really feel any different at all."

"Don't you find that a bit . . . unusual?"

"What do you mean?"

"Well, when people go through that sort of experience, they usually go on and on about their insights and how they understand it all now and so forth. You may not have been into any of the current crop of salvation therapies."

"You mean like Primal Scream?"

"Primal Scream, Gestalt, Rolfing, bioenergetics, the whole neo-Esalen grab-bag of fundamentalist psychology. There you get to yell and scream, or to sound off, or to lie on a mattress and curse your parents, and afterwards you and the therapist congratulate one another on the breakthrough and chalk up your insights on the wall, like racking up points in a game of billiards. But they all miss the boat, because they still think that experience is worth something. They operate on the premise that if you have enough experiences, some kind of cumulative effect will take place and one day you'll have somehow learned something. What's worse, they begin to get competitive about their experiences, creating a kind of World Series of breakthroughs. And it becomes just another kind of drug."

"I can see that," Martin said. "I've never been involved in any of that, but I've always had the suspicion that it was a fancy kind of masturbation."

"It is, and it is necessary for a lot of us because you do have to be able to masturbate without guilt before you can learn how to fuck or make love."

"How is Babba different?"

"Because he is pure consciousness, he never discriminates among different types of experience. And so those who stay with him gradually learn how to approach life in the same way. He never says 'do this' or 'don't do that,' but just by being in his presence, one learns how to live. It's like sitting next to a stove on a cold day. The stove just gives off heat. You sit next to it and you get warm. It's very simple. Well, Babba gives off consciousness. All the time. It isn't something he does, it's something he is. So when you go to him, no matter whether you're in a good mood or bad, whether you think you're king of the world or a worthless piece of shit, he looks at you in precisely the same way. Because he doesn't get trapped in forms or different states. He remains in that one place, that pure consciousness, that eternal energy. So when you went through your heavy emotional changes, nobody there identified with you. Nobody said 'oh poor you,' or 'what a marvelous breakthrough.' We all understood that it was a very powerful, personal experience, but we also all understood that it was just another manifestation of God, nothing to get all wrought up over."

The waitress came by with a round wooden plate. She put down the coffee, the pie and ice cream, forks, spoons, napkins. She took a breath and stepped back from the table, checked it out to see that everything was there and in place, waited until one of the men looked up and nodded his affirmation, and then turned to her next table. She had a twenty-minute break coming up in seven minutes and she was almost frantic to take her shoes off, have her own coffee, and smoke a cigarette. After that she had three more hours, and then home where her husband would be up late, studying. A thick black curtain closed over her heart momentarily and her mind lit up with a brilliant image in which she took her Friday paycheck and tips and got on a Greyhound Bus headed for Key West where she would get a room and a job and live a life in which she wasn't responsible to someone else every minute of the day, where she could stay out all night or spend weekends at the beach and not have to report in or explain. But the image passed. She was two weeks late on her period. She would probably have a baby. And that took care of the next twenty years. Her parents would be pleased, his parents would be pleased, he would be pleased, and she would smile, forget that she had any identity outside of the net of family and friends, and she would be pleased. Table fourteen needed something. A man was sticking his hand in the air like a small child in class asking the teacher if he might leave the room.

"I must say that I surprised myself," Martin replied after they had put sugar and milk into their coffee and had begun to eat and drink. "I would never have believed I could do something like that, much less do it in public. And then to be so blasé about it afterwards." He paused, fork in the air. "It's strange. I'm impressed, and yet I don't feel impressed."

"Babba says it's the difference between drinking water and drinking soda when you're thirsty. Both will quench your thirst, but the soda will leave a residue in your mouth, which will make you crave more. Truth is like water. It just does the job. And you hardly even notice it."

"I was really angry with him afterwards," Martin went on.

"For just dropping me like that. I'm afraid I had a few unkind thoughts about him. And probably still do."

"He's been called more names than you can imagine. There are times when I've been so furious at him I could have hit him with a bat. Once a man tried to shoot him. But when these things happen, you just take a breath and look at what's really happening. That man isn't doing anything. He hasn't asked you to sit with him. You go out of your own free will. And when there, he simply sits and talks. He doesn't move around very much or do very much of anything. So when you get murderously angry, you ask yourself 'where is this coming from?' It's not from him, so it must be from inside you. And then you realize once more what a guru is. He's someone who lives continually in a state of consciousness that we can only glimpse. In relationship to him, we find out our own quirks and stupidities and distorted emotions."

Robert leaned back in his chair, raised his arms over his head, and stretched voluptuously. His spine cracked in several places. He brought his arms back down, leaned forward, and looked into Martin's eyes.

"So. It's been quite a night, hasn't it?"

Martin was made slightly uncomfortable by Robert's gaze, but for the first time in his life he was aware of the discomfort, and he forced himself to look back, sharing a look of warmth and intimacy with a man.

This is a change, he thought.

"You know," he said out loud, "when we left the loft I was sure I never wanted to see him again. But now I feel very much that I want to."

"Your face and eyes are so much softer," Robert said. For a second he had let himself speak freely, as he would to another gay man, letting his feelings inform his words, without the constant subliminal habitual defense that men assume in the world of daily combat. He was somewhat shocked that he could let himself be that loose with someone who practically personified male rigidity. Martin blinked. It was something that would have made him uncomfortable even if expressed by a woman. But to hear a man tell him that, with such gentleness of voice and ease of expression, ought to have sent him scrambling back inside his cage of reaction.

Instead, he simply smiled. "Thank you," he heard himself say, and was surprised to feel his impulse to reach out and take Robert's hand, not to shake it in some stiff, formal fashion, but just to hold it, to feel its warmth, its texture, its wondrous humanity.

Three

A week of Sundays had passed. From the point of view of the immeasurable, sprawling, fantastic, blissfully indifferent universe which was but one of as many universes as it itself contained of atoms, and beyond that, where the mind, boggled beyond belief simply says, "Aw shit!" and goes fishing in a local philosophical pond where it catches itty bitty little wrigglers of wisdom, intelligence, insight, compassion, and only glimpses the big ones, mystery and enlightenment lurking behind rocks . . . from that point of view, nothing happened. Even if one were to regard things from the sun, no change would have been noticed. The planets rotated and revolved, the galactic drift continued, stray comets came and went like horny bachelors hitting every discotheque in town on a Saturday night, leaving a karmic trail blazing across the essential darkness of space. Lower still, seeing things from the vantage point of life, after two billion years, trees had attained the highest form of vital intelligence yet evolved. Below that, a loud, dirty, obnoxious species had succeeded in breeding itself practically to the point of starvation and using its tawdry evolutionary gimmicks, the thumb, the upright posture, and the big brain, to precipitate a crisis of staggering proportions, threatening to take most of the other life forms on the planet with it when it finally burned itself to a cinder or suffocated in its own garbage. At a lower level yet, in its own historical terms, the same species was mired in its ten-thousandth year of warfare.

Given all this, the relatively insignificant changes in the lives of four people living in a concrete human-heap assume their proper sense of proportion . . . to anyone that is, except the four people themselves. They shared the essential stupidity of the species, the notion that what we do or think or feel, or even whether we survive, is of any interest to anyone at all.

And yet, this life is our stage, these words our roles, this body our costume. And perhaps the teachers who articulated the final esoteric truth in all the traditions are correct, that there is no One Mind, no Ultimate Source. That there is nothing, indeed, but the simple facticity of direct perception, that the awareness of what-it-is is none other than the awareness of that-it-is. Then a soap opera would once again be a soap opera, and whether it appeared formally on a television screen or informally in someone's living room, would make no difference. An egalitarian existentialism would drive a stake through the third eye of anyone who assumed that he or she had some special or more significant viewpoint than anyone or anything else, whether it was the podium of cosmic consciousness, enlightenment, or direct communication from God.

Martin stretched, forced his eyes open, rolled off the bed and landed on the floor in a crouch. He straightened up, went to the bathroom to piss and splash some cold water on his face, and then walked to the living room where Robert had his altar. It was only a large wooden crate covered with a madras cloth. On it were Babba's picture, showing him wrapped in a grungy blanet lying next to a dirt road near an Indian village. His expression was that of a man who had just been bitten on the toe by a large ant. On either side of the photo stood a candle and an incense holder. In front of it a bowl with several pieces of fruit. Twice a day, followers of Babba's were expected to sit in formal meditation before his picture, offering him a piece of fruit and receiving his Grace in return. Since he taught that his physical presence was only an illusion anyway, a photo could prove as effective a channel for Divine Power as a body.

Martin lit the candle and the incense. He stepped back, sank to his knees, and bowed three times, hitting his head to the floor with each prostration. Then he slipped a pillow under his buttocks, crossed his legs in front of him, and with a deep sigh, began his sitting. The instructions were simple. He was to keep his back straight, his hands folded on his lap, his eyelids lowered but not closed, and to put his attention into his breathing, following the swelling and emptying of his belly with each inhalation and exhalation. He was not to become occupied with his thoughts. It was explained that they would come and go, and that he should neither try to suppress them nor indulge in them. And his heart was to become a fountain of yearning, a fireplace of flame, an open embrace welcoming Babba, the Guru, the Bringer of Light, the Godman, the living realization of Divine Truth.

After his initial meeting with Babba, Martin had become fast friends with Robert. They went to films together, they talked to one another on the phone late at night, they even went on tours of Robert's gay haunts so that Martin might lose some of his prejudice and fear about homosexuality. They went to see Babba several times a week, and after a month spent a weekend with him at an upstate New York camp that had been rented for the occasion. Without his knowing precisely when, or how, Martin crossed a line. It was just that one afternoon, as he was walking down Seventh Avenue, he realized that he wasn't looking at tits and asses, not with that perpetual frisson of clenched excitement which he had learned to control so that no more than a spasm of light flickered in his eyes. And he saw that he wasn't thinking about Julia or fretting about what he was doing with his life, but was meditating, quite spontaneously and happily, on Babba and on God. He had, to a small but noticeable degree, detached himself from manifestations and was perceiving the emptiness with which they played out the game of figure-ground. He had called Robert and told him about the experience and Robert said, "Good. The Guru's grace has been activated in you. Now it will work in you forever, no matter whatever else you do." That idea, that what flowed from Babba would always be part of him, filled him with such unbounded joy that he spent the next three days floating through his routines in a state of absolute euphoria.

Then Robert had asked Martin to move in with him.

"I won't make any passes at you, you bastard," Robert said.

"Then what for?"

"My roommate moved out. I can use someone to share the rent. You must be tired of hotel rooms. We're good friends. We are both into Babba." He counted each reason off on one of his fingers. "You'll have a private bedroom. It's perfect," he concluded.

Martin pressed his lips together, frowned, and agreed. And moved in that night. It had been an ideal situation. The two men found that they could live together without a smidgin of friction. They kept the same hours at work, and so their schedules allowed them to divide their days without conflict. They often meditated together, once Robert introduced Martin to the practice, pointing out that sitting was a marvelously subtle technique independent of its virtues as a magnet for Babba's influence. They fell into the habit of playing chess, and continued going to Babba's meetings. The one discrepancy came on those nights, once or twice a week, when Robert manifested a certain edgy restlessness, prowled the apartment a bit, and then announced that he was "going out for a bit of air." Martin knew that he was headed for the bars or the bookshops or baths, and drew a curtain in his mind over the pictures of the things he knew Robert must be doing there.

Now, as Martin sat, he wondered where Robert had spent the night. Usually the tall yoga instructor was up at six, did an hour an a half of yoga, and then sat for half an hour before eating and going to work.

"I guess he stayed the night with someone," Robert thought.

He reflected on what his feeling would have been had Julia done that. It was absurd. He and Julia had treated one another like children, forcing each other to be home each evening, to explain where they'd been. And why? Was it because of sex? If he and Robert were to become lovers, would they evolve the same sort of strangling hold on each other? It was interesting that the word "lover" was used to describe someone you had sex with. But no sooner had Martin begun to board that train of thought than he realized he was drifting again, getting lost in his thoughts, and he pulled his attention back to his posture, to his breathing, to his feelings for Babba.

Yet, some seed had been planted, for after he finished his formal meditation, after breakfast, and all during his day at work, a certain unease steadily grew on him like the sense that one might have left the oven on three days earlier when leaving for vacation. He alternately nagged at it and pushed it away, but when he found himself absentmindedly stroking his crotch while talking to a woman on the phone, the fact could no longer be denied. He was hungry. Hungry for a woman. Hungry for the smell of hair, the taste of cunt, the texture of mouth, the sound of female voice slipping over the edge of awareness into orgasm, hungry for the heft of a tight, full ass pressing into his groin.

But he was not the simple creature he once was. Before he got married, he would simply have called one of his girlfriends. While he was with Julia he would have gone home and hoped she was in the mood. And up until two months ago he might have gone to a massage parlor or taken up one of the women in the club who were usually on erotic standby. Now, however, he had his image of holiness to contend with. And even though Babba himself had indicated that once a person was enlightened there was no single pattern of sexuality he or she would follow, Martin still carried over the hierarchical prejudice which places random, anonymous promiscuity at the bottom and celibacy at the top.

"If Robert can go out and suck cocks, why can't I go find myself a cunt?" he said to himself, trying to find justification for what he knew he had to do.

Finally, he compromised. He would take a middle road between outright getting laid and downright going home and gritting his teeth. He leafed through a copy of the *Village Voice* and turned to the "Socials" section which listed all the alternatives to bars for singles who wanted a more genteel cruising ground. Lectures, public parties, discussion groups, tours. He let his eyes roam around the offerings until he found one that caught his attention. He couldn't say why, since it seemed no different from a hundred others on the page, but he went by his hunch. It was a meeting of the Humanistic Society, listening to a talk by a Rabbi on "Marriage: The Rose and the Thorn." It was at the Unitarian Church on Central Park West, and admission was three dollars.

Humanitarians, Unitarians, and Jews, Robert thought. *It ought to make a nice contrast to the steady diet of Hindus I've been getting,* and allowed himself the first laugh at himself in months. He was learning, even though he couldn't begin to understand the process in that way, that one of the uses of the Guru is as a springboard from which to jump into enticing pools.

All the way uptown on the subway, as he walked to the church, and inside the hall, the gender mood was upon him. He was brimming with male energy, the result of constant interaction between himself and Robert, himself and Babba, himself and himself. And like a Leyden jar riding a tide of electricity, he needed to discharge the tension of fullness, the bursting skin of ripeness. And woman called to him like the original Sirens singing their songs to Ulysses and all the sailors who rode by the treacherous rocks on which they perched, beautiful, long-haired, irresistible in the Sicilian sun.

It was a peculiar form of hominess, not centered primarily in his cock, although that venerable and single-minded organ, sensing that the lash of assumed spirituality and grief of separation from Julia might be lifted for the first time in months, raised its cowl and dared to sniff at the emanations of the millions of cunts that fluttered, flounced, and fretted in giddy profusion all around the town. It arose as though from a long, long nap, a bit cranky but refreshed and hungry. *This very night,* it might have thought if it could think, *I may be gorged with blood, thick, hard, mighty, running amok in the luscious wet folds of a gaping clutching loving valley between a wanting woman's thighs.* And at that, it stirred, causing Martin to smile, just as the young Unitarian minister walked up to him, held out one hand, and said, "Welcome. My name is Jim. I hope you'll enjoy our program tonight." Martin shook his hands and began to mumble something but by the time his tongue would function the minister had moved on to the next arrival, a portly man of about fifty-five who smelled like damp parchment.

Martin paid his money to a pleasant matronly woman in her early forties, plump, abandoned by any hope of eroticism, and walked into the church proper, a large vaulted chamber with chairs instead of pews and the most rudimentary suggestion of an altar. It was as though the Unitarians, in their frenzy to disavow any connection to the Christian tradition from which they sprang, made sure to destroy any evidence by which their origin might be traced. A crucifix would have been as out of place there as a male truck driver in a lesbian bar.

Martin felt awkward and displaced. Like a pilgrim driven by a vision who arrives at his particular holy land to find nothing other than surly, hungry beggars, flies, and the stares of demented children, Martin questioned the wisdom of whatever lust took him to this place.

It must be just lonely losers who come here, he thought. *Happy people, successful people, wouldn't be found dead in a place like this.* He scanned the crowd, and his spirits rose somewhat. He saw, here and there, an attractive woman. He had to remember to remind himself that he had not come strictly to get laid, nor would he avoid that possibility. He was going to continue as he had been doing, keeping his attention on Babba, on his awareness that the world of appearances was not the only reality. And at the same time stay in touch with his need, the need to do something with the growing sense of power, of centeredness that now made him feel nothing at all like the man who had lived with Julia and turned into a whiner, grumbler, and pussy-whipped bully.

Martin ambled around for a few minutes until the minister called for the attention of the crowd. He struck that pose of authority which lies at the heart of every man's ambition who enters one of the forms of priesthood, and proceeded to welcome all the people he'd welcomed as individuals now as a group. He was in a peculiar situation. Possibly the youngest person in the room, and theologically committed to the most vague, faint affirmations about the nature of reality, yet by virtue of title and property he was able to gather enough of a semblance of a pose in order to dissemble. He made several feeble jokes, announced that there would be coffee and cakes afterwards, and asked for a nice welcome for Rabbi Gelberman.

The Rabbi materialized from a pocket of gloom behind a partition next to where the minister stood. He was a short man, not quite five and a half feet tall. He wore a pair of tan slacks and an orange turtleneck shirt. His hair was cut short and his beard trimmed neatly. He looked as though he had come from the same seminary as the minister. And in fact the two had become friends when they met at an ecumenical council where it had been decided that God was something of an embarrassment to religion. The Rabbi, however, came from a strong tradition, so his revolt into modernism carried a bit more zip to it. He could even be irreverent since he was close enough to a religious sensibility that still carried traces of wonder at the fact of creation.

"How many here never been married?" the Rabbi asked.

Three people out of the seventy-odd raised their hands. One of them was the minister.

"Out of all those who have been married, how many are still with their mates?" the Rabbi went on.

Not a hand went up. The people in the room glanced around at one another, with a certain stiffness at first, and then with a growing humor. They were all in the same boat.

"A lot of thorn, not so much roses," the Rabbi concluded, and a number of people laughed.

From then on, it was progressively delightful. The Rabbi was a born entertainer. Had he not gone into the formal aspect of religion he would have gone into that informal mode known as show business. His pacing was excellent, and he moved from joy to sorrow, from laughter to tears, with the ease and regularity of a shuttle craft. He told stories of the *shtetl,* although he'd never been to Europe, and he told stories about his friends. He told stories about his own marriage, and in short order elicited contributions from the audience so that people were unburdening themselves, sharing the private pains and memories of happiness. He effected a real communion, which is the heart of true religion, and a kind of grace entered the room. The mood lightened, a gentle aura emerged, tensions were relaxed. Martin found himself thinking of the way the Rabbi dealt with spiritual stuff in contrast to Babba's approach. And he decided that the essential difference was cultural. The Rabbi was an American, a regular guy, a mortal. Babba had spent much of his life in a jungle, and his level of consciousness was not such as one might ordinarily find in a divinity school. And yet, once the juice began to flow, once people rose out of their masks and postures and let their souls mingle, then it didn't matter how the effect had been achieved.

After some two hours, the Rabbi began to wind down, and

he called a halt to the proceedings. He took a question from a woman and announced that that would be the last one, and then they could all descend, like locusts, on the food and drink. As Martin turned to look at the woman asking the question, something caught his eye. He couldn't tell what or whom, but a very brief disturbing flash went off in his head. Since it didn't seem related to anything he could identify, he dismissed it.

At the refreshment table, everyone was jolly. A good deal of group subconscious had been uncovered and dispersed and the sense of unity was high. It was destined slowly to decline again once the people started to use the energy to begin yet another cycle of behavior exactly like that which led them to this place to begin with. They were like poverty-stricken workers who suddenly come into a lot of money via a sweepstakes. For a while they expand as far as their dreams, but before very long they discover they are still loutish, uneducated, surly, mean, jealous, petty, and cruel, the only difference being that they now have a six-figure bank account.

Euphoric, temporarily released from all his disciplines, both neurotic and wholesome, Martin cast his eyes around the room. He stood alone, watching the others talking, saying things that people who have just had such an experience should be embarrassed to say, not because of the content, but because they are already sliding into a realm where awareness is put to sleep and only the mouths continue, moving, making noises. Fifteen feet to his side and in front of him, he saw the most attractive woman he'd spotted all evening. She was medium height, wearing a tight black dress and high-heeled shoes which lifted her legs just enough to accentuate the calves. Her hair was short and glowed with an accent of red. Her buttocks were superb, and he was won over. He sipped his coffee and nibbled his cake and began to sidle over to her. She was in fairly animated conversation with a middle-aged man who obviously had the same ideas as Martin. Martin felt both adventuresome and foolish, like a teenage boy at a dance. He took four or five steps, stopped, looked around, waited, then took a few more steps, all the while trying to look as though he were somehow being moved along by an invisible current. But the other man spotted him coming, and his face first twitched in anger, then fell in dismay as he saw the nature of the competition. The man was no match for the perfectly muscled, young, keen jock who was being drawn to the woman's back with ineluctable force. Martin slowed down his progress, giving the man a chance to bow out gracefully. The man's words dried up, and in a few minutes he was withdrawing, smiling, but casting glances over the woman's shoulder.

"She's magnificent," Martin thought as he got closer. His need, so long dormant, now threatened to seize him entirely, and he found an impulse to wrap his arms around the woman, cupping her breasts, pulling her high, hard ass into his crotch.

The woman half-sensed his presence, half-gathered from her conversational partner's reaction that something was going on behind her, and as Martin drew up she turned. He could not look at her directly all at once, nor could he avert his eyes. What he received was a blurred, shifting set of images. Deep-set breasts, a flat stomach, a trace of perfume, a face of sharp features.

There was nothing for it. He had gone this far, and, fighting all the shyness of the man who knows he is not verbally agile, Martin smiled with forced gusto and looked into her eyes.

"Hi!" he said.

She did not reply, but stared at him evenly, a response so cool and unexpected that it totally flustered him. Like the wallflower who has waited all night to ask for a dance in fear that he would be turned down and is then turned down, Martin suffered the hell of the loser.

He was utterly confused, not only in terms of the social awkwardness, but also because the woman attracted him so strongly, with an almost demoniac pull.

"Interesting talk, wasn't it?" Martin said, blundering forward, peering into the steam rising from his coffee cup as though he were a scientist making a discovery to change the nature of the world.

"Martin," the woman said. Her voice was calm, flat, and yet, wildly, madly, carried a trace of exasperation.

"How does she know my name?" he wondered. And he lifted his eyes, slowly, traveling the whole length of her body, until he came to her face, thinking all the time, "Maybe she's a woman

I knew years ago. Maybe she's one of my old students all grown up," teasing himself with the hope that luck had descended upon him and perhaps given him a lady who was already a bit taken by him.

By the time he looked at her face his expression was set. He was smiling slightly, almost smugly. His eyes had pulled themselves together into a subtle, sharp focus. He was ready.

He looked at her for a full five seconds before he recognized her.

Oh my God, it's my wife! he thought at precisely the same moment his mouth dropped open and he tried to say her name.

"Oh, Martin," Julia said, her midwest drawl breaking through her patina of New York speech pattern. She looked at him the way a mother would a child who has covered himself with mud for the third time in a day. It combined the ultimate patience with the ultimate exasperation, thus manifesting an irresistible vibration of parental affection and, as its more sinister underbelly, superiority.

It was the sort of look that would have unzipped the tension in Martin's hamstrings several months earlier, combining as it did an admission of guilt along with instant forgiveness. He would have melted then, succumbed, buried his face in the ancient valley between her breasts. Now, however, while all that did pass through him, while he suffered all the same reactions, some other force continued to operate within him. It was as though he had become the central character in his own movie and he could watch himself play his role out with humor and detachment. It was as Robert had noted one night: "It isn't that you become someone else, some superman, some pious thickhead. You keep all your karma, and you continue to do all the asshole things you've done all your life. But you don't put the same energy into it, and so it begins to fade, become transparent. It becomes light, ironic, brief."

"Julia," Martin said at last.

"Well, I see you remember my name," Julia replied sardonically, "even if you did have some trouble with the face and body."

"You've lost weight," Martin said.

"Fifteen pounds. And I've cut and tinted my hair."

She regarded him with an appraising eye. "What have you been up to?"

He didn't know what to say. Julia was standing in front of him. Their whole life together assailed him at once, from their first meeting in the school cafeteria, through all the months and early years of euphoria, to the growing darkness and confusion, to the last days of absolute sorrow and anger. And since then, his friendship with Robert, his devotion to Babba, while Julia seemed to fade further and further from his consciousness, until it seemed she no longer existed, had never existed. Yet, here she was. And changed somehow, somehow sharper and somehow sorter.

Her appeal was as strong as the smell of baking bread to someone who's been on a ten-day fruit fast. And for the first time he understood the erotic aspect of marriage, for this delectable woman in front of him was his wife, *his*. She was not a stranger, someone with whom the excitement of newness would be offset by the necessity of adjustment. They had already both done their worst to each other, they had married and all that that implied. So the price of admission was already paid.

He wanted to fuck her so badly it almost brought tears to his eyes. He remembered asking Babba about sex, and Babba had replied, "You already did it all as an infant." Martin had frowned in noncomprehension. Babba had continued, "When you were a baby, didn't you suck at the nipple for hours? Didn't you kiss and stroke your mother's body? Didn't you try to bury your head between her thighs?" Martin had nodded. "So," Babba concluded, "has anything changed?" This was the new ingredient. For even though his desire raged, the nascent awareness that had begun to act as a counterintelligence in his daily life was not burned. As Julia's presence pulled him with the force of a thousand-foot fall at the edge of a precipice, he clung to the memory of Robert and Babba as he would have to thick tree branches. No matter what else happened, he must not let go of his friendship and of the teaching, for then he would be a single man using all his energy to stand firm amidst the hurricane of Julia's roiling energy, and he would succeed in resisting only at the cost of defending himself against her, or he would succumb and be sucked into the same marriage they had had before.

"Oh," Martin replied after a while, "I've been working. And I'm sharing an apartment with a friend. Maybe you remember Robert. The tall yoga teacher who works at the club. And I've been seeing . . ." He stopped. For an instant he felt that it might be blasphemous to mention Babba's name. What if she laughed, or mocked?

I'm afraid of her, Robert realized. *I'm actually afraid of her. Why?* He focused his eyes and looked at her. *She's just a tiny little thing. I could break her in half with one hand. Why am I afraid?*

"Seeing . . .?" Julia added.

There was something about him that bothered her, and she couldn't tell whether her feeling was annoyance or excitement. He seemed a bit smug, and yet she found that somewhat enticing. She wondered whether he had another woman.

"A man. A teacher. A man called Babba," he said. "He's a . . . guru."

The information nonplussed her. She had no ready response, nor any way to gauge his relationship to this new situation. Martin was the last person in the world she would have expected to get caught up with some Eastern teacher. He had even refused to see a marriage counselor or a therapist. Then she made the connection. Robert. The yoga teacher. Martin was sharing his apartment. This must be part of the involvement. Once again she saw Martin's suggestibility, what she considered his inherent weakness. A bitter husband once remarked, "A woman does all she can to domesticate a man and then despises him when she succeeds." Martin was held in that double bind, although the yoke was not so heavy on his shoulders now that he stood somewhat apart.

"Oh. How interesting," she replied, noncommital, cagey.

"And what brings you here?" Martin asked.

"I thought I might meet a man," Julia said without hesitation.

An old familiar icepick poked at his entrails. And before he could remember to take a calming breath he shot back, "Horny?"

"A bit," she told him. "But not desperate. Otherwise I'd be

in a bar. I thought this might be a genteel way to feel my way around." She glanced up at him. "After all, it has been almost four months, you know."

"Don't tell me you've been celibate all that time," he said, falling into the rhythm of their joust.

"I won't tell you that," she replied.

There was a very long, icy pause. And then he broke, unable to maintain any facade of being cool. "Have you been?" he asked.

She appraised him again. The front of her body was about ten degrees warmer than the back. Standing in front of Martin was like being next to a stove. She felt as though her dress might peel right off. And she could have him if she wanted him, she knew that. If she swayed just an inch he would grab her, might fuck her right on the spot, in front of the Unitarian minister and his arched eyebrows, in front of the Rabbi and his go-go wife, in front of the tepid crowd of mediocre people who collectively couldn't muster up as much élan vital as a healthy whore on Second Avenue. But what would the terms be? Could they enter and exit cleanly? She took a breath and opened her mouth and let the words slide out without thought.

"I had one man, about two months after you left. I had him once. I didn't spend the night with him. That didn't seem right." She looked at Martin to see how he was taking the news. His face was several shades whiter, but the lines showed that he was nowhere near the danger point. She waited for his reaction.

"That seems . . . reasonable," he said. And then added, "Thank you."

"It wasn't for you, you creep," she said. "It was because of the way I felt."

"Thank you anyway," he said.

This was his equivalent of her exasperated mother ploy. This was his rendition of the Noble Husband, strong, firm, warm, accepting, and grateful. It was practically irresistible and Julia might have weakened somewhat except she remembered one evening she'd spent with Gail and they'd talked over possible scenarios that might take place when Julia and Martin finally met. Julia had said, "Oh, at one point he's sure to do his Noble

Husband number. He knows that my knees get weak when he starts gazing into some sorrowful distance." And they'd both laughed at the image. Now that he was actually there in front of her, actually doing it, the remembered humor returned to put his act into perspective.

"So," he added, "you've had sex with one more person than I have." This thrust was the hidden dagger behind the Noble Husband stance. The game was to soften her up and then slip the blade between her ribs. However, he hadn't noticed that the first half of the act did not work its usual magic, and that his thrust would be aimed at an alert and waiting opponent.

"If by that you're implying that you haven't been to bed with anyone, then I've had two more people than you."

"But you said there was only one man," he protested, as outraged as a soldier who had just stepped on a boobytrap.

"That's right," she told him. "Only one *man*."

He shook his head, blinked his eyes, looked stupid. His brains had begun to flop around inside his skull. The logical progression was beyond his ken, so his thought patterns were bogged down and his cerebral engine was whirring and whining, trying to get the conceptual wheels out of the mud.

She waited until he had gone through his entire repertoire of indicating that he didn't understand, and then she smiled very sweetly.

"The other person was a woman, darling." And, after a pause, "*Is* a woman."

"A woman," Martin repeated as though it were the first time in his life he had heard the word and was fascinated by the sheer sound of it. "You mean, a lesbian? You've been with a lesbian?"

"The next question you are bound to ask is whether or not I've become queer. Shall I answer it for you? Actually, I consider that I've become de-queered. I look back on my past life and wonder how in the world I came to the conclusion that the only way to live it is in a tight, exclusive, suffocating nasty little closed circle with a man. I can only attribute it to the power of conditioning. If you start feeding a child poison at an early enough age, she will eventually develop an immunity to it. And from the day I was old enough to understand, they began giving me dolls, telling me that I would one day be a mother, and teaching me how to play house, because one day I would be a wife, and telling me how to handle boys, because one day I'd have to capture one all my own. And women? They became rivals, enemies, bitches. I could have pleasant acquaintanceships with them, but no passion, no commitment, no meaning."

"Yes," Martin said, "Yes, I see." He spoke in a whisper, his eyes focused on some distant spot in the room. It was as though he had gone into a trance. It made Julia nervous.

"See what?" she said and twisted her head around to peer in the direction he was looking. But there was nothing there except the far wall of the large hall. She glanced back at Martin. He had the expression of a child who has finally understood the problem in mathematics given by the teacher. For an instant she wondered whether he had gone mad.

"Are you all right?" she asked stepping a bit closer to him and pulling lightly on his sleeve.

The action pulled him back to the moment. "All right? Oh, yes, yes, I'm fine." He blinked several times. clearing a film from his eyes. He looked at Julia, drinking her in.

"It's you," he said. "This is fantastic, really fantastic. Coming to this place and finding you. It's good to see you, really good to see you." And without warning he put his arms around her and pulled her tightly to him. For an instant she resisted, the surprise causing all her muscles to tense. But he was so strong, so overwhelming, and she was so truly hungry for the touch of a man, that she melted by degrees, yielding first her shoulders, then her breasts, then her belly, and finally her thighs and crotch, until she was plastered against him.

"Martin, I don't think we should," she said after a few minutes had passed. "People are looking."

"You've got so thin," he said. "And you cut your hair and dyed it. I didn't recognize you."

"I know," she told him. "You were going to try to pick me up until you saw who I was."

"Can I pick you up anyway?"

"Let's go slowly, Martin."

"Sure. How about going for coffee? If you were a strange

woman and I'd picked you up here, that's exactly what I'd do. I'd take you for coffee."

"And then?" The heat between their bodies had risen considerably.

"And then we'd tell each other stories."

"And then?"

"And then we'd try to figure out whether we were going to go to bed or not."

"You might think I was a loose woman," Julia whispered as Martin nibbled her throat.

"From what you've told me so far, you're far worse than that. Do you go to bed with men anymore?"

She pulled back just far enough to be able to step on his toe with some force. He pulled his foot back and let her go, an expression of surprise and slight pain on his face.

"Don't try to shmooze me, you bastard," she said, her voice suddenly sharp. "I came here for the same reason you did, to pick somebody up. I have my diaphragm and foam in my handbag. I was ready to actually go off with someone and have him stick his dick inside me, if he was healthy-looking and polite and showed some sense of tenderness." She stepped back a couple of feet and stared at him with half-lidded eyes, and then, incongruously, smiled, a tough, warm smile of camaraderie. "And I won't hold it against you that you're my husband, if you meet all the other qualifications."

He held his hands in front of his chest, palms forward, a gesture of conciliation. "Almost a fight," he said. "A few months ago this would have been enough to start us off for a whole weekend."

Julia began to say that she had changed, that she now didn't stand alone but had incalculable support from her relationship with Gail. The two women now saw each other four or five times a week. Two or three of those times they slept together. Gail and Eliot had married a month earlier. When Gail told him of the situation he had suffered approximately thirty difficult seconds, and then asked, "You mean I'm off the hook?" He'd had to face a bit more flak from Julia who spent the better part of one morning at the office tearing him up one side and down the other, throwing in her newly formulated opinions about a number of aspects of his business. True to form he had asked, "Can we have threesomes?" to which Gail replied, "Only if you're a very, very good boy." And added, "And also depending on what Julia works out with Martin."

But as all this went through her mind, she found herself observing Martin. He too had changed. There was a calm about him, a sense of self-assurance that went far deeper than what was usually afforded him by his muscles. She didn't know precisely what it was about him but whatever it was she liked it.

"Come on, buy me a coffee at least," she said.

She went to pick up her handbag and walked toward the door where he caught up with her. He took her hand and they headed for the exit but were intercepted by both the Rabbi and the Unitarian minister.

"Excuse me," the Rabbi said. Martin and Julia shot each other a glance of complicity, and in that instant, four months fell away.

Being tripped into a social role in which they had to assume a unity against an external force, the very essence of what it is to be a couple was activated in an instant. The four months dissolved. The distance, the pain, her night with Eliot, his friendship with Robert, her love affair with Gail, his devotion to Babba. It was an utterly terrifying, extraordinarily delicate, totally heartrending moment. It was that instant again, that single penetrating glance into the fact of each other's grave. It was all there, the transient beauty, the fleeting joy, the fragile sorrow, the poignancy of existence, the magical embryo, the mystical child, the impassioned adult, the wrinkled old woman and stooped old man, the parchment corpse, the smell of moist earth, the scrape of spades on stones, and then the transmogrification into ooze, into ick, into mulch, into bones, into dust.

Martin and Julia stood transfixed. The fantasy of their time before their marriage, the nightmare of their marriage, the dream of the months apart, all impacted to implode the present moment. The look they exchanged was so momentous that the Rabbi took a solicitous step forward as though they were children playing too close to a high voltage wire. The Unitarian minister saw a dark hotel room with flaking paint and a young, dark-skinned whore with red lips and a more copious flow from her vagina than he had seen from his fiancée any twenty-five times put together.

"You look very blissful and yet filled with dread," the Rabbi said. "Excuse me, but your embrace, your whole attitude, is so striking that . . . well, frankly, I'm bursting with curiosity. Was it something I said in my talk?"

Martin and Julia smiled, grinned, broke out in titters. Then, realizing the rudeness, turned to the small man in the black suit.

"We've been separated for four months. We're married for five years, and we've been separated. And we met here tonight. I mean, neither of us knew that the other was coming."

The minister nudged the Rabbi in the ribs. "A miracle, Ephraim. What do you imagine the others would say if they heard we pulled off a miracle tonight?"

"It's just a coincidence," the Rabbi said, "Or, as our recently popular Eastern sages might put it, 'karma.'" He glanced shrewdly back and forth between Martin and Julia.

"So this is a joyous moment, but it creates problems, right?"

Martin smiled embarrassedly. Julia looked away.

"No need to be shy," the Rabbi went on. "That's what the talk was all about, if you remember." Then, recalling himself, he stepped back. "But I'm sorry, this is an intrusion. It's just that you two, well, you put on quite a spectacle. And I wondered what the story was." He stepped back another few feet. He waved, his hand making an arc in front of his chest. "So, good luck," and then edged off the way a spectator might after having pushed through the crowd to see the accident victim lying on the pavement. He caught the minister's arm and led the young man away. They moved into a far corner where they discussed the meaning of the Minister's and Rabbi's role in a society which is attaining complete fragmentation.

Martin and Julia walked out into the night, holding hands. It was almost eleven o'clock, the air as warm and soft as a kitten's belly. Without a word, they strolled across the wide avenue and into Central Park. Old women sat on benches, young men walked

their dogs, a policeman stood in alert boredom keeping an eye
on a derelict who looked as though he hadn't slept in a bed for
several weeks. The man couldn't be dangerous to a tough ten-
year-old boy, so decrepit was he, but he might do something to
offend the sensibilities of the dowagers, to unzip his fly and piss
on the bench, perhaps, or perhaps to pitch face forward and die.

They walked to the point where the overhead streetlights ran
out. There was only one other person, a short, heavily muscled,
bald black man with two Doberman Pinschers on chain leashes.
He had the air of the truly insouciant, like an eighth-degree
black belt in Karate strolling along a waterfront dock where large,
drunken, clumsy sailors might frighten less protected mortals.
This was the beginning of mugger territory, where rapists were
said to lurk, where sociopaths giggled behind trees.

It was not a place where Martin would have ordinarily gone,
even though his superb physical conditioning and ability to kick,
jump, and move with blinding speed would make him a sorry
choice for even a pair of muggers armed with knives. But Martin
had two talismans. One was the sense of peacefulness that had
been developing in him through his association with Babba, and
the second was the presence of Julia. Being with her infused him
with such a sense of unreality that the terrors of the physical
plane had no meaning for him.

Julia was slightly apprehensive at first, but once Martin had
explained that the man with the dogs was like one of the demons
that stand guard at Tibetan temples, put there to scare away those
whose quest for truth is not wholehearted, she relaxed. And he
gave off an aura of such self-assurance that her fear shriveled
and blew away for lack of nutrients. Martin walked with her
until they came to a spot behind a row of shrubbery. He took off
his jacket and spread it on the grass. Julia sat down on it and he
sat next to her, cross-legged. It was almost pitch black.

Like two children in a closet, they were overtaken by a sense
of naughtiness. The darkness, the total seclusion in a completely
public place, the distant vibration of violence, the hum of the
city beyond the perimeter of the park like a vast and aspirated
chant, the electricity of their sudden presence together, the
rising up of the realization of the initial erotic expectation for

the evening, all combined to brush away, for the moment, all other considerations except their actual contact.

Martin took her in his arms, and in five seconds they had become a thrashing, moaning, biting, sucking, grabbing, thrusting, rolling animal, a sound in the woods, a movement under the stars. They wanted to do everything at once, to squeeze a universe of rediscovery and new discovery into the relatively limited vehicles of their bodies and minds. And the only tools they had were hands and mouths and genitals bursting with sensation.

"Oh, oh, oh," Julia whimpered and Martin thrust his hand under her skirt, slid the cupped palm up her thighs, and closed on the moist hairy center, naked, unobstructed by panties. She fell back as he kissed her throat, sucking on the point where her jugular vein throbbed, her own hands groping wildly, fluttering on his chest, scratching his back, cupping his buttocks, sliding over his hard, madly rearing cockhead.

Rain on parched earth, cool water on dry tongue, divine grace into a sinner's heart, sunshine on upturned flowers, none of these is more satisfying than the sweet surrender of female and male, shakti and shiva, cunt and cock, mind and mind. There was not a millimeter of space upon which to perch a thought, an idea, a fantasy. Their embrace was pure process, an event without a trace, a progress without a track. Like the primordial bleak black intelligence which is the true eternity in the palms of which infinities dance like dust motes before a pane of glass, their act of sheer erotic facticity manifested every conceivable conception, all of which, bound together in a maddening unity, curved into a gentle, ineffable smile.

They pulled off shirts and kicked off shoes. Then her breasts were in his hands and he pummeled the resilient mounds, pushing them flat against her ribs, pinching, cuddling, stretching, rubbing the nipples between his fingers. His lips covered one breast, and he sucked the whole bulge into his mouth, all the while licking the nipple with his tongue. He sucked her tit into him and let it slide out, trembling on the awareness of the thing, the extraordinary reality of having the sensitive, proud, shy breast between his teeth.

She arched her spine and pushed her breast into his face, at the same time pulling his head forward. Three fingers of his right hand were swiving her cunt, twirling, thrusting, pulling back and caressing her large, serrated clitoris. Her hand grasped his cock and squeezed. It was hot to the touch, and volatile, turgid, thick, explosive. They both squirmed about until they lay in opposite directions, and dove into one another like sharks cutting into the body of a whale. Her legs parted as he sank his face into her crotch. The sticky lips of her cunt parted and a white viscous trail oozed out from the bottom of the fold and trickled into the valley between her buttocks. He closed his eyes, and with his tongue wide, flat, and curved under, he licked her from hole to hole.

Simultaneously she opened her mouth wide and took his cock inside, sliding foward until the head was at the very opening to her throat. She took a deep breath, opened wider, and forced her head down until his cock slid past the curve downward into the esophagus and burst into the narrow channel down which passed food, water, and air. It was a death grip, for if he didn't move, she would suffocate. She choked on his cock until she began to grow faint from lack of oxygen, and then disgorged it, her head flying back, a mouthful of spit exploding and drooling from her lips, her belly and cunt contracting, her tongue licking the air.

"Ohhhh," he moaned, his mouth glued to her cunt, his lips touching her lips with the intimacy of a glance, his tongue steadily, patiently, thirstily licking the constant flow of secretion, and then the quick breath, the gulp, as he drank her down. His cock vibrated in the air, wild with the sudden expulsion. Her lips puckered and smacked together as she yearned toward him again. He lifted his pelvis toward her and once again his thick hot cock slid into her mouth.

They ate at one another for more than a half an hour, rising and falling, swinging through cycles of frenzied mashing, of silent nibbling, of animal devouring, of pornographic yielding and realization. They became wet, grass-stained, and their hands were voracious, digging into each crevice, exploring each stretch of flesh. A hundred times they hovered on the brink of orgasm, but each time they edged back, not consciously by design, but as part of the natural rhythm that had been established. Just when Martin thought he would erupt, pulsing sperm flooding Julia's mouth, she would drop back, change pace, take her lips away completely. And each time Julia flattened out ready to come, baring her cunt the way a cat bares its teeth, spine curved, legs stretched taut, fingers curved into claws, he would slip lower, going from clitoris to inner lips, from inner lips to asshole, from asshole to thighs.

Then, on signal from some source that was accessible only to them at that moment in that spot, they spun around, Julia rolling onto her back, Martin kneeling between her thighs. He lowered his torso as she spread her legs. His cock floated forward until the tip of it hung poised at the core of her intensity, and then he let himself sink completely, his body covering her, his cock penetrating into the spongy, slick, quivering walls of her cunt.

Then there was no question of delay any longer. The force that seized them would admit of no interference by an ego or will. They were as powerless as dry logs in a fire. There was no point in attempting to negotiate with the flame. Her thighs parted as wide as tendons would allow. She grabbed her ankles with her hands. She made him an open present of her cunt. He slipped his hands under her buttocks. He began to ride her the way an experienced mount rides a horse, by becoming one with the beast underneath instead of trying to control it. They got very silent; the only sound that arose was the steady beat of guttural breathing. She pumped into him, meeting his thrusts. Her vaginal walls contracted, let loose, contracted, let loose. His cock sang with scintillating consciousness.

And then the spurts. The tart, thick globs of the seed of life tearing loose from the tube, dying as they fly, programmed with two billion years of complex wisdom to attain the most simple result: contact; the piercing of the egg. Martin cried out, a high-pitched sob. Julia blacked out, her soul a single spasm. And the vegetative energies romped like dolphins at play, causing their spines to shudder, legs to tremble, minds to spin out of control. The orgasm went on and on, rippling, diminishing, flaring up, transforming itself into feelings and insights, and then returning to brute vibration, until they finally came to rest, lying still, breathing with long voluptuous breaths, clinging to each other like wet leaves on park bench staves in Boston on a rainy autumn day.

And like any travelers to an exotic land, they then had to face the voyage home, knowing that the trip was over, that it would soon devolve into memory, and then not even that, but a kind of formal recollection. And the force of daily life would reassert itself, and one would have to deal with things that are death to shipboard romance. They would have to become people once again, names, identities, routines, commitments, schedules, bundles of feeling, packets of conditioning, matrices of need, orchestras of want, things trailing a past into a future, almost invisible in the present. And they would have to do that knowing what it had been like to merge with the primal energy, the unimaginably mighty power of raw creation.

Understandably, there was a reluctance to break the clinch, but after a while the exigencies of the relative world got to them. Ants crawled on their backs, grass stuck to their skin, and a certain chill of nighttime made them shiver slightly. They pulled apart, with no words possible yet, and stood up to brush themselves off. Then the groping for the clothing in the dark, and the humorous efforts at dressing, hopping around, losing balance, slapping at a stray mosquito.

Finally they were clothed and composed, except that Julia still swayed a bit as she tried to walk and Martin couldn't remember from which direction they had come. They held hands, he to steady her, she to lead him back to the path.

"Do I still get that cup of coffee or is that no longer relevant now that you've had your way with me?" Her voice was light, her tone lilting, almost teasing.

They strolled slowly back into the wider context. The man with the dogs was gone, and so were most of the people who had been on the benches and walk when Martin and Julia entered. The policeman still stood, now about fifteen feet away from his former spot, and the old drunk was fighting sleep on the bench. The two times he had slipped over the policeman had walked over to wake him. It was extraordinary that a young man, in the prime of health and vigor, wearing an official uniform and carrying a deadly weapon, equipped with two-way radios and several pounds of notebooks, billy clubs, handcuffs and spare bullets, earning more than eighteen thousand dollars a year, should have nothing better to do than keep an old man from his rest. Yet it was considered normal. No one even questioned it, not even the old man.

They turned left and walked four blocks to the Dakota, now suffering a vogue, and went west on Seventy-second Street, past bakers, boutiques, Greek sidewalk cafés, a chess club, a vegetarian restaurant, and window upon window of second-story astrologers, psychics, therapists, and drama coaches. But they were oblivious of all that, being caught up in the rhythm of walking together again, of the texture of their hands, the tinglings of the experience they'd just shared in the park.

Martin stopped near West End Avenue at a coffee shop with a glassed-in enclosure that extended a quarter of the way onto the sidewalk. It was called Sahbra, and was run by an Israeli who proved that the foundation of a nation would not cure Jews of their restlessness. He was a man whose parents had been born in Europe and migrated to the United States and then gone to Israel to partake in a vision. Their second son, having killed three Egyptians at close quarters and having watched them die and begin to fester in the desert sun, decided that no fantasy of a return to the homeland was worth the continual tension and threat of warfare. He took his portion of the extraordinary energy which sustains that small state and within three years of living in New York had opened a restaurant. He was on his way to buying the building that housed it.

They went inside and sat at a table next to the window.

"First the Rabbi and now this," Julia said. "This must be our night for Semites. Interesting symbolism." She had already begun to pull herself together and was casting about for a way to extricate herself from any intimation of commitment to a reinstatement of their marital status quo. Martin was holding on to the same edge, his fingertips figuratively white with grasping the cliff of constant identity represented by his relationships with Robert and Babba. And each feared that the other would force the issue and cause a scene that would instantly catapult them back into the big bicker.

The waiter came by, tall, wearing jeans and a white t-shirt, sporting a blasé mustache which hung like tendrils of moss over his upper lip. His eyes were glazed over in an expression of longterm boredom. To place an order with him was to expose oneself to scorn, to have one's taste openly and silently examined and dismissed with disdain. He held a Master's Degree in Economics from New York University, was twenty-seven years old, and currently held four women in thrall, juggling them with careless anxiety so that he never spent a night alone nor heard a complaint about anyone else's having to do iust that. His current pique derived from his thwarted desire for the waitress, one of those maddeningly erotic types who spice the ambience of the city, women with dancers' rumps and little girl breasts and eyes that gaze perpetually on the face of fear, whose souls cry out for a pain to distract them from the terror of their condition, who end up groveling before they bottom out completely, have a child, and become Greenwich Village mothers with streaks of gray in their hair and a history that makes them smile when they recall their youth. The waiter, for all his arrogance and expertise in treating women badly, was no match for the Israeli owner, who also had money, and a willingness to use his hands to bruise.

Martin and Julia ordered humus and pita and coffee. The coffee was all they wanted but they were intimidated into ordering something else and the ground chick peas were the only thing that came easily to their lips. There was a rumble of thunder from outside, the first signal of a shift in the weather.

"Remember the lightning on the beach in Greece?" Julia asked.

"I kept missing it," he mused. "We'd made love for hours and I was falling asleep."

"And then that one flash that turned the whole room stark white."

They fell into a silence and gazed at each other across the table. They did everything in the way of holding hands except to hold hands. Behaviorally, legally, and on the surface of their feelings, emotionally, they were a married couple out for a bit of refreshment, some coffee, a look at the streets, a browse in a bookshop, rubbing auras with people. They had just made love, and they had even negotiated a skirmish at the edge of a fight. The previous four months was relegated to the past, which indeed it was, and nothing stopped them from picking up where they had left off the night that Martin walked out of their apartment. They could have it all back, the intensity, the fierceness, the attachment unto death, and the use of one another as targets for the existential fury which attacks all human creatures who have evolved far enough to be aware of their mortality but not so far as to accept it with perfect ease.

And the temptation was strong. The waiter brought the coffee and humus and bread. They did not bother to look at him. They put in sugar and milk and tore apart pieces of pita and dipped it into the soft spread of beige paste. There would be nothing to it, to have Martin return home with Julia, for them to spend the entire night fucking, for both of them to call in absent at work, and then to play for the whole weekend, three days of discharging the enormous energy that had been built up during their separation. And the next step would be easier still, for Martin to begin to move his things back in. First toiletries, then some clothes, then his papers and books, and finally the entire accumulation of possessions, now swelled to three suitcases and four boxes over the original two suitcases with which he left, a careless and haphazard addition of things that simply accrete to a person over time.

And then the accounting. The slow dance building to a frenzy of destruction in which each would force the other to deny all the beauty and truth and pleasure that had occurred during the intervening third of a year. Martin would begin to make jokes about Babba, denigrating remarks about Robert. He would tell stories, and in telling them begin to take into account Julia's possible reactions and before she could even have a response would tailor the tale to meet that expected emotion. And then blame himself for selling himself short, and then, after a flash of unconsciousness, blame her for seducing him into the trap. And Julia? Well, she would have to dismiss Gail, and put aside everything they had known with one another, everything they had promised. She would have to bear the brunt of Martin's jealousy, his snide remarks, and there would very soon come a day when Julia and Gail would no longer see one another, no longer talk to one another.

"The choices are pretty clear, aren't they?" Julia said.

"I guess so," Martin replied. "At any rate, everything is clear until I think about having to make a choice."

"Do you have to?"

"It begins with where do I sleep tonight?"

"We're at that point already?"

"In some ways, part of me treated you as having died. I guess I knew that I would see you again, but I felt that it would be like meeting a ghost or seeing an old photograph. I imagined that you would just sort of be there, shimmering, transparent, and I would feel warm and loving and filled with delicious memories. And that you would then fade again, like a dream. And now you're here. And you're real. And you're a problem all over again."

"Well, you put a curve in my road too."

Martin took a deep breath. "You mean with Gail?" He shook his head. "It's funny. But if something like that had happened before our breakup, I would have gone crazy. But after becoming close with Robert, and living with him, well, I guess homosexuality has lost its mystery and terrors for me. It's just another way of doing the same old thing, isn't it?"

"Do you have sex with him?" Julia asked, apprehensive about the answer.

"I haven't, and I don't think I will. It's funny, he helped me get over my fear, but he doesn't turn me on. We went to a bar one night, though, where I met a young boy who did get my palms to sweating a little bit. Robert tells me that that's par for the course, that I'll probably take the thing closest to women for a while, like pretty boys, and if I become serious will get involved with men. Men who are men, not children or people who dress up. So, I don't know. Maybe the physical part of it will become active one day. But the most important thing is the friendship, the closeness, sharing feelings, telling each other what we really think, and not being afraid to touch one another, even to holding hands. I never realized how lonely I was until I met Robert, how lonely for the love of a man. He says that it begins with our fathers who are afraid to show affection, who never cry or speak simply about how they feel. And so we grow up crippled. Most men suffer the sickness of never loving another man. Most homosexuals suffer the sickness of only having sex with other men. But very few learn to have it all, the warmth, and the sex, and the friendship."

Julia shook her head in wonder. "You know, if you substitute 'woman' for 'man,' you have exactly what's been happening with me and Gail. The only difference is that we sleep together a few times a week. The physical part was the big barrier and at first we did it just to get past it so we could be lovers on a deeper level. But once we tried it, I guess we just got to like it." She smiled, wrinkling her nose. "And you're right, it's just another way of doing the same old thing. But it feels good, Martin, it feels so, so good. Except that it's not enough. For the past month I've been feeling a man hunger growing in me, and tonight I coldbloodedly went out to get laid. But of all the dumb places to pick. I suppose I hoped I'd find a man so bland I wouldn't even have to notice him as he negotiated me somewhere and maneuvered his cock inside me. A Unitarian fuck, you know? No passion, no danger."

"And you met me."

"Who would have expected a Jewish miracle in a Unitarian church?"

"Yeah, God isn't dead, He's just become a little senile."

Julia sipped at her coffee and shot Martin a glance over the edge of the cup. "Speaking of which, what about this guru you mentioned? That's the very last thing I would have expected from you."

"Nobody's more surprised than I am. And I'm not sure I can even talk about it without sounding stupid, you know, like those Moon people who keep trying to get you to go to Yankee Stadium? The thing is that I'm not sure what's happening to me, and that's the most exciting part of it. And then, on another level, nothing at all is happening. I mean, I'm still me. I have the same feelings, ideas, needs, wants. I still get angry and selfish. But somehow, it's all much lighter, less heavy, less oppressive. I don't hold on to anything any more. People or thoughts or situations. Somehow, Babba's influence is working inside me at a very, very deep level. I'm beginning to see what a jerk I am, and it doesn't bother me, because I see what jerks we all are. And so it becomes humorous, predictable."

He drained his cup and tried to signal the waiter for more coffee, but the man was involved in a triangle of smoldering stares involving himself, the owner, and the waitress. She was torn between the two men, trying to figure out which one would treat her badly better. The owner had her salary, promises of a bonus and raise, age, and the advantage of an inherent nastiness, while the waiter had the fascination of the untested, the new. She was already soaking her panties with secretion by virtue of the growing tension and the obvious direction of the evening. Martin was angry at not being noticed and called out, "Waiter!" in a sharp, stern voice, the way one might call a dog back from the edge of a busy highway. The waiter turned quickly, ready to brawl. Martin flexed his body, making it quite obvious that he could tear the other man apart without increasing his heartbeat. They locked eyes and Martin fed pure superior hostility into the channel. And while they still glared at each other Martin said in a soft, clear voice, "Bring me more coffee, please." His tone was so ominous that people at nearby tables looked around nervously.

The waiter filled both their cups and retreated to a five minute cigarette break in the kitchen.

"I've never seen you do anything like that before," Julia said. "I'm impressed, but it doesn't seem very holy."

"That's part of the general misconception about what spirituality is," he told her, "one which I shared. Being spiritual means being real. Being real means feeling and expressing your feeling fully."

"What if it had come to a fistfight?" she asked, intrigued, because Martin was articulating things which she had been discovering in terms of her relationship with Gail.

"I would have tried not to damage him beyond what the situation called for. That's the paradox. You have to be free, and yet freedom is a kind of discipline. Babba says that there might come a situation in which you might have to kill someone. He said that if that happens, if it's *really necessary,* then do it with as much ease as you would crack an egg for breakfast."

"Has he ever killed anyone? Did you ask him?"

"Somebody did. He said that there was a really big, bad baboon in the part of the jungle where he lived. And that the two of them took themselves off to a secluded spot to settle things. And that the baboon never came back."

"But that's just a monkey," Julia said.

"As far as Babba is concerned, that's all any of us are. Just monkeys."

Julia began to remonstrate, and then something peculiar happened. She saw everyone in the place as though they were naked. She saw the raw sexuality of the men and women, the cocks and cunts that get covered up. She saw the capacity for ferocity, the predatory quality of the owner, the animal helplessness of the waitress. Everywhere people were eating and drinking and making noises at one another.

It's true, she thought. *If you take away the clothes and the concrete, then we might all be around a watering hole somewhere. And probably doing more interesting things than talking, like combing one another's hair and chasing each other around trees.*

Martin saw her appraising glance. "It's weird," he said. "That's the thing about Babba. Everything stays the same but you start to see it differently. And all the things you used to think were the pinnacles of the human species you see as the biggest examples of stupidity and pride."

"Maybe I could meet him," Julia said and the moment she spoke the words was drawn back to the actuality of their situation with one another. This was precisely the value of their separation, that they were cut loose to discover new truths, new ways of opening to the world. And perhaps the biggest error would be in trying to horn in on each other's realities. Maybe she should let Martin have Babba and Robert and stay away from meeting them or becoming involved in any way. And perhaps Martin should not get implicated in what was going on between her and Gail.

A veil fell between them, a thickness of darkness merely,

without substance, but real. Each second they remained together dragged them more deeply back into marriage, or marriage as they had defined it. Each word spoken was a form of betrayal to the liberty they had tasted. Like climbers on a cliff who have reached a seemingly impassable spot, they could not go higher and yet it was unthinkable to back down. The other solution, one never considered, was simply to cut all lines and leave each climber loose to follow his or her own inclination, own destiny.

"It might have been simpler if I had been a strange woman after all," she said, reflecting the structure of the mood.

"You were, once, and look what happened," he replied. "If you had been a different woman, nothing would have changed. We would have only had to do it all over again to arrive at this point. Or some variation of it. You know, quitting the jobs, going to Europe, moving to a new city, deciding whether or not to have a child, arguing, going downhill, breaking up, and then . . . what? Being apart for four months and meeting by accident in a church? Why bother? We're already here. Why start again with someone else and go through it all again?"

Julia's eyes became unusually bright. She looked at Martin as though he were a Roman candle exploding. "You're right!" she said, surprise in her voice. "You're absolutely right."

"It's the mating dance. It's only biological. That's why we do it so well. It's as programmed as the way birds dance or fish waggle their tails. And since we can do it unthinkingly, we like to repeat it. Only each repeat seems to require a new partner, which is hell on the bank book and nervous system. The trouble isn't with the mating dance, it's with what happens to the mates when the dance is over. When they settle down and try to feather the nest"

"You're really big on monkeys and birds these days, aren't you?"

"Aside from rats, roaches, and few scraggly trees, that's about all that lives in the city. Us and the pigeons."

"And that's all there is? I mean, that's the only thing available to a man and a woman? The mating dance and then the dreary ritual of maintaining the cave or the nest or whatever you want to call it?"

"The home?" Martin ventured. He bit his lower lip and stared out the window for a few seconds. "I don't know," he went on. "That's all I can see. Unless . . ." He broke off.

"Unless what?" she asked.

"It's another one of those things that I can't really put into words, because I'm not sure what it is. But is has something to do with men and men and women and women. I mean, my friendship with Robert is crucial, and primary. I couldn't conceive of going back into a relationship with you or any woman which would make me put Robert into second place behind her."

Julia sucked her breath in sharply. "But that's just the promise that Gail and I made with one another. That no relationship with a man would ever come between us. In fact, those are the conditions which she gave to Eliot before they got married."

"Eliot finally married Gail, eh?" Martin said. 'That's an interesting match. I suppose it finally came down to money and children."

"Yes," she said. "And he saw what she meant about keeping her own place, and maintaining her own life, and having her relationship with me." She considered telling Martin about her scene with Eliot, but decided it could wait until another time.

"Would that work for us?" he asked.

The question was sudden, unexpected, and harsh, even though it was the only question that really mattered between them, the barrier through which they had to pass or fail to penetrate. It might have seemed that they would have a bit more time to tool around before coming face to face with the central issue. But there comes a moment when childhood is suddenly no more, when playtime is over once and for all, when the implacable nature of reality quietly and firmly asserts itself beyond all power of any individual to contradict, when the awareness of mortality invests time with a fearsome meaning. This was the situation of husband and wife as they sat in a tawdry coffee shop and weighed the balance of their future. There was no margin within which to tease the edges of decision.

"I don't know," she replied. "But that's the only chance at all. There's no going back to the two of us locked in that terrible unrelenting embrace. I won't do that again, Martin, not with you, not with anyone. I need space, I need an identity independent of any man."

"Or woman?"

"Or woman. But I can't live without men or women, although for most of my life I've tried to live without women. Perhaps if there is both, there is the slim possibility that I can cancel the two sides out and emerge as just myself."

"I have no objections," he said. She raised an eyebrow. "I really don't," he went on. "All I want is peace, and whatever has to be arranged or shifted around to bring peace, then I'm for it. If I don't see you again after tonight, that would be all right too. But that would seem like a false peace to me, the peace that comes from hiding from life. And I think you're right. If we tried to move in together again and dropped our new relationships, we'd be at one another's throats in no time at all."

The waiter returned and dropped the check onto the table. He turned and walked away quickly, like a child who will run up and hit another child and then escape to a spot behind its mother's legs for safety. Out of habit, Martin picked up the check. They both noticed the action at the same time and laughed.

"There must be a thousand unconscious little rituals like that which bind us together in the old way of relating," he said.

"As long as we keep seeing them as such, then there's no problem," she replied. "I guess the trick is to stay awake."

They stood up. Martin left a fifty-cent tip and remarked to Julia, "Here's another one. I'm so damned conditioned I'm embarrassed to walk out without leaving a tip for that creep who waited on us."

"Then don't," she said.

His hand hesitated over the coins.

"I mean it," she insisted. "Break the pattern. Liberate yourself."

Martin smiled, picked up the two quarters and put them in his pocket. They walked to the door where the cash register was, and he paid the bill. He turned to watch the table, to see whether the waiter would go over to clean up. He wanted to watch the man's reaction. But the waiter was leaning against a far wall, his arms folded across his chest, a broad sardonic grin on his face.

He had seen the scene at the table and had psychically positioned himself to emerge with a sense of moral superiority. He was a pro, and something like this happened to him several times a day. He knew when to cut his losses and how.

Martin and Julia walked out into the street. It was now nearly midnight. There were still rumbles of thunder and lightning flashes, but they were further, more feeble, like a receding toothache. The sidewalk was still filled with walkers, people who for one reason or another did not want to return to their apartments. Some eight million human beings were stuffed into a space that might nicely accommodate several hundred thousand, and the enforced proximity, the crowding, the constant abrasive contact, had made them permanently mad, so much so that they had come to accept the most bizarre and aberrant living conditions as a way of life, with only the vaguest glimmerings that existence on the planet might be a gracious, spacious thing, a dance with elegance and passion, with calm and time in which to appreciate the transience of sensation.

"I guess we have a problem," Julia said as they turned east and strolled down the street.

"You mean 'your place or mine?'"

"Or neither your place nor mine."

"It's funny," she added. "There have been hundreds of nights when we returned to the apartment without giving it a second thought, following the rote routine of our live together, and it got to be so casual, so unthinking, that it lost all its value, all its meaning. And now that we are outside the pattern, such a simple thing as deciding where to sleep becomes a kind of exhilarating challenge."

"Any ideas?" he said.

"Let's walk," she told him.

It was the last quarter of the twentieth century as measured by Christian dogmatists. The world was beginning to concur in the judgement of a critic that "This is our worst century yet." The globe had too many people on it, and they were organized into the most cumbersome and idiotic social structures imaginable, unwieldy, ugly states that imposed uniformity on larger and larger numbers of people. All the tribes had been wiped out, all the delicate and elegant lifestyles had been eradicated. And now the species was embarking on a systematic program to destroy all life on the planet. The very city in which Julia and Martin walked had produced so much garbage that it had poisoned the sea for scores of miles around, and swimming had been banned for seventy-five miles along the shore.

Those people who tried to make things better made things worse. The ancient traditions had lost all vitality and survived as grim shells of what had once been living truth. Protestants and Catholics planted bombs in one another's homes. Whites and blacks still smoldered across genetic barbed wire. Communists and capitalists brandished nuclear weapons at one another in an attempt to prove which system could produce the higher level of human misery. And everywhere virulent morons made speeches and ran for president or led coups or piled more bodies to shore up the decaying walls of economic empire. Fascists appeared and swept up followers in the name of God. Everywhere the barbaric practices continued, the slaughterhouses boomed, the automobile factories continued cranking out unnecessary millions of poisonous machines, and square mile after square mile of earth was covered with concrete and asphalt to make room for these hideous toys of demented apes.

As they walked down Broadway, heading south, moving with no specific goal, no clear purpose, the neighborhoods changed. The folksy anarchy of West Seventy-second Street gave way to the lanky impersonal high-rises that had begun to close in on the old turf, great Orwellian nightmares without grace, charm, or concern for human scale, things built by huge machines, ordered by creatures who wore the human body but who possessed the souls of jackhammers, brutal, insistent, destructive animals for which a name has not yet been found.

At Fifty-ninth Street, yet another change. They passed Carnegie Hall, a building left over from a time when the inherent horror of Western culture had not yet hit its stride in the new land. After destroying the continent of Europe with incessant warfare, foul technology, strangling ideologies, and a greed so mammoth that even life forms in other solar systems must have wondered, they came to a land that was utterly unspoiled, inhabited by the highest form of human society ever seen on the face of the earth, a diverse people of different languages and civilizations who nevertheless managed to inhabit a land for ten thousand years without leaving a scar on the earth, without wiping out a species, without leaving vain and foolish monuments, without descending to the degeneracy of enforced uniformity.

The Europeans came, and with a viciousness made all the more ghastly because of the indifference within which it was couched, destroyed half a continent. Within four hundred years they had poisoned every body of water, polluted the very air, killed off entire species of animals and birds, and found justification on the lips of their priests to annihilate the red men, who, the sages and holy men of Christianity averred, had no souls anyway and thus could be slaughtered along with the bison, the beaver, and the trees. Where there was lawfulness they imposed laws and created lawlessness. Where there was the beauty of God's creation, they erected testimonials to Man, and turned the land into a shit heap.

Past the culture corner of Fifty-seventh Street, with its book shop and delicatessen for celebrities, a short stretch of automobile showrooms followed, now all dark, the bodies of the cars gleaming dully behind plate glass. Here the street was empty, dark, almost sinister. But in the distance there was a bright glow, like the reflection of a fire seen against the clouds. They walked toward it, toward The Great White Way, toward Times Square.

As they approached, the nature of the street changed radically. Junk stores selling obscure plastic novelties that a retarded child would be embarrassed to play with. Souvlaki parlors with great hunks of meat dripping over a flame from which Greeks who had not shaved for days sliced long slivers to put on sandwiches. Movie theatres, massage parlors, the latter offering "Complete satisfaction, Yes, *Complete!* Only Eight Dollars!" After Forty-fifth Street, the slide into manifest decadence was swift and total. The space from there to Forty-Second Street was side-by-side sex shops. Peep shows, massage parlors with even more lurid promises, movie theatres showing XXX, and tiny stores which displayed knives, pocket calculators and dildoes indiscriminately in their windows, composing a set which would have taxed the ingenuity of an expert in Boolean algebra to define.

Along the sidewalks, the quality of people would have stretched the limits of a Buddhist's capacity for compassion. Pimps, heroin addicts, muggers, killers, whores, young men who existed as nothing more than a twitch of nastiness, a festering scar, boys of no more than twelve or thirteen selling their bodies to middle-aged men with damp palms. And amidst all this, the police, stunned, stoned, overwhelmed, their eyes reflecting their inchoate stupefaction at how they could possibly be expected to halt the decline and death of a two-thousand-year-old civilization by standing on a street corner and brandishing their clubs.

Martin and Julia crossed over and went to stand underneath the Chemical Tower Building, a tall triangle of glass and brick which, when compared to the Flat-iron Building, speaks several volumes on the death of architecture in the nation. This was the spot where the crowds gathered on New Year's Eve to watch the ball drop, to signal in the new year, which is the same as the old year, except for the digits written on billions of pieces of paper from coast to coast. There several hundred thousand people get drunk and gaze fuzzily into the air waiting for the signal when they can all jump up and down and make noise. Those viewing or listening at home are switched to Guy Lombardo who still makes an effort at waving his arm although the band can play Auld Lang Syne with the perfection of a phonograph record. Then there are several moments of sentimentality and a dim flare of primordial awareness around the edge of deep unconsciousness which is the waking condition of the modern world.

"Something is happening," the collective mind says to itself. "There was something about . . . what was it? Time? Eternity? Wonder? Mystery? Awe? The Fact of Existence Itself? The Poignant Joy of Life? The Miracle of Love?"

But the shades go down very quickly, and before a quarter hour of "the new year" has passed everyone is stumbling about once more, ugly robots clanking about in the dirty grooves of their conditioning.

Martin and Julia stopped and turned to face one another. They held hands like two children about to swing round and round. They had not spoken a word for the entire thirty blocks they'd walked. There was nothing to say, and everything to say. The impact of the world they'd just passed through had both disheartened them and given them a wider perspective on their situation.

"Well, here we are," Julia said at last.

"What do they call it" Martin asked. "The Crossroads of the World?"

She smiled. "Remember how excited we were when we decided to move to the big town? New York seemed like it would be the most sophisticated, hippest, richest place in the world. And it's just a big garbage can. Nothing but unhappy people and poisoned air and noise and violence."

"Do you think we would have been better off staying in Simpsonville? Me teaching gym and you raising babies in the back yard?"

"Who knows?" Julia replied. "We might have even become swingers and saved our marriage."

"What are we now?" he mused.

"Statistics. Marriage statistics, divorce statistics, migration statistics, population statistics, income level statistics, rise-in-homosexuality statistics, people-who-have-begun-to-follow-gurus-statistics."

"Is there a chance?" he asked.

She swept the area with her eyes. The din of traffic was so loud that it was difficult to hear or speak. Grotesques lurked in little psychic crannies up and down the street. The promised storm had absconded entirely and the earlier promise of fresh air in Central Park had become a false hope, replaced by an atomosphere that might make a gas chamber seem merciful by comparison.

"A chance for what?" she replied. "You see the way things are. We're a suicidal race of creatures. What you and I are going through is nothing but the reflection of what's happening everywhere, to everyone. The whole show is folding, falling apart."

"Not all of it," he said. "Babba is not part of this. My friendship with Robert is not part of this. Your love for Gail is not part of this."

"And our marriage? Is our marriage part of this?"

"It was."

"And so? We can't go back to that?"

"We can go forward."

"Where?" she asked. "Your place or mine? Or neither?"

"Or both."

The little patterns of energy between them were beginning to dance once more. Front of body called to front of body. They hesitated, then shrugged, and gave themselves up to an embrace. It was peculiar. One might almost have expected the entire stage to collapse, for traffic to stop and the degenerates to straighten up and the air to clear, that two people could lovingly hold one another amidst the ruin of their civilization and the ashes of their dead marriage. They hugged each other tightly, her breasts murmuring against his chest, his cock whispering to her cunt.

They stepped back, still holding hands.

"I honestly don't know which way to turn," she said.

"What are the possibilities?"

She frowned at the question, taking it first as rhetorical, and then stopping to think about it.

"We could go back to Ohio and try to be normal."

He shook his head at just about the same moment she did. The suggestion was definitely a possibility but not on the level of practical reality.

"We could just turn our backs on one another and walk away and not see one another again."

"And then what?" he asked. "Each of us would find another mate of the opposite gender and begin again."

She nodded.

"Maybe your guru could whisk us away to India and we could live happily ever after in Paradise."

"Babba says he's going back to the jungle for a year or so. He says he can't stand the rat race any longer."

Julia laughed. "Did he really say that? The rat race?"

Martin nodded. "Someone taught him the phrase and he uses it all the time. He's like a child with a new toy."

"Well, we don't seem to be doing too well," Julia went on. "It's absurd to even mention your moving back into the apartment, isn't it?"

"I'm afraid so," he said, "As much as part of me wants to. We would just kill each other. And hate each other for what we had to give up."

"Well," Julia sighed, "the only other thing I can think of is going to the country and starting a commune."

"Who?"

"You and me and Robert and Gail and Eliot."

"Eliot?" Martin said. "I barely know him. I'm not sure I even like him."

"But he's Gail's husband, and Gail's my lover, and I'm your wife, so if you want me, you see, the line leads right up to Eliot."

"And I suppose Eliot has a mistress he'd want to bring also."

Martin put his arm around Julia's shoulder and they began walking again, heading west, deep into the hooker territory, the subterranean atmosphere of Eighth Avenue.

"Martin?" Julia said after a few minutes.

"Yeah?"

"What *are* we going to do? I don't mean just you and me, but all of us. All the statistics. The people getting divorced, the people deciding that they can't live with anyone at all anymore?"

"I don't know, darling," he replied. "That's a big question. I'm still trying to figure out what to do tonight."

They turned the corner of Eighth Avenue and began to walk uptown once more. On the next street over, peering down the block, Martin saw a large, red neon sign: *Dixie Hotel*. It was the place where the whores took their tricks.

He pulled Julia a bit more closely to him and guided her down the street. At the entrance, he stopped. She looked up, a bit perplexed.

"Here?" she said.

"I think it's perfect," he told her.

"But what will we do here?"

"We'll make love all night long, listening to the hookers fucking strange men through the cardboard-thin walls, and we'll be naked without clothes and without possessions and then, in the morning, we'll . . . we'll . . ."

Across the city, Robert knelt naked on a concrete floor in a bar called The Toilet while a burly man pissed on his face.

Twenty blocks away, Gail called Julia's number for the fourth time in less than an hour. She was upset because she suspected that Julia might have met a man at the meeting she said she was going to, and was beginning to feel the first twinges of insecurity, and had already begun to mistake the sensation for that of jealousy.

In a penthouse overlooking the city, Eliot stood by the parapet of his sun deck and sipped at a martini. He was tingling with the rare joy of conscious solitude.

And in a spacious room in an antique apartment on the upper East Side, Babba watched a Joan Crawford movie on color television while he puffed on a pipe filled with potent and aromatic hashish, shaking his head from time to time and wondering if any of the thousands of people who called themselves his followers and devotees had even begun to get the point.

The earth continued to turn and Julia's question was gently whisked into the night. Martin had no answer. And so they stood there, uncertain, hesitant, filled with need and suspicion, like children at a horror movie, afraid to look yet unwilling to look away, peeking through their fingers at the screen.

While, from across the street, two pimps talked about the incongruous couple and made rapid estimates on where they might have come from, why they were standing there, and what they would do next. The conversation ended with a fifty-cent bet as to whether the man and woman would go into the hotel. They leaned against the building, picked their teeth, and waited to see which way the species would turn.

About the Author

MARCO VASSI was, without a doubt, the foremost erotic writer of our generation. Praised by Norman Malier, Kate Millett, Saul Bellow, and Gore Vidal, he was not only the ultimate sexual explorer, but a literary craftsman whose own life experiences became the stuff of his fiction—expanded, of course, by a grand imagination and a full sense of the absurd.

Tragically, Vassi died from pneumonia after he had contracted AIDS.

OPEN ROAD
INTEGRATED MEDIA

Open Road Integrated Media is a digital publisher and multimedia content company. Open Road creates connections between authors and their audiences by marketing its ebooks through a new proprietary online platform, which uses premium video content and social media.

www.ingramcontent.com/pod-product-compliance
Lightning Source LLC
Chambersburg PA
CBHW020844260626
47169CB00003B/1126